Lifting Courtney in his arms, Darius carried her into the bathroom, where he turned the shower on full blast.

Taking no time to disrobe, he settled them both under the downpour of water. Courtney moaned as the warm spray caused her robe to cling even more tightly against her body. She slowly slipped the robe from around her shoulders and let the water carry it the rest of the way downward.

With increasingly assured hands she reached out and tugged at the opening of Darius's robe. His soft moans let her know that he was enjoying this experience every bit as much as she was.

Darius tenderly lifted her into his arms, holding her securely. "Wrap your legs around my waist, baby," he encouraged huskily. Turning his back to the water, he moved closer to the shower's wall with Courtney still in his arms and wrapped around his body.

Fear once again swelled in Courtney, but in a matter of seconds it dissipated. Darius's hands stroking her wet, exposed flesh caused any bit of fear to fly free from her mind and body. There were so many mind-numbing, amazing sensations assailing her that she could only concentrate on the w_____us was so lovingly besto_____

Books by Linda Hudson-Smith

Kimani Romance

Forsaking All Others
Indiscriminate Attraction
Romancing the Runway
Destiny Calls
Kissed by a Carrington
Promises to Keep

LINDA HUDSON-SMITH

was born in Canonsburg, Pennsylvania, and raised in Washington, Pennsylvania. She furthered her educational goals by attending Duff's Business Institute in Pittsburgh. The mother of two sons, Linda lives with her husband, Rudy, in League City, Texas.

After illness forced her to leave a successful marketing and public relations career in 2000, Linda turned to writing for healing and as a creative outlet. Dedicated to inspiring readers to overcome adversity against all odds, she has published twenty-six acclaimed novels. During Harlequin's 60th anniversary party held in Washington, D.C., Linda received an award for her twenty-fifth published novel.

For the past eight years Linda has served as a national spokesperson for the Lupus Foundation of America. She travels around the country delivering inspirational messages of hope. In 2002 her Lupus Awareness Campaign was a major part of her book tour to Germany, where she visited numerous military bases.

Linda is an active supporter of the NAACP and the American Cancer Society. She is also a member of Romance Writers of America and Black Writers Alliance.

To find out more about Linda Hudson-Smith, please visit her Web site at www.lindahudsonsmith.com.

Promises to Keep

ESSENCE BESTSELLING AUTHOR
Linda Hudson-Smith

KIMANI
ROMANCE

MAY YOUR LIVES BE FILLED WITH LOVE AND HOPE

This story is dedicated to people all over the world.

May all of your needs be met in abundance.
May your hearts' desires be fulfilled.

May you find love and hope in all that you do
and everywhere you go.

KIMANI PRESS™

ISBN-13: 978-0-373-86166-8

PROMISES TO KEEP

Recycling programs
for this product may
not exist in your area.

www.kimanipress.com

Printed in U.S.A.

Dear Reader,

I sincerely hope you enjoy reading *Promises to Keep,* my inspiring new love story featuring two entrepreneurs, the lovely Courtney Campbell and handsome Darius Fairfax. Their story will take you on a whirlwind romance from the U.S. mainland to the windswept shores of Hawaii.

The connection that develops between Courtney and Darius just goes to show that we can't predict where and when we'll find true love.

I am very interested in hearing your comments and thoughts about this story. Please enclose a self-addressed, stamped envelope with all your contact information and mail to Linda Hudson-Smith, 16516 El Camino Real, Box 174, Houston, TX 77062. Or you can e-mail your comments to lindahudsonsmith@yahoo.com. Please visit my Web site and sign my guest book at www.lindahudsonsmith.com. You may also read my newsletters and meet other published authors, aspiring authors and other creative spirits at thewritersworld.ning.com.

Enjoy,

Linda Hudson-Smith

Chapter 1

"You ten o'clock appointment has arrived," the receptionist, Monica Long-Norman, said to her boss, Courtney Campbell, over the intercom. Monica was a pretty lady with a sweet personality, standing five-foot-six with dark shoulder-length hair, cut in blunt layers.

"Mr. Fairfax?" Courtney asked, her dark green eyes sparkling like emeralds.

"You are so right. Are you ready for him?" Monica queried.

Courtney laughed. "Give me a couple of minutes. I need to tidy up my desk and file away the work-in-progress contract for the Davies-Wilcox wedding reception."

"Buzz me when you're done, Courtney. By the way, a March chill is expected."

Monica was Courtney's employee, but the two women had become dear friends. The owner was also close to her other staff members, but she and her right-hand assistant, who wore several different hats in the business, had developed an airtight bond.

"Thanks, Monica. I heard the dreary weather report earlier. I won't be long."

Courtney cradled the phone and gathered all the papers into a neat pile before returning them to the labeled folder. Unfulfilled contracts were filed alphabetically in her antique cherrywood desk.

Removing from the top desk drawer her hairbrush and makeup, Courtney rushed into the bathroom to do some primping. She then dried off her hands with a paper towel. Making repairs to her golden-brown complexion, she stood at the mirror and applied translucent powder over the shiny spots on her face. While engrossed in her catering projects, she had a habit of twirling slender fingers around her long, reddish-brown curls, which she brushed neatly back into place. She then applied a fresh layer of berry lip gloss.

Back at her desk, Courtney rang Monica. "I'm ready for Mr. Fairfax."

Approximately five foot five in stature, weighing 105 pounds, Courtney waited for her client to walk through the door. The second her eyes fell on the fabulous-looking Darius Fairfax, her breath caught. The man with sable-brown, close-cut, wavy hair was fine with a capital *F*. She put his height at six foot two and his weight around 170 pounds or so. His athletic build supported a solid mass of rippling muscles.

Trying to recover from an instant, undeniable attraction to this man with loads of sex appeal, Courtney extended her petite hand. "Welcome, Mr. Fairfax. I'm Courtney Campbell, owner of The Party People. Please, let's sit down so we can discuss your event." Moving over to the cherrywood table, she pulled out two chairs and respectfully waited for Darius to be seated first.

Courtney handed him a catering packet. A fork, knife and spoon joined together, circled by a wreath of colorful flowers, served as the company's logo.

Darius quickly leafed through the envelope, surprised by the extensive offerings. "Very impressive! How long have you been in business?"

Courtney dared to look right into a pair of intriguing topaz eyes. As her breath caught again, she stifled a gasp. "A couple of years, but we've only operated at this location about six months. Business has been extremely good. We remain optimistic."

Darius nodded. "Congratulations. What made you decide on catering?"

Courtney flashed him a bright, white smile. "Been around it most of my life. My paternal grandmother ran a successful catering operation right out of her own kitchen. I learned from her the majority of what I know about this exciting, rewarding business."

Darius smiled warmly, revealing a beautiful set of well-maintained teeth. "Grandmothers. I feel sorry for anyone who didn't grow up around one. I have fond memories of mine. Nana Fairfax and Grandma Sheridan's spirits are now at home with the Lord, but they live on in my heart. Is your grandmother involved in your operation?"

Courtney's eyes lit up. Any mention of her incredible grandmother touched her emotionally. "Not so sure I could've done this without her. She helps me out a lot and is a whiz at keeping the books. Very much a confidant, Alma Campbell is on my payroll. My grandpa, Harrell Campbell, works for me, too. He loves to chauffeur our clients to and fro. My maternal grandparents have been deceased for years now. They passed on when I was a toddler, so I don't have any vivid memories of them."

"It's nice to know both your grandparents are on board." Darius's eyes brimmed with sentiment. "I'm sorry about the deceased ones. What about your parents?"

The conversation had turned more personal than she was used to when dealing with clients, but she wasn't put off. "Divorced, yet they're very good friends. Neither one has remarried. My father, Maurice, an LAPD officer, lives here. Chelsea, my fashion-designer mom, lives in Paris. I moved in with my grandparents during the divorce."

"I imagine it's nice if everyone can get along, especially when children are involved." A moment of sadness hit him—and he paused to ponder quietly.

"I've never planned a large, upscale social event," he said. "This one is extremely special to me. It has to be top-notch. I'll be personally involved in every aspect of the planning, relying heavily on you and your expertise. There are a few things I may want to handle on my own. We can get to those items as they come up. The finest surprise engagement party money can buy is the end result I'm after. Cash up front; no expense spared."

Any notion Courtney had of possibly getting to know honey-brown-complexioned Darius better after their business arrangement was fulfilled was quickly dashed. A surprise engagement reception didn't exactly need an explanation. *Spare no expense* didn't require one, either.

"As I mentioned, we offer both partial and full-service contracts. The latter covers a variety of services. We're running a spring-fling special for April and May."

"Full service," Darius responded without hesitation. "Spring fling, huh? Nice."

Even though Courtney felt profoundly disappointed over his engaged status, Darius's last remark and his cash up front comment had her smiling beautifully. Cash and carry was her favorite way to do business.

"You've come to the right company to get your event needs met, Mr. Fairfax. In addition to catering services, decorating, hosting, bartending, DJ and waitstaff are at your fingertips. We can arrange reliable transportation to and from the events via late-model Town Cars and stretch limousines. One-stop-shop is what we love to boast here at The Party People."

"Just how old *are* you?"

Courtney wrinkled her nose. "Three years shy of thirty."

The diamondlike sparkle in Courtney's green eyes mesmerized Darius, causing his heart to quiver. Not only was she an intelligent woman, she was softly pretty, as opposed to beautiful. He saw that she had an amazing spirit, one that radiated from deep inside. Her fabulous figure had inspired him to indulge in more than a mere glance.

Darius couldn't help wondering if Courtney was involved in a serious relationship. Since she wasn't wearing a ring, he assumed she wasn't married, yet he still couldn't be sure. A lot of his male friends would go bananas for a shot at dating her. He was amused by the way she had referenced her age, making him three years older than her *three years shy of thirty*.

Courtney handed Darius an application form. "After you

fill this out, we can discuss your vision for the reception, Mr. Fairfax."

As Darius filled in the blanks, Courtney was already thinking about the kind of reception he might like, based on the way he carried himself. Once she learned pertinent information about the prospective bride, she'd figure that into the equation. The form had a box to fill in for favorite colors of both bride and groom and their favorite flowers and greenery.

"Here you go," Darius said. "For the date, third or fourth week in May is good."

"The dates are good for us."

She was impressed that he'd filled in every single blank. Many future brides failed to fill in all the spaces. Men often left blank the most important areas. It surprised her when couples didn't know the more intimate details about future spouses. She'd make it her business to know everything about a man she loved enough to take his last name. Likes and dislikes revealed a lot about an individual.

The bride-to-be was named Candice. No surname was supplied, but Darius was the client. Her birth year made her six years younger than her fiancé's thirty years.

"I see Candice's favorite colors are lavender and green. I can work wonders with those combinations. Adding splashes of silver here and there will make those hues pop."

Courtney opened her company's brochure to the section on centerpieces. "We also do amazing creations with flowers and balloons. If you don't see what you want in here, we can create something special and unique, customized to fit your vision."

"Angels have to be a part of the table decor. Candice collects them."

"Angels with silver, glittery wings will work beautifully as centerpieces."

"Can we center the angels in some sort of floral arrangements?"

Courtney made note of his suggestion. "You're quite creative yourself. I saw on the application that you're a filmmaker."

Courtney had scrutinized Darius's paperwork more closely than normal because she'd found herself wanting to learn everything there was to know about the gorgeous man with the deep, seductive voice. Before she'd found out he was engaged, her mind had wandered all over the place, earning him the top spot on her *hot* chart. She was still intrigued with him, yet she'd be ever mindful of his completely off-limits status.

As a Hollywood filmmaker, screenwriter and producer, Darius was the owner of a production company on the rise, D.F. Film Productions, Inc. Courtney was thoroughly impressed by his credentials and the list of references it hadn't been necessary to provide.

"My plans are to establish myself as a major force in Hollywood. D.F. Film is geared more toward producing screenplays written by and featuring African-American characters and other minority actors. I'm also interested in novel-to-film adaptations. However, I consider projects offered by all ethnic groups."

"Sounds like you know exactly what you're after."

"A lot like you, I'd say. You've certainly pursued your dreams to fruition."

"I'm not all the way there yet. Catering is in my blood. I couldn't have gone in another direction if I'd wanted to."

"We obviously share similar dreams. In my opinion, there's not enough work for minorities in Tinseltown. I'm determined to address that critical imbalance. Keeping veteran actors of color on the big screen, as opposed to filling jobs with young stars of tomorrow, is another one of my goals. Veterans lend credence to any film. A mix of old and new artists lighting up the silver screen is one of my strongest visions."

"Good luck, Mr. Fairfax. I'll be rooting for you."

"Thank you for the vote of confidence." Darius looked down at his watch and instantly got to his feet. "I'm afraid I've got to go. Is it okay if I call you tomorrow to schedule another appointment? This engagement party has to be the event of the year."

"I can have Monica reschedule you on your way out."

He shook his head. "I have to check my calendar first. It's best if I call back."

"My business card is in the packet. My cell number is also available in case clients have to reach me after normal business hours. Thanks for choosing The Party People to cater your event."

Darius smiled. "You're welcome. I couldn't have chosen better."

It was commonplace for Courtney to walk her clients out to the reception area and see them to the exit. Escorting Darius out made her positively giddy with pleasure. Her wild attraction to an engaged man was silly, dangerous and couldn't be acted upon. *How would she override these dizzying, heartfelt reactions?* Reining in her mind and body wasn't difficult. Getting her heart to tag along might be a bit of a problem.

Darius looked back at Courtney. Winking, he smiled and strode out the door.

Blowing on the tips of her fingers, Courtney shook her hand out. Laughing from deep within, she deposited herself in a chair. "Talk about sexy and hot! That indescribable man caused a major heat wave up in my office. Is he not gorgeous?"

"He *is* fine!" Monica laughed at Courtney's to-die-for expression. "What type of party is he interested in?"

Poking out her lower lip, Courtney shook her head. "Engagement party. *His.*"

Monica smiled sympathetically. "Sorry about that. He's a real turn-on. If I wasn't married, I would've enjoyed flirting with him. But I love being married to hunky J. R. Norman." She looked down at the appointment book. "Normally I ask clients what kind of event they're interested in, but this entry isn't in my handwriting. Someone else took his call and forgot to initial it. I'd definitely remember that sexy voice."

"Mr. Fairfax's voice *does* caress the soul. I wonder what his whispers sound like." Both women laughed. "It matters who booked him for proper credit, but I'm thankful he showed up. He hasn't signed a contract, but I'm confident he will."

Monica looked closely at the telltale glint in her boss's eyes. "You're terribly smitten. How will you manage to work with someone you're so obviously attracted to?"

Courtney grinned. "I am a professional, sweetie. I know how to keep my game face in place."

Monica grinned. "You are the consummate professional! Since J.R. is out of town, you want to stop by Club 21 for a drink or two after work?"

"Sorry, not tonight. I'm beat. Let's shut down at four o'clock instead of five. We've come in an hour early and stayed late every day this week. And we have to work the Wilkerson-Banks lingerie bridal shower tomorrow."

"I'm glad I have to work this event because I'd be home alone anyway. J.R. probably won't get in from Atlanta until midnight."

"That's what happens when girls marry boys in the band," Courtney remarked, laughing. "Unfortunately, for me, my calendar only includes the social events I work. Maybe one day I'll find the right man and eventually settle down. How nice would that be? Darius wants a May date. Pencil him in for the third week of May."

"Got it." Monica smiled. "Your Mr. Right is lurking out there somewhere. I'm glad J.R. plays the majority of his gigs in the L.A. area. When they hit the big time, he'll be gone a lot more."

"As much as I'd hate to lose my right-hand employee, I hope you're still planning to travel with your husband when his big break comes. You have to protect your personal interest. Women love the boys in the band, even the married ones."

"They absolutely love drummers. Found that out a long time ago."

Courtney nodded. "Not only is J.R. a great drummer, he's so good-looking. I guess other band members get their fair share of fans, too."

Monica smiled. "Fans are one thing. Groupies are another. I'm blessed to have such a loyal man."

"You sure are." Getting to her feet, Courtney walked toward her private office. "I could sit and listen to you chat all day about your wonderful husband, but I've got lots of work to do. See you later. Hope I can suppress all sizzling thoughts about Darius Fairfax."

"You'd make a striking couple," Monica cooed.

Courtney smiled. "I kind of thought so, too. Candice is one lucky woman."

* * *

Courtney let herself into her recently purchased Hollywood Hills three-bedroom residence. She had yet to put her personal stamp on her 3,200-square-foot home. The decor she had in mind would one day reflect her serene, warm and colorful personality. She had extensive plans for her space, but limited time to make them a reality.

Totally blank, swirling ecru-textured walls were featured throughout. Only the master suite, laundry and kitchen were fully furnished. Surfing online had given her some terrific decorating ideas: a mix of antique, European and modern-day furnishings was her dream for ideal living quarters. Courtney planned to purchase items for the formal areas as soon as possible. The emptiness had begun to get to her.

She had already decided to eat leftovers from the tasty meal her grandmother had prepared yesterday: roast chicken stuffed with cornbread dressing, plus a vegetable medley of steamed broccoli, pearl onions and cauliflower along with a side garden salad. She planned to shower, eat and go straight to bed. The day had been a long, tiring one.

Just as Courtney slipped into the beautifully draped king-size bed, her cell phone rang. Her first thought was not to answer it. She then thought of her clients, as always. Someone might have a problem and need her help. She immediately reached for the cell.

"Sorry to call so late, but I was wondering if you'd come to my office tomorrow to get started on the event plans. I know it's a Friday and I'll understand if you can't."

Darius hadn't identified himself—and he hadn't needed to. She recognized that sexy voice instantly. Courtney took in a deep breath to try to settle the butterflies in her stomach. "I'm working an early-evening event tomorrow. We're contracted for three hours. I can meet you afterward."

"Good. I'll order take-out food for us to eat in my office. Okay with you?"

"Well, yeah, I guess so. I'll make sure I don't eat too much

Promises to Keep

at the shower. It'll be hard to do. Several of my grandmother's specialties are on the menu."

Darius chuckled softly. "I don't want you to miss out on Grandma's delicious cooking. Hope you won't mind if I eat while we work. I know I'll be ravenous by then."

"Not a problem. Six-thirty is good for me. If something unexpectedly pops up, I'll call right away. Otherwise, I'm there."

"Six-thirty it is. Is there anything special you'd like to drink?"

"Whatever you have on hand will be fine. I'm not hard to please."

"If it's true, you're the first woman I've met who can lay claim to that."

"There are plenty of us out there. Talk to you later, Mr. Fairfax."

"Darius works just fine for me. Is it okay if I continue calling you Courtney?"

"Absolutely! Have a great evening, Darius," she said, trying on his request for size. She liked the way her tongue caressed the pronunciation of his name. Courtney disconnected before he had a chance to say another word. Talking to him turned her on every bit as much as seeing him face-to-face. She moaned softly.

Darius cradled the phone, unable to believe how wildly his entire being reacted to Courtney. He felt like a starstruck lover. *How was that possible?* He didn't know her, yet he was drawn to her the moment he'd stepped into her beautifully appointed office. Courtney's melodic, slightly husky voice made him want to hear it over and over again. Her pretty face and sexy body were desirable, but it was more than that for him.

No woman had affected Darius the way this one had, especially not on a first meeting. He hadn't been able to think of anything but Courtney since he'd left her office. He had a ton of work on his desk, but concentrating on anything but her was difficult. His steamy thoughts of her were totally inappropriate. He knew he had to snap out of this dream world.

As the intercom on his desk buzzed, he instantly picked up the receiver and pressed the red button. "Yes, Jasmine, what is it?"

"There's a Mr. Meyer Chandler on the line for you. He says he's from See-Through Films. Should I put the call through?"

"I've been waiting to hear from him. Remember his name. It's an important one."

"It's already stored in my memory bank. I'll transfer him to your private line."

Jasmine Parker, Darius's administrative assistant, was young and pretty, possessing a nearly flawless brown-sugar complexion. It was rumored by other employees that she had a big crush on her boss, but that simply wasn't true. Jasmine never gave any hint of her purported love-jones for him. Her longtime boyfriend was a professional football player, a linebacker.

Darius never thought of Jasmine as a possible romantic interest. At twenty-one, she was too young for him, though she acted very mature. It didn't matter that she had the kind of body that stopped men dead in their tracks. Jasmine was smart as a whip and ran his office with extreme professionalism. She stayed on top of everything. He loved giving her well-deserved bonuses and a semiannual raise. Jasmine gave a whole new meaning to the term girl Friday.

Darius pushed the button on his private line. "Meyer, how are you? It's good to hear from you," he said with tremendous enthusiasm. "I'm glad you called."

"I'm fine. I've been eager to get in touch with you. I've done a lot of research on you and your company. You run quite an impressive operation. Your stellar reputation precedes you. You come highly recommended by the powers that be."

Darius beamed. "Thank you. That means a great deal coming from someone like you. So do you think we might be able to join forces on a few movie and television projects in the near future?"

"By all means, Darius. I'd love to hear whatever you have in mind. When can we get together to discuss some ideas?"

"Why don't you set aside a few dates and times when you're available. Then call my assistant, Jasmine. She'll check my schedule against yours. I want to make things convenient for you. I'd like this meeting to happen as soon as possible."

"I appreciate it, but I should be the one trying to make it convenient for you. You're the one who's set this town on fire."

Darius was pleased with what he'd just heard. "I'd like to think so, but I haven't set off enough alarms yet. I look forward to hearing back from you."

"Count on it. Is sometime next week too soon?"

"Not at all, Meyer."

"Talk to you soon, Darius."

Once the line was cleared, Darius buzzed Jasmine on the intercom to tell her about his conversation with Meyer. "Do everything you can to set up an appointment on one of the dates and times he or his assistant gives you. If you can't find any free space for next week, let me know. We'll go over my schedule and do some clever juggling."

"No problem," Jasmine assured her boss.

"Thanks, Jasmine."

"You're welcome, D.F. Buzz me if you need anything else."

Several of Darius's employees and associates referred to him as D.F., but Jasmine had been the first one to call him that before it caught on. In front of colleagues he was Mr. Fairfax, yet he prided himself on creating a relaxed atmosphere among his employees.

Darius finally managed to clear his head of thoughts of Meyer Chandler and Courtney Campbell to tackle the mountain of paperwork before him. There were quite a few tasks he didn't trust to anyone else. He listened to the input of others and received advice from his attorneys and other advisors, but the final decision on how to handle important matters was always his. D.F. Film Productions, Inc. was his baby. He had conceived it inside his brilliant mind and had given birth to what was now a cutting-edge, lucrative company.

Courtney looked cool and relaxed in fashionable melon-colored pants. A navy blue silk shirt and cute, semidressy sandals in the same navy hue complemented the slacks. Her shoulder-length hair hung loose and was salon fresh, with a high-sheen finish. She had taken charge of the bridal shower festivities from the moment she and Monica had walked through the front door of Sonya Wilkerson's posh high-rise condo.

The Party People had been awarded full-service contracts for the bridal shower, the bachelor and bachelorette parties and the couple's wedding reception. Courtney had worked closely with Sonya's wedding planner to ensure that the future bride was happy with all the arrangements.

Courtney set her briefcase on a bar stool. After opening the lock, she removed several packets of papers. She handed Monica a stapled set. "Let's go over the catering list, line by line, to make sure everything has been delivered."

Courtney always inventoried all items to avoid the type of embarrassment she'd endured early on in her career. The cake, of all things, hadn't been delivered for a fortieth birthday party. An employee had failed to put it into the delivery van. Fortunately, the missing chocolate confection was discovered early enough so it could be retrieved in time. Courtney hadn't fired the delinquent employee, but she had issued a sensitive yet firm reprimand so it would never happen again.

"It's all here," Monica sang out. "Now let's do our usual last-minute check on the decorations. I recall seeing dozens of helium balloons on the order form."

"You're right. They're stored in one of the bedrooms. We need to bring them up to the front and float them upward. I asked for long ribbons to be attached for easy retrieval." Courtney looked down at her watch. "Sonya's guests should start arriving any minute now. She plans to make her grand entry twenty minutes after the start time."

"One of those, huh?" Monica remarked.

Courtney shrugged. "It's her party."

"And she can cry if she wants to," Monica joked.

Courtney giggled. "In the meantime, let's get those balloons hovering."

Courtney and Monica laughed upon seeing the bedroom ceiling covered with silver and blue balloons, inscribed with the names Sonya and Justin. The ladies each began to grab hold of the ribbons. Once they had several in hand, they realized they had too many to fit through the door at one time. Laughing all the while, the women caught and carted balloons from the back bedroom up to the front rooms. Courtney and Monica tried to make each event they worked a fun-filled adventure.

The doorbell rang just as the last batch of balloons was released.

"Time to rock and roll. Let's get it done." Courtney hugged Monica before she was off and running to act as hostess until Sonya and her bridal party arrived.

The party was in full swing and Courtney was delighted to see how happy her client was with everything. Sonya had repeatedly thanked her and praised the employees for their expert handling of the party. She was delighted knowing that her wedding reception was in the capable hands of The Party People. They had delivered far above Sonya's expectations—and this wasn't even the main event.

Two and a half hours later, Courtney pulled Monica aside. "Do you mind handling the last half hour or so alone? I made an appointment to meet with Mr. Fairfax at his corporate offices."

"Not a problem. The initial contract was for three hours. Are we billing Sonya for the extra time?"

Courtney frowned slightly. "No, but you'll be paid time and a half. I wouldn't ask you to stay later if I couldn't pay you. The guests look like they're starting to wind down. Sonya has a dinner to attend later on, so it should be over soon."

Monica looked embarrassed. "Paying me to stay over the allotted time is not necessary. It was just a question that came to mind. I know we've charged in the past for overtime and the clients are made aware of it up front, before signing the contract."

"Some people you charge and others you don't. Sonya isn't someone I'd want to hit with overtime. She's a wonderful client. Now if she were one of the moody grouches we sometimes get, we'd probably charge her for every additional second," Courtney said with a wicked grin.

Monica laughed, too. "Go on and get out of here. You don't want to be late for a date with the gorgeous Mr. Fairfax."

"Date! Hardly. I'm meeting with the soon-to-be-married Mr. Fairfax," Courtney countered, lightly pecking Monica's cheek. "I'm out."

Chapter 2

After a gentleman said Darius would be a few minutes late for the meeting, Courtney was ushered into his private office to wait for him. As she looked around, she was simply astonished. The panorama of Hollywood from the picture window behind Darius's desk included a bird's-eye view of Capitol Records. This was certainly a high-rent district.

Crystal-clear glass and gleaming chrome furnishings breathed high-tech energy into the room. The circular glass desk dominated the space. A high-back chair, crafted from fine silver leather, was supported by chrome arms and legs. The remarkable decor was like nothing she'd ever seen before. It belonged to a futuristic era. Chrome and glass bookshelves, tall and impressive, were for more than show. The white carpet beneath her feet felt thick and plush. Posh sofas and chairs created an elegant ambience. The office, beautiful and luxurious, was manly, yet subtle enough for a woman.

Exquisitely framed pictures on Darius's desk caught Courtney's eye. She moved nearer to take a closer look. A single eleven-by-fourteen color photo of a woman made her mouth drop open. Unable to pull her eyes away, she couldn't help staring.

Talk about beautiful.

The lady with a caramel complexion was positively stunning. Any man would love to hold and caress the slim, petite body, dressed in an alluring, cobalt-blue silk dress. In another picture of the same size, Darius wore a dark, double-breasted suit. He stood directly behind the lady, his fingers locked together at the middle of her waist. Satiny ginger-brown curls nestled back against his broad chest.

Candice, Courtney easily surmised. This beauty had to be Darius's Candice. What a lucky woman, she thought, hoping Candice treated him as wonderfully as she would if he were her man. Though she didn't know if he deserved special treatment or not, she somehow felt he was worthy of whatever goodness this world had to offer. He seemed genuinely kind and compassionate.

In an eight-by-ten picture was a lovely woman with a nearly flawless coffee-and-cream complexion. Her midlength, dark brown hair was sprinkled with salt. Standing next to her and much taller than the woman was a handsome, stately-looking man, who called to mind the expression *silver fox.* Every strand of his wavy hair had turned completely silver. The couple looked into each other's eyes with adoration. His parents, she surmised.

Darius slipped quietly into the room. Unnoticed by Courtney, who appeared focused on the pictures atop his desk, he watched her. As he drank in her natural beauty, his heart started to race. The effect she had on him was profound, something he'd never experienced before. The view from behind was sexy, spellbinding and thrilling.

Feeling someone's presence, Courtney turned and saw Darius standing there.

Impeccably dressed in a light gray, pinstriped suit, a pink silk shirt, with a complementary white, pink and gray silk tie, Darius exemplified a successful tycoon. The fashionable attire looked exquisite on his fine physique.

Courtney smiled brightly. "Good evening, Darius. It's nice to see you again."

Darius smiled gently. "The feeling is mutual. Would you like something to drink?"

Courtney nodded her assent. "Cold water would be nice. Thank you."

Darius walked over to his desk and picked up the phone, punching in the red intercom button. "Jasmine, please bring in a few bottles of ice-cold water and a platter of fresh fruit. I'm starving and way past ready for my dinner order."

"Right away, Mr. Fairfax."

"Thanks, Jasmine. You're the best."

Instead of sitting down in the swivel chair behind his desk, where he conducted most of his business, Darius opted for one of the plush microfiber sofas. He wanted to make Courtney feel at ease.

She took a seat. One click of her thumb opened the brown leather briefcase. "I'm letting you call all the shots," she reminded him, smiling softly.

"In that case, we're ready. Have you come up with any other inspiring ideas for the surprise engagement party?"

"Based on the things we discussed yesterday, I think I have a couple of good ones. Since I can't confer with Candice, I only have your brain to pick." Reaching into her briefcase, she removed a few sheets of paper and handed them to him.

"I sketched a few ideas for centerpieces to include the angels you mentioned."

A light knock came on the door before Darius could respond. The door opened and in walked Jasmine. She set a metal tray on the rectangular chrome table situated in one corner of the vast room.

Jasmine was dressed beautifully. Courtney thought she was stunning; her attire had class and style. She imagined guys giving off shrill wolf whistles whenever Jasmine walked into a room or strolled by. Clad in a red silk blouse and slim navy skirt, the young woman was a looker. A wide red patent-leather belt spanned her slender waist.

Getting to his feet, Darius was eager to introduce the two dynamic women.

"Jasmine Parker has been my administrative assistant for the past couple of years. I can count on her when I can't rely on anyone else. A one-of-a-kind employee, she's loyal to me and committed to running the office to the best of her ability. I'd be lost without Jasmine," he told Courtney. "She agreed to stay on until our meeting is done. This young, innovative lady has a great future ahead of her in film."

Courtney took Jasmine's extended hand. "So nice to meet you, Jasmine."

"Same here," Jasmine assured Courtney, smiling sweetly.

A couple of light pleasantries were exchanged between the two women before Jasmine turned her attention back to her boss. "Do you need anything else before your dinner arrives, Mr. Fairfax?"

"I'm good for now. Thanks, Jasmine."

"I'm just an intercom buzz away." She smiled at her boss then quickly excused herself and hurried out of the room.

Courtney's eyes followed Jasmine until the door shut. The lady was intriguing.

"It looks like you surround yourself with beautiful women." Courtney wanted to swallow her tongue. What a provocative thing for her to say to a client. It was asinine.

"I'm assuming you're talking about Jasmine for one, but who else are you referring to?"

Cheeks aflame with embarrassment, Courtney pointed at his desk. "The ladies in the photographs are also stunning."

"Ah, Candice and Mom. They *are* beautiful. Candice's inner spirit matches her physical beauty." He suddenly grew silent, his eyes misting. "Candice needs protecting. She's very fragile. I try hard to make sure she's always happy."

Courtney looked concerned for Darius. He looked so sad all of a sudden. "A surprise reception should make her happy. I'm sure she'll be pleased." She wanted to ask him more about his mother, but something told her not to. The fact he hadn't offered any personal information about her, not even her name, was enough to deter Courtney from making any inquiries.

"I'd do just about anything for Candice, including laying down my life. I'm her fiercest protector. Our relationship is immovably strong and refreshingly honest. I'm beyond certain that no one can ever come between us. We are in each other's blood."

Darius's comments gave Courtney chills and goose bumps. She'd never heard any man voice his feelings for someone in such an emotionally moving way. Whatever Candice had or didn't have, she had a fiancé who loved her, a man who was willing to die for her. How many women were able to say that? Courtney could only imagine what it might be like to have someone communicate with her in such a profound way. That he hadn't included his mother in his statement had Courtney thankful she hadn't opened up what might be unpleasant for him. She just didn't know what was what.

Courtney thought about the one and only serious romantic relationship she'd had in her adult life. Unfortunately, the liaison had turned out to be a huge, painful disappointment and failure for her. She often thanked God for bailing her out of the toxic situation before she'd fallen hard for Michael Scottsdale, a corporate executive.

Unwittingly, excruciating heartbreak had been waiting for Courtney around every corner. By the grace of God, she'd been led onto another path, but only after she'd taken an unfortunate detour to Michael's cheating, unfeeling heart. Many women had fought hard in the trenches to become number one in the life of this successful man—in hopes of winning him over. Just as many ladies had lost the battle, including her. Yet losing had really turned out to be a win for her in the end.

All the endless, lonely nights in Courtney's life were as much her fault as anyone's. Safeguarding her precious heart had become as important to her as breathing. She preferred to be alone than to have her leisure time filled with a meaningless relationship. Loneliness was sometimes a hard row for her to hoe, yet she had finally found peace in merely sharing her time with girlfriends and others with whom she'd forged mutual bonds.

Courtney spread out on the coffee table several sheets of paper that outlined her plans for Darius's special event. Everything had been illustrated in painstaking detail. "Please take a minute to look at what I've come up with."

"My time is yours. That's why I asked you to meet me here in my office."

Courtney nodded. "In that case, I'll wait for your comments."

A knock came on the door again. Just as before, it opened and Jasmine stepped inside. Walking across the room to the corner table, she set down the tray and left the domed top in place. "Can I get you something other than water to drink?"

"Water is fine." He looked up at Courtney. "What about you?"

Courtney nodded. "Water is perfect for me, too."

Darius smiled warmly at his assistant. "Thanks. The food smells wonderful."

"It came from Miss Lilly's."

He grinned. "Cube steak, gravy and mashed potatoes?"

Jasmine laughed. "Your favorites are what I always order from Miss Lily's. Hot applesauce and a salad are there, too, along with thick wedges of cornbread and sweet potato pie. If you need anything else, just let me know."

"I will," he said. "Thanks again."

Darius stood and moved over to the table, inviting Courtney to join him. Once she was seated, he sat down and said a humble blessing over his meal. Picking up his fork, he took the first bite of cube steak, closing his eyes to savor the delicious taste. The meat was tender and the thick, dark gravy was seasoned perfectly.

Scooping up a forkful of mashed potatoes and another piece of steak, he held it up to Courtney's mouth, shocking her silly. He noticed the reluctance in her eyes. "You just have to taste this wonderful dish. Please indulge me. You won't be sorry."

Despite her surprise, Courtney took the proffered food. She wasn't keen on eating off his fork, but she did so rather than making a fuss over it. It was the closest she'd come to sharing a kiss with him. She decided not to deny her desire to taste the full, sensuous-looking lips that had wrapped around the fork first. She suppressed a satisfied moan. "It *is* delicious! Where's this restaurant located? I'll have to give it a try."

"Perhaps we can go to dinner there together. I'd love to take you to Miss Lilly's."

Not sure of an appropriate response to such an inappropriate comment, Courtney said nothing. It was wrong of him to ask her out to dinner. Maybe Candice *didn't* have a man who loved her. Or perhaps his suggestion was perfectly innocent. It was possible she'd read too much into his remark. She quickly convinced herself that had to be it.

As he picked up one of the sketches, he drew in a deep breath. "Did you say you sketched these designs?"

"I did. I love art. There was a time when I thought I might pursue it as a career, but learning all I could about catering kept me too busy to take on anything else."

"There's no reason why you can't do both. These sketches are exquisite. You have quite a creative eye."

"You think so?"

"I know so. I've taken a few art courses in my day. It dovetails with my desire for filmmaking. They're both artistic talents. I love sketching. Sculpting, too."

Courtney nodded. "That's great! Which sketch of mine do you like best?"

He pointed at the drawing with the angel's wings fully extended. "It's beautiful. I love the soft shades of lavender you chose. The wingspan suggests a flight to me, a journey into paradise, which is where I hope Candice will always live."

You can make sure of that by sharing paradise with your precious Candice.

"Where is paradise for you, Courtney?"

Courtney lowered her lashes momentarily. "I haven't given it any thought."

Darius looked totally surprised. "You've never thought of paradise, of what it might be like or what you'd want it to be like?"

Courtney did everything she could do not to grit her teeth. *Why did Darius care about her paradise? Why was he pushing her on the issue?* She hadn't given up on living an idyllic lifestyle. She just tried very hard not to think about it. Her illusions about heaven and love on earth had been shattered a long time ago. Love and happiness would come as a complete surprise if either found her, since she simply wasn't searching for them.

He looked closely at Courtney. "I seemed to have hit a nerve. Who hurt you?"

Getting up from the table, Courtney walked across the room and stood at the window. As she looked out at what many would happily refer to as paradise, she fought to keep her emotions in check. As she glanced toward the Hollywood Hills, she saw the sun playing hide-and-seek with the jagged mountain range. The colors in the sky were the same soft ones she'd used to sketch one of the angels amid a lovely floral arrangement.

Courtney suddenly stiffened. Darius was right behind her, close enough for her to hear and feel his breathing. As his hands came down gently onto her shoulders, she balled her fists tightly. *What did he think he was doing? Why was he touching her so tenderly?*

He felt her go rigid and backed off. "I'm sorry," he whispered. "I shouldn't have gotten so personal. I promise not to do it again. Think we can get back to work?"

"I'd like that very much. I came here to work, Darius."

"I understand. Can we sit back down now?"

Instead of a verbal response to Darius's question, certain that her voice would quiver, Courtney claimed a seat on the sofa, hoping she could get back to the business at hand. He had unnerved her and her wild attraction to him only made things worse. Under different circumstances, she might have answered his personal questions with a daring remark or a passionate kiss. But he was a man about to be married and they shouldn't be getting personal, period.

End of story.

Darius looked over the catering catalogues once again. "Candice loves seafood, but I'm afraid of it spoiling, not to mention the smell. What do you think?"

"All foods can only be kept out for certain periods. Seafood is kept on ice when it's out. My staff and I will see to it that nothing is left out past the recommended time. Cooked seafood doesn't smell bad. What types are you interested in?"

"Shrimp, cracked crab and lobster are her favorites. If I decide not to go with seafood, what other suggestions do you have?"

Courtney handed Darius a few menus she'd already put together, boldly typed on parchment paper. "Give yourself time to look these over before making a final decision. We have time. Maybe you'd like to get other opinions or even consult Jasmine."

Darius smiled. "You're very thorough. I feel I can trust your judgment. Too many opinions can sometimes cloud a vision. I'll stick with your suggestions, but there's one thing I'd like to say. I don't want to order any alcoholic beverages. You may think it's an unusual request, but Candice doesn't drink."

His request wasn't such an odd one. She'd catered plenty of events where no alcohol was served. "I understand your request better than you think. You're in charge of whatever we order. Once my staff knows our clients' likes, we're known for making the right choices."

"Sounds like you've got it going on." He loosened his tie and popped open the top button on his silk shirt.

Courtney wished she wasn't thinking of what was under that shirt. She knew his chest was broad. *Was it covered with hair?* She'd like nothing better than to suckle his nipples and lick them like Popsicles. The idea of his areolas hardening beneath her tongue caused moisture to form at the core of her femininity. By the color of his skin, she imagined his nipples to be either a medium shade of brown or slightly darker.

"Hello, are you still with me?" Darius sang out, laughing at her dazed expression.

Courtney quickly returned to the here and now, fighting hard to hide her embarrassment. Losing herself to sexy thoughts of him had to stop immediately. "I'm still with you. Just thinking of a few more ideas," she lied. *Ideas of how I can seduce your fine body until you give in and eventually beg for mercy.*

Courtney and Darius worked together for another hour and a half. They talked shop, mixed and mingled menu items and swapped ideas on the decorations. The color scheme and angels were definites. He chose the angel with the full wingspan, opting for lavender for the floral arrangements, just as he'd suggested from the beginning. He consulted her on a theme for the invitations, telling her he wanted gold-embossed angels on the front, but he was interested in handling the design himself.

Courtney put everything back into her briefcase then closed

and locked it. "I'll call you after I pull this all together. We can meet again when it's time to get your approval. I hope you'll love what we do for your reception. It's coming together in my mind and now I need to get it sorted out on paper. Then we can draw up a contract."

"You *are* thorough and confident. I like people who run their businesses efficiently."

Courtney blushed, smiling at the same time. "Thank you. I like people who are willing to give credit where it's due. When my customers are happy and satisfied, they recommend us to family, friends and colleagues. That helps the business grow. All my clients become salespeople and advertisers for my business if they're treated right. Pleasing our clients is our top priority. If anything goes wrong, I'll do my best to fix it."

"Touché, my fair lady. You are indeed something else, a powerful force."

Excited by his sincere praise, Courtney grinned. "Good night, Darius. Have a nice evening."

"You, too." His eyes narrowed as he watched her walk to the door and leave.

Darius felt like he'd just been steamrolled and bulldozed, all at the same time. Courtney Campbell was one hell of a woman. *Where had she been hiding all his life?* Women like her didn't come a dime a dozen. This intriguing lady was one in a trillion, one of the rarest kinds. God had surely broken the mold and tossed it after creating her.

Courtney slipped into the driver's seat of her Lexus. Once she started the engine, she laid her head on the steering wheel to give herself a few minutes to settle down. Darius had her so high she wasn't sure if her feet would ever touch down on earth again.

The man is engaged to a beautiful, sexy woman, one whom he clearly adores.

The sobering thought did little to quash the euphoria Courtney felt inside. There was no harm in a bit of daydreaming about the finest man she'd ever met. She knew full well that Darius was romantically unavailable to her. That didn't mean he couldn't star in her fantasies every now and then.

Promises to Keep

Once she met Candice, Courtney hoped all these dizzying thoughts about him would vanish. The fiancée was real enough to her, but Courtney hadn't met her face-to-face. After becoming acquainted with Candice, Courtney was sure dreams of Darius would die down and eventually disappear altogether.

This fine brother and his fiancée have promises to keep, promises to each other.

Clad in a navy blue double-breasted pantsuit and a red silk top, matching it with red leather heels and bag, Courtney had attracted a lot of male attention from the moment she'd entered the large ballroom inside the beautiful Hollywood Westin Bonaventure. She had spotted her brunch companions immediately but decided to check out the food offerings first.

The decorations set off the buffet in such a beautiful yet healthy manner. The deep purple eggplants and green, orange and yellow squashes exuded vibrancy. Various types of whole and sliced plump red tomatoes infused the table with even more color, as did a variety of fresh melon slices, red and green grapes and golden pineapple chunks. There were too many delectable items to choose from.

Sauntering over to the omelet station, Courtney checked out all the available ingredients. She then requested from the white-capped chef an all-vegetable omelet, consisting of button and sliced mushrooms, black olives, yellow squash, zucchini, chopped asparagus, slivers of green peppers and diced tomatoes.

J. R. Norman pulled out Courtney's chair and then reclaimed his own. A physical fitness enthusiast, his body was tight and muscled, his waistline tapered. His complexion was soft and dark and his thick moustache was kept neatly trimmed. Sporting a close-cropped haircut, his waves were dark brown sprinkled with a bit of gray. By all standards, J.R. was a good-looking man and eminently charismatic when he decided to pour it on. Courtney liked how real and up-front he was and how deeply he loved his wife.

Monica had fallen in love with the professional music teacher and drummer in a matter of weeks, surprised to learn he'd fallen just as hard for her. Six months later they'd taken their vows in front of family members and very close friends. No bride was any more stunning than Monica on her special day. Courtney had been her maid of honor.

With a plate piled high, showcasing all sorts of delicious-smelling food, Monica was seated to her husband's left. Dressed in a white pantsuit and a yellow silk shell, she looked gorgeous. Yellow patent-leather shoes and a matching purse complemented the stark white suit beautifully. Monica was a vision of loveliness. At times it was hard for J.R. to take his eyes off his woman.

A quick look at Courtney's dish made J.R. laugh. "Is that all you're eating?"

Courtney gave him a sideways glance. "I'm just starting out. There's not a lot of room on this table so I didn't want to fill too many plates at once. Don't worry. My $34.99 will not go to waste, especially the way I love breakfast food."

"I hope not," J.R. countered. He looked over at his wife's plate. "Now this sister knows how to pack it. What amazes me is she doesn't gain an ounce after eating a ton of food."

"J.R.," Monica scolded lightly, "you should never talk about a woman's weight in front of her or any other ladies. It's rude and insensitive. And leave Courtney alone."

J.R. hunched his shoulders. "I call it like I see it—and you already know that about me. What do you think, Courtney?"

Before Courtney could respond, she felt a warm hand on her shoulder. "Had I known you liked this place, I would've invited you to join me. I eat here often. Hello," he said to J.R. "I'm Darius Fairfax." He then nodded at Monica. "I'm one of Courtney's clients," he told J.R. "She's handling an engagement reception for me."

J.R. wiped his right hand on a white linen napkin before extending it to Darius. "You got the right lady for the job. So nice to meet you, man. Care to join us?"

"As a matter of fact, I'd love the company. I'm alone. Since I haven't filled a plate yet, I'll do that first. Thanks for the invite." With that said, Darius strolled off.

J.R. looked right at Courtney, though she felt as if he were looking right through her. "What's up with this Darius Fairfax? He may be getting married, but he definitely has a thing for you.

What'd you do to that man to make him go off the deep end? He's spellbound. The brother couldn't take his eyes off you."

Monica tried to reel her husband in, but his fishing expedition was already too deep. Courtney hadn't taken the bait, yet he felt he had a right to reel her in. Monica looked on as he continued firing questions at her boss, barely giving her a chance to respond.

"J.R., you know I love you, but please put a lid on it. There is nothing between Darius and me. He's a client and I'm his hired gun, with major firepower. Got it?"

J.R. nodded. "Yeah, and so has he. The man has it bad for you. Don't be surprised if he backs out of this commitment. He can't possibly love another woman and look at you like you're the queen of his heart. Sparks are flying every which way between you two. Mark my words, ladies. Anyone care to make a wager?"

Monica gave Courtney a pleading look, hoping she could ignore her husband and forgive him. It was like he'd suddenly lost all his marbles. Courtney returned a nod of understanding. J.R. wouldn't say these things in front of Darius. He'd never embarrass his wife or her. The three friends very much respected and relished their closeness.

Upon Darius's return to the table, he sat down next to Courtney. As his arm accidentally brushed against hers, she felt a rush of heat. If it wouldn't be so telling, she'd fan herself to cool the hot flames singeing her skin.

Discreetly, Courtney surveyed Darius's attire. Though dressed more casually than when she'd last seen him, he still looked like a man of means. He wore a black blazer with a gold royal crest and his light blue silk shirt was open at the collar. The revealing bit of thick chest hairs made her want to see so much more of his sexy attributes. A sudden thought of him standing under the shower naked caused her to gasp.

Darius looked at Courtney with concern. "Are you okay?"

She managed a believable smile. "I'm fine. Something must've gone down the wrong way. It's okay now." Things were definitely going down the wrong way, but she had no clue as to how to redirect them. Gushing over an engaged man was simply insane.

Noticing the tiny beads of sweat on Courtney's forehead

didn't convince Darius that everything was fine with her, but he thought it best to let it ride. The last thing he wanted to risk was embarrassing her in front of her friends.

"I know Monica works for Courtney, but what about you, J.R.? Are you employed by The Party People, too?" Darius inquired.

"I work for Courtney on occasion. If she has clients who need a band, we accommodate her if we're free. However, I'm a music teacher at Rutherford Junior College. I also teach private keyboard and drum lessons to youngsters. Writing music is the part of my career I love best."

Darius smiled broadly. "That's good to know, man. Have you ever written music for a film or television?"

J.R. shook his head in the negative. "Can't say that I have, but I'd sure love to give it a try."

"Let's set up a meeting before we leave here. I'm the owner of D.F. Film Productions, Inc. My offices are here in Hollywood. Have you heard of my firm?"

"Who hasn't heard of your company?" Impressed with Darius's success, J.R. wondered if he might help something extraordinary happen in his music career. "Great things are said about what you're doing for blacks in theater arts. I'm awed by what you've taken on. The power people in Tinseltown are not easy adversaries."

"I try not to see them as opponents. My desire is to partner with some of the best producers and directors working in this city. There's enough for all of us in the world of entertainment. And we always need music."

"I'd love to hear what you're looking for. Monica always said that might be just the right ticket for me. She's my wife, and she means everything in the world to me." J.R. leaned over and kissed Monica full on the mouth.

Darius grinned. "The way you two look at each other made that an easy call. Body language tells its own story. Love between two people reveals itself in a number of ways. The lack of love between partners is just as easy to read."

"Yeah, I know," J.R. remarked. "Love is loud and clear, with or without vocals."

Darius's eyes suddenly flickered. "I like that! People in love are blessed. It's a thrill to watch actors communicate love in a romantic story without saying a word."

Talking about love and romance had gotten to Courtney, a hopeless romantic who had yet to experience a genuine loving relationship. The man of her dreams was out there, but she had no idea when he'd show up. If he did appear, she wasn't sure she'd recognize him immediately.

Glancing at Darius, she recalled her heart reaching out to him the moment she'd laid eyes on him. Unfortunately for her, his heart and love already belonged to another.

Chapter 3

Gathering together the papers she needed for the staff meeting, Courtney slid them into a manila folder and headed toward the conference room. She was early, but the extra time would give her a chance to sip a cup of coffee and go over her notes again. There was much to discuss this morning and the staff had a lot on its plate, literally.

The months to come were filling up quickly and quite a few dates had been booked up to the end of the year. Several Christmas parties, both day and evening events, were already on the December schedule. Deposits had been obtained.

Remembering when she only had one or two events scheduled in a single month made Courtney laugh. Even when dates were scarce and far and few between, she never thought about giving up. Anything worth having was worth working hard for.

Courtney entered the conference room and set down her briefcase at the head of the table. *Monica—sweet, highly efficient—Monica stayed on her toes.* From the looks of things, as usual, her assistant had set up the conference room for the staff meeting sometime before she'd left the office on Friday. Copies of the meeting agenda had been placed on the long table in front of each high-back leather chair and cups of pencils and pens were within easy reach.

A quick glance to her left revealed a linen-covered table fully stocked with both regular and flavored tea bags, dry packets of creamer, sugar, various artificial sweeteners, plastic stirrers, regular-size napkins and foam cups.

Mini flavored liquid creamers were kept inside the office-size refrigerator, along with bottles of water and several kinds of regular and diet sodas. Single-serving-size juices, such as tomato, V8, cranberry, apple and orange were available, too, along with fresh lemon, lime and orange wedges.

Pretty sure the coffee station was ready for use, Courtney walked over to the built-in counter and pulled out the coffeemaker's filter tray, which was indeed filled with dark crystals. After filling the water well, she plugged in the electrical cord then pressed the red on button. Reaching into the cupboard above where the machine was located, she pulled out one of the black ceramic mugs adorned with the company's gold-embossed logo and waited for the coffee to brew. After pouring her java, she sauntered over to the conference table.

Just as she sat down, her cell rang. "You Are Not Alone" played and made her smile, inviting sentiment to well up in her heart.

As Courtney instantly recognized the voice on the other end, her eyes danced with light. "Good morning, Darius. How are you?"

"I couldn't be better. Sharing Sunday brunch with you, J.R. and Monica was a pleasure for me yesterday. Listen, Courtney, I need a big favor. Think you can go to a club with me on Thursday evening to hear a band? I'd really like your opinion on the group who call themselves Rest Assured."

Courtney chuckled. "I already like the catchy name. What time are you meeting them?"

"It's not an official meeting. I just plan to show up and listen. J.R. already has a gig booked on the event date. Eight or so is when I'd like to get to there. They go on at nine, but I always like time to unwind. They're performing at Club 21."

"My employees and I drop in there after work from time to time. Let me look at my calendar and get back to you."

Unprepared for the jagged disappointment sluicing through him, Darius winced. He was used to women telling him they were available at his beck and call, though it wasn't something he encouraged, desired or demanded. Courtney, on the other hand, made it seem as if she wasn't the least bit interested in him on a personal level—and he was more than bothered by that. She was a true enigma, and he actually liked that about her. Generally speaking, figuring out someone instantly wasn't very challenging or exciting to him.

Getting to know Courtney Campbell outside her corporate persona was a challenge Darius wished he could meet head-on. The lady was so intriguing that it was hard to keep his mind fixed on one of the finest engagement receptions he had to pull off.

Monica was the first employee to pop into the conference room. Dressed in pink designer jeans and a fashionable top in a dark shade of coral made her look cool and comfortable. She smiled as she rushed by Courtney, who was still on the phone, to claim her favorite seat at the table.

"Say, Darius, our staff meeting is about to start. I need to end this call. I promise to try to get back with you before the lunch hour is over. Is that okay?"

"It's fine. In fact, let's discuss the reception some more over lunch. I've been given a Web site for the band. I'll check it out and print the important criteria to bring along."

Sucking in a deep breath, Courtney mentally wrestled with her reluctance to accept Darius's invitation versus her desire to be near him. *It's only lunch. You do have to eat.* "Where would you like to meet for lunch?"

Deep regret assailed Courtney's common sense the same moment the words left her mouth. Being alone with this irresistible, engaged man was dangerous. The riotous feelings he evoked inside her should serve as a serious warning: *Danger dead ahead.*

"Roscoe's Chicken and Waffles on Gower and Sunset is the first place I thought of. If Monica is free, please invite her, too. She kept us laughing at brunch. I like both her and J.R. I get the feeling they're very genuine, down-to-earth people."

"You nailed that right! They're the most sincere people I've ever met. I'll share your invite with Monica and see if she can make it. Does twelve-thirty work?"

"Perfect. See you then."

Wanting to hear his last breath, Courtney kept the phone up to her ear until he'd clicked off. As she looked around the room, it appeared that almost everyone was present. There were a few staffers missing, mostly part-timers, but she expected them to skid into the room any minute now. Everyone knew tardiness was a major pet peeve of hers.

Courtney smiled brightly as Alma and Harrell Campbell came through the door. Her grandmother had said she wasn't sure if they'd make the meeting or not, but Courtney was pleased to see them. As her grandparents took seats, Courtney blew kisses their way, showing exactly how she felt about Grammy Alma and Papa Harrell. Love was written all over her face and it shone brightly in her eyes.

After demonstratively greeting her family members, Courtney made her way over to them, gave out warm hugs and planted kisses on their cheeks. Smiling with contentment, Courtney watched as Monica dashed around the room to get coffee for the elder Campbells, whom Monica loved as if they were her own kin. Once she filled the mugs, she came back to the table and handed the dark, hot liquid to Alma and Harrell. Monica then returned to the counter to pour a cup of coffee for herself.

Courtney walked over to the podium and opened her manila folder. Another quick glance around the room confirmed that everyone was present and accounted for.

"Good morning to all of you. It's nice to see your sunshiny smiles. The uplifting weekend zipped by us with the speed of lightning. Now we're here to share in our Monday morning blues session. Hopefully, we won't have any." As Courtney pulled a comical face, everyone laughed. Her sense of humor made the staff meetings fun.

"We'll discuss old business first and then go over the items we've yet to complete. I hope all of you have evaluated the events you've worked. Writing reports can be tedious, but it helps us pinpoint our strengths and identify weaknesses. Cheryl, let's start with you. How did the Bevins' twenty-fifth anniversary party go?"

Cheryl Dawson, an attractive, fair-skinned female, tall with a slender body, stood up and approached the podium. She was a genius with numbers. Everyone called on her after receiving a final head count for the events they worked on. She almost always suggested just the right amount of food items and beverages to order.

Cheryl smiled warmly. "The Bevins' event was a big success," she said into the microphone. "We know how hard it is to pull off surprise parties, but the family members in charge managed to keep the couple totally in the dark. No one could've faked their reactions. Everyone who responded to the RSVP showed up. We succeeded in all areas. The handling of the event received an A+, according to the feedback surveys."

The staff clapped in response to Cheryl's positive report as she sat back down.

Courtney moved back to the podium. "Congratulations on the hard work to Cheryl and her great team! We wish every event earned such high marks. An A+ is rare."

For the next hour, Courtney sat and listened to the other staff members' assessments of the events they had handled. Not a single one was a disaster, but neither were any as perfect as Cheryl's. There were several B grades and a couple of Cs. The staff discussed in depth things that had and hadn't run smoothly.

Taking thorough notes helped Courtney identify problem areas with an event, which gave her an opportunity to make improvements. Working out all the kinks was a job she relished and also paid very close attention to.

Courtney smoothed a hand down her white dress slacks before slipping back into the matching suit jacket. The lavender silk shirt was a great color to complement her complexion and it beautifully offset the white Evan Picone crepe pantsuit.

Standing in front of the mirrored dressing table, she refreshed her makeup and tended to her full lips, brushing on a clear gloss. Combing her hair back in place came next. Satisfied that she looked her very best, she left the bathroom and headed back to the front of the restaurant to wait for Darius. Monica had already made other plans for lunch and her grandparents had had to leave immediately after the meeting adjourned.

The moment Darius spotted Courtney he couldn't help smiling. She hadn't seen him yet, so that gave him a few seconds to indulge himself in a bit of girl-watching. He loved the outfit she had on and he also thought the lavender color complemented both the stark white material of her suit and her warm skin tone. He noticed that the lavender shoes she wore had low heels, as opposed to the stiletto styles a lot of women preferred. She walked with confidence; he noticed how high she held her head.

What was going on inside her mind was only one of many things he'd love to explore about her. *What made her tick? Who was the woman beneath the business persona? What would make her smile the brightest and bring her the most pleasure? What kind of man turned her on? What did Courtney Campbell want out of life and love?*

So many intriguing questions without answers. Darius vowed to find out everything about the mysterious Courtney. She seemed to have a lot going for her. It was important for him to know her every desire and what fueled them.

Settled in at a window booth the hostess had led them to, Courtney and Darius looked over menus while waiting for the waiter to appear. Both had eaten at Roscoe's Chicken and Waffles countless times, but they still perused the offerings closely.

"I think I'll just have a side order of wings. I'm not that hungry," Courtney said.

Darius glanced up and made eye contact with her. "I noticed at brunch you don't seem to eat much. Are you dieting?"

Courtney chuckled. "J.R. and you must've put your heads together on this subject. He also questioned what little I had on my plate, but I don't feel I undereat. I've certainly overdone it a number of times."

Darius laughed. "Who hasn't overdone it?"

"For the most part, I'm simply not a big eater," Courtney explained. "I also get full pretty quickly. The portions on my plate have nothing to do with dieting, though I do try to eat healthy. But when it comes to breakfast foods, I can eat like a horse."

Linda Hudson-Smith

"There's nothing wrong there. What about having a salad with your wings?"

Courtney shot him a cool glance. "I *had* planned to order a salad. Do you suggest what foods Candice should eat?" Courtney wanted to remind him that he had a fiancée to be concerned with. What Courtney ate or didn't eat shouldn't concern him one bit.

"Sorry if I hit a nerve. That wasn't my intent. To answer your question, I do concern myself with what Candice eats. She's a diabetic, who tends to ignore her health issues as if they don't exist. Her diabetes is a big concern for me. Unfortunately, I have the tendency to become overanxious, especially with folks I care about."

Slightly embarrassed by her odd behavior, Courtney bit down on her lower lip. "I'm sorry. I didn't know about Candice's health. I can see why you'd voice concern."

His eyes softened as he looked across the table at her. "I try not to call attention to what others eat, but sometimes I end up doing it anyway. It's only because I care."

"Point well taken," she said, hoping they'd move on and leave this topic in the dust. "Does anything on the menu have your palate worked up?"

"The chicken and waffles is my favorite dish. I always say I'm going to try something else, but I never do. I don't come here as often as I'd like, but that's by choice. Too much of anything isn't good for anyone. I'm hyper enough without all the syrup."

A male waiter arrived at the table just as Darius finished his remark. He quickly suggested that Courtney's order be taken care of first. Once the waiter had written down both of his patrons' meal choices, he left.

Darius pulled from his briefcase the information on the band he'd downloaded from his computer. He handed Courtney the paperwork. "I'd like you to look these over. I'm considering using this band for the reception if they're free on our May date."

Courtney took hold of the paperwork and laid it aside. "When you spoke about the band, I didn't know you intended to hire them for the reception. I thought when you went with the full-service catering package you were content to have us take care of the entertainment. Why the sudden change of heart?" she asked rather pointedly.

Darius wasn't sure, but he thought he'd heard a sharp edge in Courtney's tone. *Had he offended her? If so, he'd insulted her unwittingly.* "I'm still committed to the full-service contract. A friend just happened to tell me about this band…and I thought I'd check them out. It seems I've stepped on your toes, unintentionally so. *Because* of our contract, I actually wanted to see what you thought of this particular band."

Deep down inside, Courtney regretted her quick, testy reaction. It wasn't like her to speak before gathering all the facts. She hadn't meant to come off as churlish, either. It wasn't as if he hadn't already mentioned the band to her. She had misinterpreted his intent by thinking he'd planned to use them for another event that she wasn't handling for him. "Looks like I got it all wrong," she admitted. "Thank you for valuing my opinion. That means a lot to me."

"Does that mean you'll meet me on Thursday to check out these guys?"

Courtney grinned, impressed by how clear he made things. "You never miss an opportunity to go after what you want, do you? *Piranha* comes to mind on occasion."

Stunned by the remark, he raised an eyebrow. "Is that really how you see me?"

"Yes."

Darius was somewhat puzzled by her coolly spoken assessment. "I admit to going after what I want, but it's never at the expense of anyone else's feelings. I seize an opportunity when it presents itself, but there's nothing underhanded about my motives. And I'm definitely no killer fish."

This man had a way of keeping Courtney way off balance. He had just shattered the image of him she'd conjured in her mind. Still, there was the question of a fiancée he seemed to conveniently forget he had.

"Forgive me, Darius. I don't know why I keep trying to sum you up in a word or two and then lump you into one category or another. It's obvious that you're not an easy man to define. It's also apparent that you're every man and it's all within you."

Darius couldn't keep from laughing. "So now you're comparing me to the song 'I'm Every Woman.' Only *you* could've come up with that one! The fact you're even trying to define me is flattering. But I think you're delving way too deep. I'm very easy to explain. I'm not a mystery."

Like hell you aren't. Darius was a man of deep mystery. Courtney had a feeling he knew how to get exactly what he wanted. She also thought he knew how to keep whatever he was after once he got it. If he wasn't engaged, she'd love to be the woman he desired, the one he'd commit to forever.

Courtney hated being this delusional over a man. And any thoughts of him and her together were definite delusions. She was very clear on that. Willingly admitting that she was badly smitten wasn't easy for her.

The waiter arrived back at the table and served their meals. He then made sure the couple had everything they needed before taking off again.

Courtney and Darius ate in silence, each lost in thoughts of what lay ahead of them for the rest of the day and beyond. For some time, Courtney had been thinking about taking a week off work and disappearing to an island paradise. She knew she couldn't leave town until after the Fairfax reception was a wrap. She was very interested in the success of all her events, but she wanted to make Candice and Darius's reception the event of the year.

Courtney had a hard time deciding what to wear to Club 21 for her meeting with Darius. Before she met him, she hadn't given much thought to clothing choices. She had simply concentrated on a professional look for the office and dressy attire for special events; casual worked best when she was enjoying some rare leisure time.

Looking too sexy had suddenly become a worry for Courtney, so she traded the outfit she had finally decided on for something a lot less provocative.

What was the point in trying to entice a man who was taken?

A crisply creased pair of white denims, a cool red-and-white-striped top and a casual blazer in white brushed cotton replaced her sexier attire. She wasn't big on using a lot of makeup, but she'd used even less than normal for this evening outing. She didn't want to look like a plain Jane, yet she didn't want to make herself too attractive.

Despite Darius's marital status, he flirted openly with Courtney and it didn't seem to bother him in the least. Someone had to keep a level head in this deal. It would be too easy for her to give in to the strong desire she had to be in his arms, but thoughts of the beautiful Candice always reined in her emotions. She wasn't a man stealer or a home wrecker.

Sliding out from behind the wheel of her dark blue Lexus, Courtney handed the valet key to the attendant who'd opened her door. In turn, he gave her a numbered ticket to retrieve her car later.

As she stepped inside Club 21, Darius was the first person she saw. She liked that he was waiting for her to arrive. He came over to her and greeted her warmly, then directed her to a table he'd reserved for the evening.

Darius pulled out a chair for Courtney. "We have a perfect view of the bandstand from here. We won't miss a thing."

Courtney smiled. "You sure don't miss a beat. I like how you handle your business."

He grinned as he claimed a chair. "Honey, for me, this is as much pleasure as it is business. I'm seated with a great-looking woman and if the band delivers all I've heard about them, this should be one magnificent night."

For all the fuss she'd made to play down her looks, Courtney knew she had failed at dampening Darius's spirits. He seemed just as excited as he always did in her presence.

"What would you like to drink, Courtney?"

"I only drink wine, and sparingly. A glass of rosé, please."

Darius stood and then summoned a waitress. Courtney noticed that he was dressed more casually than she'd ever seen him and he still looked like a million bucks. The man wore his clothing as well as any male fashion model. Everything appeared to fit him to a tee. The dark sports coat worn over a soft pink, open-collar shirt made him look dashing, just as the dark designer jeans did.

Ladies might glance at Darius's expensive attire for a moment or two, but their eyes would no doubt linger on his handsome, clean-shaven face and sexy body. He was breathtaking in more ways than one. His intellect was also very stimulating to Courtney. They talked about anything and everything and she was impressed with how tuned in he was to current events. He also loved to talk politics.

Courtney's resolve weakened more and more every time she got together with Darius. She was glad the reception was close at hand. Once it was over, she'd never have to see him again. The thought pained her terribly, but their business would soon be concluded. If by chance he contracted her company to cater any other social events, she'd make sure to assign his account to another employee—anyone but herself.

After their wine was delivered to the table, the club manager enthusiastically introduced the band. Glad that she was no longer the main focus of Darius's attention, Courtney sat back in her chair, hoping she could relax. Being in his company kept her on pins and needles and she'd lost count of the number of times she'd wondered what it would be like to sample his luscious-looking mouth.

The first number the band played brought Courtney up out of her seat. There was no way to sit still when such soul-stirring sounds got her going. Forgetting she was in the company of a client, she let her hair all the way down, dancing and gyrating right in front of her seat. Her sexy movements sent Darius's imagination racing in a myriad of directions.

As a man who'd confessed to seizing an opportunity when one presented itself, Darius took hold of Courtney's hand and guided her onto the dance floor. There, in the middle of the room, he let the music seep into his soul and completely overtake him. The music was of the feel-good variety. All they had to do was open up their hearts to it and let it in.

Courtney noticed that she and Darius weren't the only ones who'd rushed to the dance floor. It appeared that practically everyone in the club was busy getting down. The music had the patrons in the groove and ready to rock away the entire night.

Feeling totally relaxed and at ease with Darius, Courtney danced like she'd never danced before. No longer was she afraid of her feelings for her dance partner. If nothing else, Darius would make a wonderful friend. She'd rather have him as a friend than not have him in her life at all. She didn't feel as if she were betraying Candice because that wasn't in her plans. She and Darius just happened to be two decent people with a lot in common.

Turning a wild attraction into a friendship wasn't a criminal act.

Who could fault them for being friends?

As the fast-paced music changed to a much slower pace, couples slipped into each other's arms. When Darius brought Courtney in closer to him, she didn't back away. He kept their bodies at an acceptable, respectable distance, but that didn't quell the fiery heat surging between them.

Friends slow-danced, too, Courtney told herself.

Darius came back to the table with the leader of the band and a couple of other band members. He immediately introduced the guys to Courtney and asked them to have a seat and join them for drinks on him. The band happily accepted his invitation.

Terry played guitar, his sleek style lathering up the dancers, causing them to act maniacal. Mitchell was a genius on the saxophone, playing as though his very life depended on the sounds coming from his instrument. Richard could wail on the drums, making them communicate beautifully with the soulful rhythms. The bass guitarist, Stephen, seemed to completely lose himself in the sweet chords he played so well. Every single guy in the band was a superb musician.

"You guys are really great! The music is so pure and sweet, yet funky and soulful," Darius said.

Terry nodded. "Yeah, it's always like a big party when we get together. We're truly blessed."

"I can see why," Courtney contributed. "I'm kind of shy when it comes to dancing, but you guys had me letting it all hang out before I even knew what had hit me. Do any of you know J. R. Norman?"

Everyone responded to J.R.'s name at the same time. It sounded to Courtney as if he were very much respected by his fellow musicians. They all had something positive to say about him. Terry even commented about how great Monica was, which had Courtney wondering why her friend had never mentioned this fabulous band to her.

Darius set his wineglass down. "Guys, I know you have to get back to the bandstand in a few minutes, but I'd like to know if you can possibly play at a surprise engagement reception."

Terry stroked his chin. "If it's a Friday or Saturday, we're more than likely booked already. Our weekend and holiday dates fill up rather quickly. Spring and summer months are rough, too."

"Can you check it out during the next break and let me know?" Darius asked.

Terry nodded in the affirmative.

"We'll never land them, at least not for the upcoming event," Darius said to her after the band left the table. "How difficult would it be to change the event to a late-afternoon affair to accommodate their schedule?"

"The invitations aren't printed yet, so that shouldn't be a problem. I might have to rework the staff schedules. All of my top coordinators are assigned to your reception. While everyone on my staff is great at what they do, there are those who've been with me a long time. These employees know exactly what my expectations are. Like you, I doubt the band will be free, but it never hurts to hope and pray for a miracle."

The urge to take Courtney into his arms and kiss her passionately nearly overcame Darius. This woman had him on fire and there was nothing he could use to douse the flames.

Courtney was glad that the atmosphere was dim. She hoped the soft, subtle candlelight concealed the blush she felt burning on her cheeks. If Darius could look into her eyes, he'd easily see how smitten she was with him. If only she were walking in Candice's shoes. She had an idea of how wonderful that might feel. Darius was always very attentive to her and he was sweeter than the purest honey.

"Courtney," Darius softly whispered her name, "I'll be back in a couple of minutes. Will you be okay out here alone?"

"I'll be fine, Darius. Thank you."

"You're welcome." He got to his feet and walked toward the men's room, looking back at her with every few steps he took.

Courtney suddenly had a numbing, cold feeling surrounding her. She always felt overly warm when Darius was around. He'd already had a profound effect on her. She tried to force her mind into thinking of him as nothing more than a friend, but her heart wouldn't cooperate. It was as if her mind, body and soul had all turned against her. She looked over at the exit. If only she had the nerve to get up and leave. A disappearing act would more than likely lose her a client, but it would surely save her virtue.

Wasn't that better than losing her heart to someone who was unable to accept it?

Outside of Club 21, Darius took Courtney's car keys from the attendant's hand and then opened her door. "Thanks for meeting me here this evening. I hope you had as good a time as I did. That band is something else. I haven't heard music played so well in a long time."

"Yeah, it was just great. They took us back to the days of our parents' music, but I couldn't even identify where all the sounds came from. There was a time it sounded like someone was whistling across the top of a soda bottle."

Darius laughed. "You picked that up, too, I see."

Courtney reached for Darius's hand. She started to shake it, but instead, she lifted it up to her mouth and planted a light kiss on the back of it. "Thanks for a beautiful evening. Drive safely. Good night."

Darius's words had been ambushed before they got stuck in his craw. Saying something clever would've been nice, but his brain wasn't coherent at the moment. The kiss to his hand had completely stunned him, giving him an inkling of what might've happened had she kissed him on the mouth. The silly notion to never wash his hand crossed his numbed mind. No kiss had ever affected him the way Courtney's had, a kiss lighter than a whisper.

As Courtney's car drove away, Darius stood stock-still for several seconds. When he moved toward his car, a snail could've bested him had it been a race. In less than two months, he had nearly become a fool over a woman. He shook his head to try to clear the cobwebs from his mind. He shouldn't be thinking this way, but he had to find a way to keep their relationship from coming to an abrupt end on the third Saturday in May.

If friendship was all they could have, so be it.

Chapter 4

Courtney and Monica hustled around the office, making sure everything was shut down and locked up for the evening. Courtney still had to stash in the floor safe the checks and cash she and Monica had just tallied. The company used spreadsheets and generated receipts electronically, but every now and then a handwritten receipt was given out for anything under fifty dollars.

A bank run was only made once a week, normally on Friday afternoons. The Wells Fargo Bank branch the company patronized was located just a few doors down from the office. Courtney, Harrell, Alma and Monica were the only ones authorized to handle bank and credit union transactions. Courtney and her grandmother wrote and signed all company checks, while monitoring all incoming and outgoing expenditures.

"Too many fingers in the pie could ruin it" was a motto both of them swore by.

Courtney looked at her watch. They had less than an hour to make it to a special meeting Darius had set up. J.R. had been invited, too. According to what Darius had told Courtney, he wanted her and her friends to meet a man he was keen on doing future business deals with. He'd also said he had a proposition involving Courtney's company, which he planned to discuss during the meeting. Darius led her to believe this was an extremely important get-together.

"He didn't give you any clue as to what this meeting was about?" Monica asked Courtney while shutting down her computer.

"Just that it was important. I hope it's something good for the company. I can't get involved with just anything…and Darius is nothing less than extraordinary as a businessman. He has incredible visions for his company. If he wants to involve The Party People in something he's doing, I'm willing to see if I can get behind his ideas."

"Girl, you're just too savvy. Remember all those negative remarks about your visions? You certainly proved those naysayers wrong—and you did it in record time. Just think how far you've come this past year."

Courtney nodded. "It's also hard for me to believe. I often think about all the bank managers who turned me down for a small business loan. Thank God for federal credit unions. If Papa Harrell hadn't been a military veteran, I couldn't have landed a loan there, either."

"You had strong, brilliant visions for the business and you already know I think your grandparents are the best visionaries around. They're good to you and for you. As your employee and your friend, I get to cash in on the benefits, too. I love all three of you."

Courtney smiled. "I know how you feel about us. They do, too." She frowned. "Do I look okay?"

"You look beautiful, as always. For a girl who hardly ever worries about her attire, you sure have been overly concerned about it lately. What's that all about?"

Courtney rolled her eyes back. "I just asked a simple question about my appearance."

Monica gave her boss a slanted glance. "Your tan pantsuit hardly has that 'off the rack' look. The spicy-orange shell brings in just the right amount of color, along with the complementary juicy-fruit-orange leather pumps and bag. You're a fresh breath of spring, looking as if you're ready to get down to business. The simple but elegant diamond pendant and studs add more sparkle to the glow of your skin and personality. There!"

"Thank you." Courtney smiled softly. "Your kind but rather long assessment of my outfit put me at ease. I know I've been out of it lately. I'm almost ashamed to admit it. Looking good for an engaged man is absolutely insane. Yet, when I'm dressing, I often wonder what Darius would think of this dress or that suit."

"You and I both know that's pitiful. You know exactly who you are, therefore the clothes you wear highlight your personality and spirit just right. Enough said?"

"Enough said," Courtney echoed, "especially if we plan to get out of here to be on time for the meeting. I'll secure the safe and be ready to go in a couple of minutes."

"Sounds good to me. I'm going to hit the ladies' room and freshen up my makeup. I also need to call J.R. back."

"He probably just wanted to remind you about the meeting," Courtney offered.

"You're probably right. He's excited about discussing business with Darius."

"I'm trying not to let it get to me. Excitement or dread, we'll know after we find out what Darius has in mind."

Jasmine smiled. "Welcome to D.F. Film Productions, Inc," she said to Monica and J.R. "It is nice to see you again, Miss Campbell. I'm glad you found time to take this last-minute meeting. Darius was really pleased all of you could make it. Have a seat. I'll let him know you folks are here. Can I get any of you something to drink?"

All heads shook in the negative, followed up by a *No, thank you* from each of them.

"Okay, then." Jasmine didn't push the issue. Darius already had her phone in a nice-size spread from one of his favorite nearby eateries, Jacoby's Deli.

"Please feel free to have a seat. Make yourselves at home. Mr. Fairfax will be with you shortly."

Darius looked up at Meyer Chandler, CEO of See-Through Films. "The rest of the group has arrived. Do you have anything else you want to say before we convene in one of the conference rooms?"

Meyer shook his head. "I'm sure I'll have more queries after the next segment of our meeting."

"In that case, please come with me."

Darius got up from the table and walked to his office door with Meyer following along behind him. Darius opened the door and gestured for his guest to precede him. As he made his way to the reception area, he actually felt a little nervous. Knowing he'd soon see the lovely Courtney Campbell caused him to brace himself for the impact sure to come. Her mere presence hadn't failed to level him yet.

Smiling warmly, J.R. got to his feet, meeting Darius in the middle of the room. "Great seeing you again, man, but I didn't know it'd be this soon. Both Monica and I were surprised by your invitation. We're eager to hear what you have to say."

Darius chuckled. "And I'm eager to say it." He turned to face Courtney and Monica. "Ladies, I'm glad to see you. You're both looking lovely." Briefly, he laid his hand on Meyer's back. "This gentleman is Meyer Chandler from See-Through Films." Darius introduced Meyer to everyone, giving his guests' first and surnames.

Meyer smiled at Courtney and shook Monica's and J.R.'s hands, his grip firm.

"Now that everyone's been introduced, let's go down this hallway and get settled into the conference room." Darius looked back at Jasmine. "Please have drinks brought in right away. About forty-five minutes from now, you can have the food delivered."

"As you wish, boss," Jasmine said, her tone soft and melodic.

Darius ushered his guests down a long corridor and into a well-appointed conference room equipped with the latest in office furnishings and state-of-the-art electronics. A fifty-six-inch Kuro plasma television was mounted on one wall.

Rushing around the table, Darius pulled out two high-back leather chairs for the ladies. Once everyone was comfortably seated, Jasmine rolled a portable serving cart into the room, loaded with all sorts of soft drinks, juices and a clear ice bucket. She pushed the cart to the rear. Smiling brightly then backing out, she nodded before closing the door behind her.

Darius folded his hands and set them on top of the table. "First I want to thank each of you for working your schedules around this last-minute meeting. I'm so happy you could attend. Everyone here knows I'm a filmmaker. I'm currently working on a few special projects that Meyer and I are collaborating on. Both our production companies are fairly new, and it's our intention to pool our resources and begin producing under one umbrella. Have I grabbed everyone's attention so far?"

Eager to hear what might come next, they all nodded.

"I'm actually writing a romantic screenplay," Darius continued. "The story line focuses on weddings, specifically June brides. We're considering several distinctive ceremonies." Darius paused to gauge the responses. Since no one appeared to be on the verge of cardiac arrest, he continued, his eyes directly connecting with Courtney's. "Your catering business will figure heavily into this romantic story line."

Meyer's gaze drew in Monica and J.R. "Monica, from what Darius has said about your role in Courtney's company, we're looking at both you and your boss to consult on the catering and wedding planning portion of the script. J.R., we're interested in having you score all original music. And we hope to get Rest Assured involved, as well."

"However, you'll be *the man,* the point man, the leader who answers to us," Darius said to J.R. "While we'd like a variety of artists to perform songs on the movie sound track, we want you in charge of music development. Of course, there are still a lot of issues for us to discuss and resolve, but I think we can come together on this."

Darius had paid J.R. one of the highest professional compliments he'd ever received—and the look on his face showed he was ecstatic over it. "I feel confident we can do it," J.R. said, beaming. "This is a dream come true for me."

"With Meyer and me combining our resources in this venture, we'll have more than enough funds to handle a project of this scope. You will not be working for free. All salaries will be figured into the budget, along with everything else we'll need to handle in a job of this magnitude. The contracts will be negotiated and renegotiated until we are all on the same page. That I can promise," Darius assured everyone.

Courtney's heart felt like it was doing jumping jacks. All she could do was stare openly at the two up-and-coming movie moguls. What they'd said so far had already piqued her interest tremendously.

Darius looked happy and relieved to have gotten his ideas out in the open. "The floor is now open for discussion. I'm anxious to hear your opinions on the project. All constructive criticisms and comments are welcome. However, I don't handle negativity very well."

Excited about all the information Darius had related, Courtney shifted around in her seat anxiously. "Can you explain in a little more detail where my company fits into all this?"

Darius smiled. "My plan for your business is twofold. First of all, your operation will be the one we'll use as the model for the catering company in the story line. Second, if you're willing, we'd love for you to provide the catering services—meals, snacks and drinks for the cast and crew while we're shooting the film—if we can agree on the terms."

Not only would Courtney agree to sign on herself and her company to these remarkable ideas, she was sure that every red cent these corporations invested in her catering business would get a two hundred percent return in services.

Courtney Campbell was a winner and she'd lend that winning spirit to whatever job she took on. Her heart and soul would be poured into this project. "I'm intrigued with the entire idea. In fact, I can actually imagine a story with a bevy of June brides."

Maybe I can create beautiful, fairy-tale visions, just like the ones I've dreamed of for my own wedding day. Yeah, right! Like that's ever going to happen. Courtney had mentally staged her wedding day countless times. But she first had to have a man fall in love with her and propose marriage before she could bring to life her vivid mental images.

Monica placed her hand over her husband's, her heart bursting with pride. "J.R. composes the most beautiful songs. We've also written dozens of love ballads together. I think you're making an extremely wise choice in using J.R. for this project. He'll do you proud. You can count on him to give it everything he has."

Admiring the deep love he saw in Monica's eyes for her spouse, Darius smiled at her. She hadn't said a thing about how she'd fit into the plans. She was selfless, he thought. It seemed that as long as her J.R. was okay, she was absolutely fine. "There's no doubt in my mind about J.R.'s creativity and his ability to handle the job we've tapped him for. Out of all the people I'd considered for this position, he was the first person I thought of. Once I heard him play with his band, I knew."

Shocked by Darius's last remarks, Monica eyed J.R. wryly. "You never told me he came to hear you play. Why not?"

"I didn't know." J.R. shrugged. "Just like you, I'm hearing that for the first time. Where'd you see me play?" J.R. asked Darius.

"The lounge at the Roosevelt Hotel. I was absolutely amazed at your sound. You're a brilliant drummer."

His eyes widened with disbelief, and J.R. looked at Darius as if he'd never seen him before. "I had no idea you were there."

"Well, the pleasure was all mine!" Darius looked over at Monica. "As for your roles, I've thought of you co-owning the business with Courtney. Since you are her right-hand assistant and one of her dearest friends, joint ownership is a perfect fit for the story line. Like everything else, there are a lot of details for us to iron out."

Courtney looked puzzled. "When you're talking about the roles, you *are* talking about using real actors, aren't you?"

Darius snickered. "Do you honestly believe there's somebody out in the world who can play you two ladies better than you can play yourselves?"

Monica's mouth dropped open. "Are you talking about us acting in the film?"

Hunching his shoulders, Darius turned up his palms. "Why not? I like working with new actors, as well as with veterans. All I'm asking is that you do what you do every day at work and at play. Do you think you can't handle it?"

Laughing softly, Monica fluffed her hair and pursed her lips provocatively. "I know exactly how to do *diva!* Oh, this is so exciting!" Monica did everything but jump up and down on the chair she could barely sit still in.

Wanting to hear Courtney's opinion more than anyone else's, Darius glanced at her. "What about you? Think you can portray yourself on the big screen?"

"I'd love to play myself or coach another woman to play me. I've never dreamed of acting."

"My money is on you playing yourself, which has little to do with acting, Courtney. I'm confident that you'll bring something to the silver screen that's never before seen," Darius said. "You and Monica will make a dynamic duo."

Monica blew Courtney a kiss. "For someone who's just met us, Darius seems to know us so well. We are dynamic, together and apart. I love you, Courtney."

"Love you, too, Monica."

The meeting was interrupted when Jasmine and two young men came into the conference room. Platters of deli sandwiches, salads, chips and other accompaniments were set down on a buffet-style table aligned with the back wall.

"Why don't we get our food and bring it back to the table. I promise not to talk with my mouth full," Darius joked, laughing.

Instead of resuming the lively topic they'd been discussing, Darius kept quiet, content to wait until everyone had finished eating. He discreetly stole glances at Courtney every chance he got. When she talked, he listened intently to every word she said. He saw how solid the friendship was between her and Monica. The two women touched each other often, either by simply pushing back a strand of loose hair or briefly joining hands. They exuded respect and love for each other.

Courtney waited for Darius to return to the conference room. After adjourning the meeting, he'd asked her to stay on so he could talk to her about the engagement party. Since she had ridden there with Monica, she'd mentioned calling a cab to get home. That was when he'd insisted on driving her. Promising to get right back to her, he'd left the conference room to escort the others to the reception area.

Reaching into her briefcase, Courtney pulled out the file on the Fairfax event. She quickly scanned her notes. Everything was right on schedule. Unless Darius wanted to change something, she had everything under control. She did need to ask him about the invitations he was designing. They should go into the mail at least ten days before the surprise reception. Courtney looked up when Darius reentered the room, butterflies fluttering throughout her stomach.

Darius sat down. "I want to go over the plans for the reception, but I first want to know what you really think of the movie idea. Your expressions were hard to read when we discussed it as a group. Is there something you'd like to add?"

Courtney was surprised by his remark, thinking she had shown plenty of enthusiasm over his announcement. "I have nothing to add. I think it's a brilliant idea. I'm excited about it and I love how you've worked my catering business into the story line, not to mention hiring us to handle the catering on the set. You already know how Monica and J.R. feel about it. I can't wait for the project to begin. In the meantime, it won't be long before we'll finish up your event."

"I'm looking forward to that day. I can hardly wait to see Candice's face. She's excited easily, so this surprise will be over the top for her. Thanks for the fine job you've done thus far. I'm confident that everything will run smoothly."

"That it will. Everything is right on schedule. However, I'd like to know if you've come up with the final design for the invitations."

"The design is done. The invitations will go in the mail as soon as the printer delivers them, in plenty of time. The mailing labels are printed already."

"Good. Glad you're on top of the invitations."

He grinned. "On top of it, huh? Exciting choice of words!"

Blushing, Courtney found it hard to meet Darius's eyes. She'd like nothing better than to have him on top, but that'd have to happen in a different lifetime.

Courtney handed Darius her checklist for his event. "The list will tell you where we've we been and where we have to go.

Nearly everything is done. As for the bride's parents, you haven't mentioned them. Are they aware of the event?"

"Yes, most everyone is."

Darius fell mum as he looked over the list, reading all the notes Courtney had written down in detail. Her handwriting was beautiful, very legible. He liked how thorough she was.

Darius smiled. "Just when I think I can't be any more impressed by you, you prove me wrong. Your work ethics are remarkable. You should teach a class on how to run a business. Your communication skills are impeccable. Working with you on this film will be an experience I'll never forget. I already feel it."

Courtney's eyes softened, filling with moisture. "Thank you." She didn't dare say another word, not as choked up as she felt.

Darius consulted the clock on the wall. "It's getting late. Let me get you home. I'm sure you're ready to take a long soak or a steaming hot shower so you can relax."

And, oh, how I'd love you to journey there with me. Courtney gathered the papers she'd removed from her briefcase and slid them back in place. She got to her feet. "I'm ready to go home if you're ready to go."

Courtney was more nervous than she'd ever been when she was alone with a man. Darius had asked to come inside and check out her recently purchased home, claiming he also had a keen eye for interior decorating. *Was this man's list of credentials endless or what?* She had a feeling he'd be tops at whatever job he tackled. He was so astute.

She disabled the alarm. "Let's start here in the marble foyer and work our way to the back of the house." She opened a hall closet to her left and set her briefcase inside.

Darius's eyes drank in every inch of the Italian marble foyer designed and fashioned in a variety of rich earth tones in a striking diamond pattern. The vast amount of space was large enough for a decent-size table and a single chair nesting on each side. Surprised by the lack of furniture, his mind went to work filling in the empty spaces.

He gave her a puzzled look. "Why so bare?"

Courtney shrugged. "No time to shop for the things I want. I'm very particular. I've looked up furnishings on the Internet to get an idea of what to do with this much space. Visiting a few quality furniture stores might really help me get a feel for things."

"Have you ever heard of Buy Direct? I'm a member. If you don't mind, I'd love to take you to a showroom. There's one in Sherman Oaks. What's your weekend schedule like?"

"I only have one event, a baby shower at noon tomorrow. Hallelujah! We have a retirement dinner at 7:00 p.m., but Monica and other staffers are covering it."

"How long do you expect the baby shower to last?"

"It'll probably run about two hours. According to the hostess's wishes, the food will be served first. That's all we have to take care of. We should be out of there by 2:00 p.m.—possibly earlier."

Knowing he should carefully word the request he had in mind, Darius stroked his chin thoughtfully. "Where should I pick you up?"

Courtney failed to hide her surprise. Although he'd asked a lot about her schedule, she hadn't expected him to make her shopping needs a priority. "You don't have to do that. I can look up the warehouse online."

"You won't be as impressed. Let's settle on visiting the warehouse around three-thirty. Is that cool?"

Oh, no, Courtney thought, groaning inwardly. She couldn't keep putting herself in the lion's den. Darius's offer was a kind one and she did need to furnish her house, but she was concerned about spending more time with him than was necessary. She wondered how she'd handle working on a film with him. They'd be thrown together day after day and for hours on end.

Yeah, but other people will be present; safety in numbers.

She sighed in concession. "Okay, you win. What if I just meet you there?"

Darius shook his head. "I hope you don't see us as at odds. This offer wasn't made for one of us to win or lose. I'd rather pick you up. Now that I know where you live, it's not a big deal. My condo is not too far from here."

"Three-thirty," she happily conceded, mentally admitting how much she liked spending time with Darius. He certainly was an interesting specimen. Besides, her fascination with him would end when the vows were taken.

Darius smiled. "Now that we have that settled, I'd love to continue the tour of your charming digs. I already suspect this palatial home has strong character."

"Loads of character, Darius. Every nook and cranny was thoughtfully crafted by the architect. That's why it's so important to me to fill it with signatures of grandeur."

Darius nodded. "Powerful notion, one I believe you'll convey in a telling way."

Strolling leisurely, Courtney guided Darius from the foyer and into the formal areas. Separated by an impressive archway, with intricate etchings in gilded frames, the living and dining rooms were gracefully spacious.

"These two rooms are so elegant." Darius mentally measured the breadth and length of the space. "I'm already imagining the tones I'd use. I'm a lover of color but various shades of whites or lightly tinted beiges in antique satins or brocaded materials are what I envision for the sofas and dining room chairs. Gold or silver accents could be used as a counterbalance."

"Interesting concept." *You have no idea how interesting.* "The colors alone speak to character. I've been thinking of pulling up all the carpets and installing hardwood flooring in both formals. Spills would be easier to take care of on hardwood."

"You'll have to come see my place. You can get a lot of good tips and ideas from my decor. I had the same thoughts about carpet versus hardwood. I went with top-of-the-line marble tile for my formals. It's even easier to care for than ceramic tile."

"Hmm, I think I'll look into marble. I love my foyer. All I have to do is run a dust mop over it and then a wet sponge mop to take care of it. I hate vacuuming."

He grinned. "You don't have a housekeeper?"

"My company is doing well, but with no furniture in the house, other than in the master suite, how would I justify hiring a housekeeper on a weekly or monthly basis?"

"I love having a housekeeper, but I see what you mean."

Courtney took Darius outside where the pool and Jacuzzi were located. The patio had piped-in music and was designed with

Promises to Keep

white pillars on all four corners. An abundance of tiny blue-and-white lights had been strung around the patio areas and on the trees.

The pool was obviously well-maintained. The aquamarine waters were sparkling and the Jacuzzi was nice and clean, with not a single leaf in sight. He quickly shut off the vivid image of himself and Courtney naked in the Jacuzzi. He couldn't allow himself to go there, not with the project they were about to embark on. Who would ever have thought he'd become so intrigued with the woman he'd hired to handle his catering? Beyond intrigued, he thought. She had him going on all cylinders. Perhaps he had some serious reconsidering to do. Time was of the essence.

Smiles came so easily to Courtney when she was with Darius. His mind worked very much like hers. She had already decided on the very same colors he'd mentioned for the formal areas. It was as if she'd somehow received an important vote of confidence on her decision.

Courtney definitely believed in divine intervention. Maybe God had put Darius in her life to fulfill certain purposes. No two paths were ever crossed without rhyme or reason. You might not know why folks were in your life at first, but you'd eventually discover and learn the lessons someone dropped in to teach.

Courtney hoped she wasn't just making excuses to be in Darius's company, especially on occasions when it had nothing to do with their contract. He also had big plans for her company. It was already on the map and she knew the areas of service could always be widened. One office in one city was fine for now, but she had dreamt of her company becoming known statewide. She used to think it was a bit grandiose on her part, until she reminded herself of the same businesses launched in cities in all fifty states.

Southern California today with tomorrow always on the horizon.

"Can I trouble you for a cup of coffee before I leave? That is, if you have time."

"Come on in the kitchen. I don't drink coffee in the evening, but I could sure use a glass of chilled juice."

"Maybe I'll join you in what you're having."

Darius followed Courtney back through the French doors, from where they'd entered the patio area. A little more time in her company was pleasing to him, more than it should be. He was certainly grateful that she hadn't rejected his idea to stay longer.

Chapter 5

Monica checked out Courtney from head to toe, telling her to turn around and show herself off. "You are stunning! Your filmy dress is hot enough to set a man on fire. I love how beautiful you look in mint-green. Girl, I've already seen several fabulous-looking men checking you out. Maybe you'll find a good man tonight—the right man."

Courtney raised an eyebrow. "I don't know of a single hard body that's lost on me."

Monica laughed heartily. "That quick-on-the-draw, sarcastic tongue of yours never sleeps, does it? It would have been something to reckon with in the wild wild West."

Laughing, Courtney slipped her arm around Monica's waist. "Is it sarcasm or sharp wit?" She hugged her friend. "Did J.R. get a chance to see you in this fabulous peaches-and-cream fashion statement?"

"Yes, for a hot minute." As she'd insisted from Courtney, Monica twirled around and around, ending her twirl with an off-balance curtsy. "Oops," she yelped. "You almost had to pick me up off the floor. Wouldn't that be a frightening sight?"

"Only if your butt had hit the floor with a thud," Courtney joked.

With her eyes nearly bulging out of her head, Monica bumped Courtney with her shoulder. "Look who just walked in. Take in all that sweet, delicious-looking eye candy, will you? I wonder who the other guy is. He's almost as fine as Darius Fairfax."

Courtney took her eyes off Darius long enough to see who was with him. "Since we're working for the gorgeous Mr. Fairfax, I'm sure we'll be introduced to his strikingly handsome buddy. He's definitely eye candy, too, if you ask me. Maybe the good man you mentioned being lost has just been found."

"I'm feeling you. Girl, you need to go for him. He's sexy and gorgeous! Just hope he's single and available," Monica said, finding it hard to take her eyes off Darius's friend. "That one must hit the gym a couple of times a day. Look at his chiseled body!"

"I see it. I'm not blind, girlfriend. He *is* a super hottie," Courtney marveled.

Darius's eyes suddenly zeroed in on the lovely Courtney.

Lord, please help me. She is the most beautiful woman I've ever seen and she's definitely styling and profiling that pretty, ultrafeminine dress. He loved the soft color.

Darius slowly walked over to where Courtney stood with Monica. He'd never wanted any woman as much as he desired the beauty in pastel-green. Unfortunately, the feeling was anything but mutual, yet she'd become a part of his every thought, a part of the world he moved around in.

How did she get in his blood so easily? And how would he get to her? With all that was happening in his life, his feelings for her were quite scary. *He had no right to feel this way. One commitment in his life, his business, was more than enough.*

The butterflies in Courtney's stomach were going bananas with longing. The closer Darius got to her, the more her belly fluttered. He was quite dashing in a traditional tuxedo, looking like a sexy model gliding down a runway.

Should any one man be allowed to possess so many wonderful attributes?

This one had both worldly and sex appeal. If only Candice weren't in the picture, Courtney thought, wishing she didn't dread meeting the woman of his dreams.

The manly scent Darius wore wafted beneath Courtney's nose. As he leaned in to kiss her cheek, she wished he was aiming for her mouth. She could only imagine what his kiss would do to her, something she thought of way too often. "Darius," she said lowly, "it's your big night. I hope everything goes the way we planned. Along with you, the entire staff wants Candice to be thrilled. When will she arrive?"

"In a few minutes. I plan to go out and meet her to escort her inside. I want the lights out and then turned back on the moment we walk through the door. I'm feeling like a kid in a candy store. I can't wait to see her beautiful face when she sees all of her relatives, friends and colleagues in one place, not to mention the fascinating decorations and the wonderful foods yet to be served. You and your staff have done a superb decorating job. The place looks like a fairy tale!" He looked down at his watch.

Courtney knew this was the last time she'd be alone with Darius—and it saddened her. No more lunches, dinners or late-evening meetings for them. It would all come to an abrupt end tonight. Darius would have the perfect surprise engagement party and Candice would have the man Courtney pined for, the man she wished could be all hers.

"I'd better get out to the elevators. I hope you'll save a dance for me. We both know how good the band is."

Darius leaned in and kissed Courtney again. This kiss was right at the corner of her mouth. The desire to turn her head and capture his mouth was much more than she could stand to think of. Never would she be so bold to engage him in a passionate kiss, but her thoughts and dreams could be as daring and heated as she desired.

Her excitement over such an innocent display of affection from Darius let Courtney know she'd done the right thing. It had been an issue for her ever since she'd made an important decision. What she'd thought she should do had just been confirmed for her. If a slight kiss like the one Darius had given her could excite every part of her physical and spiritual makeup, then she had behaved wisely.

Inside her suite at the Renaissance Hotel, located only blocks from the hotel where the reception was held, her bags were packed for an entire week of vacation. She was tired and bone weary of dodging her strong feelings for someone else's man. She had a reservation on the earliest morning flight to Hawaii. At 7:00 a.m. she should be flying through the air, heading for the colorful paradise she'd thoroughly researched.

Courtney's grandparents and Monica were the only ones who knew about her plans. All three were happy for her, feeling she deserved a week off to relax and have some fun. Monica had tried to get her boss to take two weeks off, but it would be a miracle if she didn't end up canceling her vacation plans altogether.

As Courtney watched Darius disappear from the room, she sighed, feeling a plethora of mixed emotions. When he walked back into the ballroom, he'd have his fiancée on his arm. It also meant he'd announce his deep love for Candice to everyone present, including her. No longer could she deny the reality of Darius's future with Candice. The deal would be signed, sealed and delivered before evening's end.

Tears unexpectedly welled up in Courtney's eyes. Surprised that she was this emotional, she looked around the room through blurred vision. Regardless of how high her emotions ran, she was proud of what she and her employees had orchestrated to near perfection. Everything was in place, as it should be, just as it had been planned out.

Courtney was proud of everyone employed at The Party People.

The five-tiered cake, adorned with cherubs, sugar roses and ribbons, frosted with butter-cream icing, was in the center of a beautifully decorated table. A silver fountain, flowing with liquid gold, represented the finest sparkling cider money could buy.

Formally dressed waiters and waitresses worked every inch of the large room, carrying around silver platters of appetizers to offer the guests. Decorated with handcrafted angels, candles and flowers, linen-dressed tables with lavender organza-covered chairs were all set for the time when hot entrées were later served.

Under normal circumstances, Courtney stayed to the end of an event. But this one was too painful for her. She didn't want to see Darius with Candice or hear him profess his love for her in a room full of people they were close to.

Courtney knew Monica would understand if she slipped out before the party was over. She wouldn't be lying if she said she didn't feel well. Not only did her heart hurt, it felt as if it were shattering like glass.

Courtney silently admitted that she was madly in love with Darius Fairfax—and she had fallen rather quickly. If it wasn't the first time she'd laid eyes upon him, it was their second or third encounter. It really didn't matter. She was in love with a man who'd never love her back, a man she'd never have and hold until death parted them.

Before Courtney could find Monica to tell her she was leaving, the lights flickered off. It was too late to make a quick getaway. Soft lighting would further romanticize the room in another few seconds. Hell on earth would arrive with her in attendance. Nearly blinded by her tears, Courtney made a mad scramble for a dark corner closest to the exit.

As soon as Darius and Candice came in, Courtney planned to discreetly slip out. No one could make her stay and hear the words she knew would tear her heart to shreds. *Why me?* She figured she wasn't the only one whose heart had been unwittingly broken under similar circumstances, but she wished hers wasn't counted among the statistics.

Courtney couldn't blame Darius for what she was going through. Though he had flirted with her, kindling her desire for him, there was never any doubt that he was about to be married. After all, he'd hired her company to cater this special lovefest.

The lights came up and Courtney rapidly swiped away her tears. Making her face a mask of happiness despite her sad heart, she managed to put on one of the brightest smiles she had. All the while, she slowly inched toward the exit, making it a point not to look over at the happy couple. That was one picture she didn't want in her memory bank.

Darius held on to Candice's hand. "Welcome family, friends and colleagues. I proudly present to you my adorable baby sister, my only sibling, Candice Fairfax, and her wonderful fiancé, Roderick Kelly, M.D. Congratulations to Candice and Roderick on their recent engagement. Eat, drink and be merry. Have fun dancing the night away. This is a special time as the happy couple celebrate their unconditional love!"

Stunned by what she thought she'd heard, Courtney opened her eyes just in time to see Darius take Candice into his arms, hugging and kissing her like she was a piece of fragile china he was afraid he might break. The love he felt for her could not be denied. He loved her as a sister; not as the woman he planned to spend the rest of his life with.

Blinking eyes wide with bewilderment, Courtney went over in her mind what she'd just seen and *had* heard Darius say. The idea of Candice as his sister had never crossed her mind—and he'd never spoken of a kinship bond. No one else in her employment had mentioned it, either, so she was sure nobody had known.

Why, why hadn't Darius made his relationship with Candice clear to her from the start? This was strange; strange but oh, so wonderful.

Courtney's heart cried out joyously. Darius wasn't engaged to be married and Candice was betrothed to Roderick Kelly, whom Courtney had never seen until she'd spotted him coming through the door with Darius. The man Monica pegged as being lost was anything but unclaimed.

This man and woman had found in each other the partners of their dreams.

Monica came over to Courtney and pulled her aside. "Did you hear all that? Darius *isn't* engaged. Why do you think he didn't tell us?"

Courtney shrugged. "I don't know, but I'm wondering about it. My heart rejoiced at his comments…but now I'm not sure how I should react to the news. This sister doesn't know what to think."

What was behind Darius's reasoning? Was he just another

game-playing brother? Courtney would've really liked to know the truth of the matter.

Monica gave Courtney a warm hug. "Well, we can't sue him for not telling us his personal history. I thought you'd be so happy that he's not engaged."

Darius looked all around for Courtney, wondering where she was. Spotting Monica, he rushed over to her. "Hey, friend, where's the other angel who waved her magic wand over this event? I couldn't be any happier with what all of you have done."

Monica politely thanked him for the compliment. "She's busy making sure everything is running smoothly. That's what you hired our hardworking Courtney to do."

"Everyone who had a hand in this reception worked very hard," he said, bursting with praise.

Monica couldn't help smiling at the charming Darius. She thought his decision not to say Candice was his sister was a little weird, but who was she to judge him? He might have had good reasons for keeping his blood relationship with her a secret. Her boss hadn't said anything negative, yet Monica had clearly seen that she didn't know how to react to the personal information he'd withheld.

"There she is now," Darius said. "I need to tell Courtney once again how much I appreciate her work. I'd recommend your company in a heartbeat. Thanks, Monica. You're one of the jewels set in the extraordinary crown of this amazing catering business. I'll see you later."

"Okay, Darius. I'm thrilled that you're pleased. J.R. is sorry he had a gig tonight."

"He called me earlier with his regrets. We'll be meeting again soon. Let me catch Courtney before she walks out the door. She looks ready to take flight."

You have no idea. Monica's eyes followed Darius as he rushed away to try to catch up with Courtney.

Darius cupped his hand under Courtney's elbow. "You're not leaving, are you? It's still early. And we haven't had that dance you promised."

Courtney knew she'd made no such promise. "I'd like to dance with you, Darius."

If Darius wanted to dance with her, Courtney saw no reason not to grant him his wish. Until this night was over, he was still her client. Before the truth had been revealed, she had been hoping to maintain a friendship with him and the possibility of a working liaison.

Were those things still possible for them? Just as she saw no reason not to dance with him, she couldn't come up with a single reason to cut all ties with him, either. Still…

A romantic slow song softly floated on the air. Darius instantly brought Courtney into his arms, just as he'd done at Club 21. As he held her tenderly, she closed her eyes. As though she had no control over her responses to this highly energetic sexual being, she relaxed her body and followed his smoothly executed lead.

"At the risk of sounding like a broken record, I have to say it again. You and your staff did a stupendous job," Darius whispered to Courtney. "Candice is so pleased. She and Roderick want to meet you. Are you cool with that?"

Courtney smiled. "I'd love to meet your sister and future brother-in-law."

Less than a half hour ago Courtney had dreaded meeting Candice. Feeling like a hypocrite, she was ashamed of herself, but she wondered if she could accept things for what they were.

No matter what happened between them now, it was in both their best interests to take time to figure it all out. She and Darius should get to know each other as individuals. They should not be thinking of starting any kind of relationship blindly, especially a friendship.

Friendship should be the first goal in all relationships.

Why hadn't Darius told her he wasn't the groom? This question weighed heavily on Courtney's mind. She didn't know why it carried so much weight, but it did. She had to be careful not to overanalyze this, though. Time away would be good for her.

The couple continued to slow-dance through the next song. They quickly changed gears to accommodate the faster-paced selection that followed. Courtney had felt so good in his arms.

She found comfort in his holding her so tenderly, but she couldn't explain the fear she felt running through her.

She already loved Darius. But what if he couldn't return her feelings? She'd have a full week to ponder the seismic shift in their relationship, along with where it might go from here. The timing of this vacation was perfect.

Darius slipped his hand into Courtney's, guiding her over to the head table. Upon reaching their destination, he leaned over and kissed his sister on the cheek. "Candice and Roderick, this is Courtney Campbell, the genius behind this fabulous shindig. Courtney," he said, "I'm pleased to introduce you to my sister and future brother-in-law."

Roderick got to his feet and then extended his hand to her. "I'm not sure I have the right words to describe the handling of this event. So all I'll say is that Candice and I are delighted with everything. I can't imagine our engagement party being any nicer. Great work!"

"Thank you, Roderick. I'll pass that on to my staff." Courtney felt so good inside as pride filled her heart.

"Please do," Candice requested, her voice as soft as the brush of a feather. "It is wonderful to meet the lady behind this exquisite setting. I hope my brother wasn't too difficult to work with. I happen to know he's a perfectionist."

Courtney smiled broadly, her eyes moving back and forth between the engaged couple. "Fortunately or unfortunately, Darius and I have that perfectionist trait in common. He was one of the easiest clients to please I ever worked with. No matter what we call him, he desperately wanted this evening to be absolutely splendid for you both."

Tears welled up in Candice's eyes. Then she stood up and flung her arms around Darius's neck, hugging him tightly. "Darius and I are all the family each of us has. Our parents and grandparents are deceased. There isn't a more loving brother anywhere in the world. As far back as I can recall he has taken excellent care of me."

"Okay, okay, baby sister," Darius said, holding up his hand to get her to stop. "This night is not about me. It's all about you and Roderick and your love. I just wanted you two to meet Courtney."

Candice clapped. "Courtney, if you have any business cards, I'd love to pass them on to my friends."

Courtney appeared astonished by Candice's generosity. "That's so kind of you. I'll make sure you get a stack. Referrals are always appreciated. It's time for me to get back to work. It was a pleasure meeting you both."

"Same here," Roderick said. "Hope to see you again soon."

"Oh, we'll see Courtney again, all right," Candice added. "I'd love to use The Party People for our wedding reception. I'll get together with you on the details as soon as we work everything out."

Courtney smiled broadly. "It'd be an honor to handle your wedding reception. I'm blessed to be way ahead of the game. Since I know quite a bit about your preferences, thanks to Darius, I can start putting together some ideas to store in my laptop."

Candice gently fingered the extraordinary centerpiece made for the head table. It was much larger than all the others, adorned with lavender rosebuds and baby's breath. The angel's wings, sprinkled evenly with silver glitter, were spread wide.

"You already have my approval on the angels, Courtney. They're handcrafted beautifully. I've never seen anything like these before. Darius told me they were your own creation. I love the elegant design. Instead of silver wings, for the wedding reception I'd prefer gold glitter."

"Gold it is. Working together with you on your reception will be our pleasure." Courtney's eyes rapidly darted around the room. "Please excuse me. One of the waiters is summoning me. I'll try my best to drop by the table before evening's end."

Courtney hastened over to Walter Taylor, one of the best waiters she employed. "Is something wrong?"

"I'd like to know if we should start putting out the evening entrées. There isn't a time inserted on the schedule."

Courtney consulted her watch. "Right now is perfect timing. I'll have the host ask all the guests to be seated until the meals are served. You know I don't like setting out a plate where no one is seated. We can always announce it if we have extra meals."

Walter winked. "Thanks, Courtney. I'll get all the staff together to start serving."

"You also deserve to be thanked, Walter. Thank you for all your hard work." Standing on her tiptoes, she kissed Walter's cheek before taking off to help oversee the meal service.

This was one of very few hotels that allowed the ballroom to be leased out and to have catering brought in from the outside. Each of the three ballrooms had fully equipped attached kitchens if patrons wanted to prepare the food there. A host of private halls and party facilities did business that way, but four-star-plus hotels normally required food to be prepared by their own catering department.

Darius was well acquainted with the hotel owner, and he loved supporting his friends' businesses whenever possible. Courtney hadn't known about this facility until he'd taken her there. She'd never seen such an exquisite facility and she quickly added it to her list of specialty banquet halls.

Just as the last plate was placed upon the table, Courtney decided it was finally time to slip out unnoticed. Overly pleased with the outcome of the event, she knew her official duties were done. Closing her eyes for a brief moment, she thanked the Lord for giving her the strength to get through it. She was proud of all her events, but she was bursting with pride over this one. Deep emotions had tugged at her heartstrings as she'd indulged in these special preparations. She hadn't fallen in love with a client before this event and she knew she'd never fall so deeply for anyone ever again.

The heels Courtney wore kept her from running down the hall, but nothing could make her look back. *Please don't come after me. Let me leave with my dignity intact.* She felt incapable of saying another word to anyone, especially Darius. The man was pleased with the job she and her staff had done. That was the end of it for them.

With her purse and light wrap in hand, Courtney stepped outside and hailed a cab to drive her the few blocks to the hotel.

Cabs weren't plentiful in L.A., not like they were in New York. She felt lucky that one had happened by so quickly. Had she not been in such a hurry to get lost, she would've called a cab from inside to ensure a ride.

Once comfortably seated in the back of the cab, Courtney unzipped a section of her purse and removed a twenty-dollar bill. The cab wouldn't cost nearly that much, but she was too grateful to begrudge the driver a decent tip.

Stripping out of her dressy attire, Courtney moved briskly through the hotel suite and made it to the bathroom, where she had already turned the shower on full blast. Thoughts of Darius occupied every corner of her mind since she'd left the reception. Getting away for a brief respite was exactly what any doctor would order for her.

Why hadn't Darius told her who was getting married? That was the one question she had failed to come up with an answer for. Courtney's mind switched back and forth between rewind and fast-forward as she stepped into the downpour of steamy water. Back to the beginning, when she'd first come face-to-face with Darius—that was crystal clear in her mind. Fast-forwarding to the announcement this evening was harder on her than rewinding.

Tossing her head back, Courtney welcomed the hot water cascading down her body, hoping it might wash away these uneasy feelings she had about Darius not being up-front. He was a man she trusted, a man she'd come to care for deeply, and she didn't want that to change.

Darius's flirting made perfect sense to her now. Although he could definitely have taken it too far, he hadn't done so. She didn't know how she might've responded had he actually gone beyond mild flirting.

What would she have done had Darius attempted to kiss her? Knowing how she felt about him, would she have been strong enough to deflect the flirtatious advances, or would she have simply given in to her strong desires to kiss him back?

All the guilt she'd felt over wanting to be with him had been for nothing. Why he'd kept her in the dark about the upcoming nuptials was the big question—one she might never get the answer to because she didn't think she could ever ask him.

Why had secrecy been Darius's choice over simple candor?

Courtney wondered if she should rethink her decision to work with Darius on the film project. It would no doubt affect Monica and J.R., who were looking forward to sharing creative time with the filmmaker. Somehow she had to make it clear to her friends that no matter what her decision was, she didn't expect them to follow suit. No way could she ask them to give up on any of their dreams of success.

For all intents and purposes, she and Darius were talking about entering into a business deal, a very serious undertaking for everyone involved. Still, she wouldn't fault the Normans if they wanted to work with him, even if she chose not to.

They weren't in love with Darius. *She was.* That alone made things complicated.

Could she trust him? Or should she subject his integrity to close scrutiny?

Once Courtney walked out of the shower stall, she slipped into a fluffy terry-cloth bathrobe supplied by the hotel. Sitting down at the dressing table, she stared into the mirror, hating herself for allowing this matter to throw her. As sure as she was alive and breathing, there was no concrete evidence that the man had ever set out to deceive her. Not an ounce.

Courtney didn't believe Darius had forgotten to mention his blood relationship with Candice. *He had intentionally withheld the information. But why?* Had she called him on his flirting when it had first happened, perhaps she would know the answer.

Then Courtney thought that maybe she was simply being unfair, that she was giving too much weight to this issue. She realized there wasn't anyone to blame for how attracted she was to Darius. The experiences she'd had with him were brand-new for her. Michael Scottsdale paled in comparison to Darius Fairfax. Courtney could only hope that Darius wasn't as unscrupulous and unfeeling as Michael had been.

Darius's scent was present when he wasn't. There were times when she knew what he intended to say before he said it. She believed they had more in common than not. Did she dare deny herself the opportunity to get to know him better?

Could something that felt so good and wonderful end up hurting her?

Hearing the song playing on her cell caused Courtney to rush out of the bathroom and grab her phone off the nightstand. "Hey, Monica, what's up?"

"I'm a little worried about you. Are you okay?"

"I'm fine. Just took a hot shower and now I'm ready to slide between the sheets. I need to set the phone for an early wake-up call. How did things end at the reception?"

"It all went just fine, but don't concern yourself with anything else about work. The moment you took off, you were officially on vacation. Darius asked about you several times. I nearly let him know you were staying at the Renaissance Hotel because he looked so miserable after he realized you'd left the reception. I figured telling him would've been grounds for my termination."

"I'm glad you didn't tell him where I was. I know how charming he can be. Don't worry about me, Monica. The strong survive."

"Please don't hate me for asking this, but I feel compelled to. Are you in love with Darius Fairfax? Before you answer, I want you to know that I believe you *are*."

Courtney sighed heavily. "I plead the fifth...and for so many reasons. Let's just leave it at that, okay?"

"I get your drift. Any changes to your itinerary?"

"Not a chance. Everything will go as planned. I'll call you when I'm settled in."

"Please call. If you don't, you know I'll lose sleep over it, if not my mind."

Courtney laughed. "You won't have to lose a thing because of me. I promise."

Monica cleared her throat. "Another question for you...and I hope you don't plead the fifth. What about the business project with Darius? Are you still game?"

"I hear what you're really asking me and I know how hard it is for you to ask about it. Listen, no matter what I do, we can't let it affect your future. If you and J.R. want to work with Darius, go right ahead. It won't harm our friendship or our working relationship. As for me, I'll be taking everything into consideration."

"Thanks, Courtney. J.R. is really caught up in Darius's plans. It would kill him to let go of this project, though I know he'd do it for you if you asked. What Darius has planned for me is totally separate from what he's talked about for J.R. If you decide to pull out, I may, too. We're in this friendship together, for life."

"You will do no such thing, not if you really want to work on the project. Our relationship is so much stronger than that. We'll talk tomorrow. I love you, Monica."

"Love you back, Courtney. Don't forget to call me."

"I won't. Have a good night's rest." Courtney disconnected the line then punched in the code for her grandparents' home number. Looking around the hotel room, she waited for someone to pick up on the other end. "Grammy, it's me, none other than your favorite and only grandchild. You sound sleepy. Did I wake you?"

"I was dozing. Papa is watching some crazy horror show on television. You know how I hate to deal with anything that seems cultish. It's nice of you to take time out to call us. How'd the reception go?"

Courtney smiled. "According to Monica, everything went just as planned."

"What do you mean, 'according to Monica'? Weren't you there?"

"I left early. If everything wasn't running smoothly, I would've stayed."

"I hear disappointment in your voice. I've known you long enough to feel it when things are out of whack with you. Come on, baby, tell Grammy Alma what's really happening, although I can probably guess."

"I left because I was worn out."

"You left because of your deep feelings for Darius Fairfax."

Courtney was shocked. "What do you mean by that?"

"Sweetheart, this old lady can recognize the look of love a mile away. I see it in your eyes when you talk about him. Couldn't take the engagement announcement, huh?"

"Grammy, you won't believe this. He's not engaged. Candice is his sister."

"What? His sister?"

"It looks like he decided to keep his personal business to himself. He was throwing the engagement party for Candice and her fiancé, Roderick, who is a plastic surgeon. Monica and I have discussed it."

Alma laughed softly, glad her granddaughter wasn't making a big to-do about nothing. "Did he ever say flat out that he was the one getting married?"

"I can't say that he did. He only said he wanted it to be the event of the year. But he talked about how much he loved Candice and how happy he wanted to make her."

"Wouldn't any loving brother feel that way about his sister?"

Courtney groaned loudly. "I see your point."

"Why should what he said or didn't say bother you one way or the other?"

"Grammy, you already know the answer, don't you?"

"Baby girl, I certainly do. Since Mr. Fairfax is not engaged, I'd think you'd be jumping for joy. What's the problem?"

"I guess there shouldn't be one, yet I may need to be cautious in how I proceed with him."

"Why?"

Courtney thought about it. "I don't know why I feel the way I do. Honestly."

"Especially when you should feel so relieved," Alma remarked.

Courtney couldn't come up with a single reason to be cautious around Darius. He had hired her company to do a job and had made good on his contract by paying in full. "You definitely have a point, Grammy. Goodbye, now. I'll miss you while I'm away. I'll stay in touch."

"If you didn't need a good rest, I'd encourage you to hang around to snag the single Darius Fairfax. He's ripe the picking. Have fun, love. God will be with you."

"God bless you, Grammy. Kiss Papa Harrell for me. Love you both."

Chapter 6

The Kahala Hotel and Resort was a top-notch hotel on Oahu, named one of the top ten Pacific Rim resorts by *Condé Nast Traveler* magazine—Readers' Choice. The resort evoked Hawaii's nostalgic era of timeless elegance. The 338-room resort offered its guests direct beach access and featured panoramic views of the Pacific Ocean, Diamond Head crater, Ko'olau mountain range and a private lagoon with six resident bottlenose dolphins.

Mailani Starks, the desk clerk, introduced herself as she handed Courtney a navy blue folder. The packet included colorful brochures and lists of the hotel's amenities and other pertinent information. "Welcome to Kahala Hotel and Resort, Miss Campbell. We are happy to have you as a guest. It's the pleasure of the entire staff to serve you. I see by your reservation that you've booked one of our oceanfront Koko Head suites for six nights. You'll love our Kahala chic luxe, residential-style accommodations."

"This is my first time to Hawaii and I'm already in love with it. How long have you lived here, Mailani?"

"I was born on Oahu. My mother is Hawaiian and my father is African-American. He was stationed at Hickham Air Force Base when he met Mama. We lived here many years. Whenever Dad had to go overseas, he always managed to get reassigned here until he finally retired."

Courtney smiled. "You *are* blessed! Do you still live with your family?"

"I've been on my own for two years. Soon after I graduated from the University of Hawaii, Honolulu, I landed this great job and moved into an apartment nearby."

Mailani activated two magnetic key cards, inserted them into a small folder then handed it over to Courtney. "Your suite is on the beach level, 1110. Your luggage will be delivered to the room by the time you get there. If you need anything at all, please don't hesitate to call."

Inserting the key card into the slot, Courtney waited for the green light to appear before she tried to open the door. As she stepped into a lavish, apartment-size hotel suite, her breath caught. Her eyes were immediately drawn to the sliding-glass doors. The drapes were pulled back to reveal a breathtaking, panoramic view of the entire resort and the vibrant-blue Pacific Ocean, white with froth atop huge crashing waves. The unusually large patio was securely enclosed with white iron railings.

After depositing her purse onto one of four plush off-white chairs, Courtney crossed her arms and stared out into paradise. Courtney instantly thought of Darius. It was only yesterday that she'd learned that the man of her dreams wasn't engaged. She wasn't sure how to feel about that or what it meant for her. Still, she couldn't help imagining him and her together in this wondrous setting. Suddenly, she shivered. Shimmering through her mind was a vision of him oiling down her body with sunscreen. She could actually feel his tender hands kneading her flesh.

Several minutes passed before Courtney managed to tear herself away from the hypnotic view whose spell she had fallen under. First on her agenda was touring the magnificent suite.

Her spacious accommodations included a separate living room with a powder room. A parlor and furnished lanai faced into the tropical trade winds, affording Courtney even more spectacular views. The mellow white and soft beige Asian-style sofas and matching chairs looked comfortable and inviting. Everything she had seen thus far exuded class, elegance and style. This resort was a mere ten minutes away from Waikiki.

A rectangular dining set with four chairs was fashioned in glass and bamboo. Beautifully framed pictures of Hawaiian ocean views, beach scenes and sunsets graced the stark white walls. Earth-tone carpeting was thick and plush. A personal bar, refrigerator and mini home entertainment system only added to the comfort, along with a forty-inch flat-screen LCD television.

Courtney was happy to see that her luggage had indeed been delivered, as she stepped into the bedroom. The king-size bed was draped in an ivory goose-down duvet and Egyptian combed cotton Frette linen. Exotic-looking Polynesian ceiling fans hung overhead in all the residential areas of the suite. A cozy, cushy divan upholstered in an exquisite-looking beige fabric was situated at the very foot of the bed.

Courtney planned to nap after a quick shower, but only for a short time. There was a lot of territory to explore and she was eager to stroll around this fabulous resort. She didn't plan to waste too much time sleeping, though she'd come here to rest. Upon opening the bedroom's slatted sliding closet doors, she saw a lavish white chenille robe and a pair of white slippers.

Floris of London toiletries and complimentary sun-care products nested in a seashell basket on top of the granite counter in the beautifully appointed bathroom. Opening the clear glass-and-brass shower door, Courtney turned on the water and adjusted the temperature to her liking.

While checking out the rest of the bathroom, Courtney removed the lei, a resort gift, from around her neck and deeply inhaled its bold floral scent. She then hung the fresh flower chain on the doorknob of the linen closet. Unhurriedly, she stripped out of her comfortable but chic traveling attire. Before leaving the bathroom, she lit several candles placed in a variety of unique holders set on the ledge of the Jacuzzi tub.

Back in the bedroom, after flipping open the suitcase situated on a luggage rack, Courtney pulled out a set of pure white cotton short pajamas to wear after her shower. After removing her intimate apparel from the smaller bag, she stored them in a drawer of the mirrored bamboo dresser.

Deciding to save the rest of the unpacking for later, Courtney made her way back to the bathroom, where she stepped into the shower. Throwing her head back, she sighed deeply, feeling comfortably grounded in her calming yet uplifting surroundings.

Tranquility eased through Courtney, allowing her to completely relax.

What would it be like to have Darius in Hawaii with her? Was he as romantic as he had boasted?

Although Courtney had thought Darius had been talking about Candice and him, she'd still gotten caught up in his vivid stories of romantic intrigue. Maybe some of his ideas had merely come from a lively imagination, not from any real experiences. Either way, she'd love for him and her to engage in endless mornings and nights of sweet romance and the hottest, most incredible lovemaking.

"Hot, steamy sex," she chanted softly, "the type of no-holds-barred sex that makes the hair stand on end. Was there any other kind of lovemaking?"

Courtney moaned softly as she envisioned her body entwined with Darius's in a passionate embrace. She licked her lips in a provocative manner, wishing she had him there to unleash her tongue on. Just the thought of kissing him, tasting his chocolatey sweetness, brought her tremendous pangs of pleasure. Maybe when she got back to California she'd seek him out and lobby for that kiss. Laughing at her own silliness, she continued to lather her body with the lavender-and-strawberry-scented shower gel.

Instead of slipping into bed, Courtney walked into the lanai and slid back the door to let the warm, stirring trade winds flow in. The sound of the surf provided the perfect peace-invoking melody for her to relax. With her nudity wrapped in the chenille robe, she stretched out on the plush lounge chair. Breath-stealing, she thought, looking out across the vast ocean, which appeared to go on and on, with no end in sight.

Courtney tried to keep her eyes open, but she knew she was failing. Her lids felt way too heavy for her to keep them lifted. Slowly, she surrendered under the increasing fluttering pressure.

Hush little baby, don't you cry. The words Grandmother Alma had once sung to Courtney every night at bedtime lulled her into a state of unconsciousness.

Give in. Giving up was okay.

The weather in Honolulu was beautiful. The sky above was as blue as Courtney had ever seen it. White, puffy clouds floated softly in the ether, no rain in sight. Lying on a chaise lounge a few feet from the water's edge, her well-protected skin soaked up the rays. One brochure she'd read warned about the burning sun, saying it was at its hottest around three in the afternoon. It even suggested wearing a hat.

The bright blue-and-yellow bikini Courtney wore was nearly dry after only a few minutes under this kind of heat. She had taken a brief swim in the ocean before stretching out on the chaise. Feeling the intense rays of the sun, she got up and headed back into the water. Although she'd badly needed some downtime, she had found it hard to rest. The light nap hadn't lasted thirty minutes. The excitement about touring the island and her romantic thoughts of Darius kept her from calming down.

"Courtney," a strong male voice called out.

Upon hearing her name, she turned around, firmly planting her feet in the wet sand. Smiling, she waved at Jonas Marshall, the airline pilot she'd sat next to on this morning's flight. Being booked at the same resort had surprised them. It was a place his airline used for employee layovers. He had a great sense of humor and she had enjoyed his company. For a while, Jonas had actually taken her mind off Darius.

While alone at the Hollywood hotel last night, the man Courtney loved had come back to claim her, torturing her with the sweet, innocent memories they'd made. Every second they'd spent together had been relived in her mind all during the night.

"I see you're ready to test out the water," Jonas said, drawing nearer.

"I already took a quick dip. The ocean temperature is bathwater warm and it feels wonderful. Are you coming in?"

"Sure am." He looked around him, pointing at the chaise with a towel spread out on it. "Is that where you're hanging out?"

Courtney nodded. "That's my bag and towel."

"I'll join you as soon as I put my gear down. Mind if I take the chair next to yours?"

"Not at all," Courtney said without reservation.

What in the world are you doing, girl? Don't go and get in over your head again!

Courtney heard the warning voice inside her head and she had an honest response. She thought Jonas might make her a great friend, but she wasn't romantically interested in him. He hadn't given any indication that he felt romantic toward her, either; she hoped he didn't. He was nice and good-looking. His well-toned body rippled with muscles. The last thing she wanted to do was to encourage him beyond friendship.

Darius didn't love her, but that hadn't stopped her from falling hard for him.

Jonas joined Courtney in the water, where they swam about and frolicked.

A half hour later, Courtney swam back to shore and sat in the sand. Wishing she'd put her wide-toothed comb into her beach bag, she dragged her fingers through her hair. The hotel had a salon, but she planned on washing her hair daily and keeping it in a ponytail or a loose bun. She'd also packed a few curly hairpieces to jazz up simple styles.

Jonas joined Courtney a few minutes later, drying himself off with a towel. "What are your plans for your stay in Hawaii?"

Courtney shrugged. "I don't have any that are set in stone. I came here for a much-needed rest, but I've already decided there's too much to see and do for that. I'm considering tackling the Polynesian Cultural Center. I hear it's an all-day adventure."

"It is. And it gets even better once the sun sets. A lot of activities go on out there after dark. I can never get enough of that place. If you don't do anything else, you have to experience a Hawaiian luau. The center offers that, too."

"How often do you come here, Jonas?"

Jonas chuckled. "Often. My route is between L.A. and Honolulu. Besides my place on the mainland, I own a condo on

Maui, so I go there a lot, too. My layover isn't as long this time so I decided to just stay here on Oahu. It's a very short flight to Maui, another incredible place. It's too bad you don't plan to visit any of the other islands."

"Not this time around. This is actually my first time in the state. In fact, this is the only real vacation I've had since I opened my own company."

"What kind of business do you have?"

"Catering. People always encouraged me to do what I love and to do a lot of it. My grandmother did catering right out of her own kitchen and I loved helping out."

"That's a very lucrative business…if it's handled properly. People who love my barbecue tell me I should sell it. The biggest fear I'd have is someone accusing me of having caused a case of food poisoning. If I just continue to give my ribs away, I won't have that to worry about."

"You have to be insured to run any kind of food business. It's costly, but necessary. My company has finally started turning a profit, enough so I no longer feel the pain of a high insurance premium. Things are going really great for The Party People."

"Great name for a catering business. I like it."

"Me, too," she said, chuckling. "I love planning and throwing parties, from small ones to elaborate affairs. I'm finding out that many folks want someone to do it all for them. And my company offers full service—and we do it very well."

"Sounds smart."

"My employees and I think so. I've got a wonderful group of people working for me. That's why it does so well. When did you decide you wanted to become a pilot?"

"The same day my parents bought me my first model airplane. As soon as I put it together, I began dreaming about flying. I started private lessons when I was sixteen. Flying is freedom. Piloting small aircraft for recreation is what I love most."

"Where in southern California do you live?"

"I'm a beach bum. Manhattan Beach is pretty close to LAX, so my town house is near the job. I keep thinking about buying a house, but I'm never sure I need that much space. If I had a family,

I'd definitely own a home. As a single guy, condo and town house living is fantastic. I recall you saying you live in Hollywood."

"I love living in Tinseltown! I purchased a foreclosure property and got a really good deal. My single-story home has about 3,200 square feet of living space and a three-car garage. That's more than enough room for this single girl."

"As beautiful as you are, I'm surprised you're still on the market."

Courtney wagged a scolding finger back and forth. "That's a horrible phrase, one I detest. I'm not a piece of meat bought and sold in a marketplace. I don't like being referred to as something on the market. Why do you see me that way?"

Jonas's almond-colored skin reddened slightly. "Sorry. I didn't mean to offend you. I don't see you that way. I guess I've just heard it said that people are on or off the market when talking about their relationship status. I do not see you as a piece of meat."

Smiling, Courtney got to her feet. "I'm going to stretch out on the chaise and soak up some more sun."

Jonas looked regretful. "Am I responsible for running you off?"

"No, Jonas, you're not. I just want to get dry and laze about for a little while."

He nodded his understanding. "Is it okay if I join you after another swim?"

"You're perfectly welcome to."

Taking a folded towel out of her oversize straw satchel, Courtney began to dry off her arms and legs. She then reached back into her bag for sunscreen, which she rubbed on all the areas of her body she could reach. Yawning, she stretched out on the towel-covered chaise.

The scenery before her was breathtaking. As she looked out over the ocean, she thought of the phone calls she'd missed from Monica. The second call had been missed while she was in the bathroom after landing at the airport earlier in the morning. When she tried to get Monica back, the voice mail came on.

Why Monica hadn't left any messages was a mystery that worried Courtney. Because of the time differences, she planned to phone Monica later on. She had bought a calling card to keep in touch with her family and friends, though it had initially been her intent to be totally out of pocket. Perhaps that was the reason Monica hadn't left a message for her. Maybe she thought her boss wanted to be left to her own devices.

Hoku's, with its indescribable beachside setting, offered panoramic views of the Pacific Ocean from every table in the multi-level restaurant. Consistently ranked as one of Hawaii's best, the restaurant was widely praised for its innovative fusion fare, melding Hawaiian, Asian and European flavors.

The stunning strapless white, black and red flowered sarong-style dress Courtney wore hugged her gentle curves and showed off the luscious swell of her breasts. She wore red and white hibiscus flowers in her loosely pulled-back hairstyle. The seashell necklace and earrings were a nice complement. On her right wrist she wore a cuffed bracelet crafted from shiny hammered silver.

Eating dinner alone wasn't Courtney's preference, but she didn't have a choice. This was her first night in Hawaii and she wasn't about to call room service. After she gave her name to the hostess, Courtney took a seat to wait for a table for one. She hadn't missed the raising of the hostess's eyebrows when she'd stepped to the podium. Courtney figured that in a romantic setting like this, guests rarely ate alone.

Who in Sam Hill came to Hawaii alone, anyway?

"I did," Courtney whispered hoarsely. "And I'm sure there are plenty of others."

Well, I'll have romance in my life one day. Someone out there is perfect for me. I just need to be patient and wait on God to find him and send me one of His angels.

Courtney did believe there was a Mr. Right for her. She also knew she was the perfect Miss Right for some lucky guy.

The hostess came back to where Courtney sat. "The gentleman over there asked if you'd like to join him." The hostess pointed out the man who'd invited her.

Courtney looked in the direction where the hostess pointed. Jonas. Without giving it a second thought, she stood up. "I'd love to join him. Thank you."

"Great, Miss Campbell. I hope you have a wonderful dining

experience. Please come with me. It's my pleasure to escort you to the table."

Jonas stood as Courtney and the hostess arrived. Instead of pulling out the chair right next to him, he chose the one across from him. "I'm glad you agreed to have dinner with me. You looked uncomfortable."

"I'll leave you two," the hostess said. "Your waiter will be right along."

Courtney thanked the hostess before she sat down. Her smile for Jonas was sunshine bright. "Thank you for asking. I felt kind of out of place and weird dining alone, but I'd better get used to a table for one while I'm here."

"Why *did* you come alone?"

"Why not? I'm single and free. I spend a lot of time by myself. I don't have a steady man in my life because it just hasn't worked out that way."

"Jonas." The shrill but happy voice came from a lady rapidly advancing on him. Positioning her hands on each side of his face, she planted a passionate kiss on his mouth.

Then she spotted Courtney. As she looked from Jonas to the woman seated at the table, the glee in her dark brown eyes disappeared. "Jonas?"

Courtney jumped to her feet. "Hi," she said cheerfully, "I'm Courtney Campbell. I was about to eat alone and Jonas invited me to join him. We met on the flight here from Los Angeles." With that said, Courtney reclaimed her seat.

The lady appeared uncomfortable. "I see. I'm Arlene Mayfair. Jonas and I have known each other a long time." As the mahogany-complexioned woman sat down, she gave Courtney a halfhearted smile. "Nice to meet you…"

Leaving her sentence unfinished made it easy for Courtney to guess what Jonas's friend might've said.

The moment Jonas sat back down, Arlene slipped her hand into his. "It's so good to see you. How are you?"

Jonas nodded. "I'm great. I wasn't sure if you'd gotten my message."

"That's obvious," Arlene remarked, a distinct chill in her voice.

Courtney stood again. "Guys, I'm sorry for intruding like this. I didn't know Jonas was expecting you, Arlene. I'll go and see if I can be reassigned a table."

"No, Courtney, that won't be necessary. I invited you to dine with me because I didn't like the idea of your dining alone." He made direct eye contact with Arlene. "You owe Courtney an apology. You're assuming things you shouldn't."

Arlene looked both abashed and contrite. "I am sorry, Courtney. I hope you can forgive my rude behavior. I didn't handle things in the right way." She extended her hand. "Hi, I'm Arlene Mayfair. It's a pleasure to meet you, Courtney Campbell."

Courtney smiled broadly. "I'm honored."

Courtney wasn't sure about Arlene's pleasure, but she'd have to make the best of this situation. She could always move back to the table originally assigned to her, but that wasn't an appealing prospect. She had starting feeling lonely not long after she'd settled into her suite. It hadn't taken her long to figure out that Hawaii was for lovers. Not only did she not have a love interest with her, she really had no one to talk to. Jonas was merely a stranger who'd sat next to her on the plane: there was no semblance of a spark between them.

Arlene cleared her throat. "Are you here in Hawaii alone, Courtney?"

Expecting Arlene to guffaw at her response, Courtney reluctantly nodded. "The trip was a last-minute decision resulting from major fatigue. Lots of work and no play."

Arlene looked as though she doubted Courtney's statement. "You wouldn't be running from love, would you? That's the impression I get."

Her mouth agape, Courtney stared coolly across the table at Jonas's friend. The last thing she wanted to do was show aggression toward Arlene, but she wouldn't stand by and allow herself to be antagonized for no reason. Her comment had been right on the money, but it was voiced coldly, unkindly and with the intention of inflicting pain. Even if Arlene believed Courtney was running from love, she didn't have to say so.

Jonas looked thoroughly embarrassed by Arlene's remarks.

Courtney couldn't hold against Jonas his friend's rudeness.

Deciding to meet the problem head-on, she squared her shoulders and looked Arlene dead in the eyes. "As a matter of fact, I am here to escape love. The truth is I'm in love with someone who doesn't share my feelings. In fact, I'm in love with someone who doesn't even know how I feel. Yes, I came here to lick my wounds, but I'm also in dire need of rest. Are there any other personal things you'd like to know about me?"

Arlene had the good grace to look ashamed. "I'm sorry. I shouldn't have pried into your personal affairs."

Narrowing her eyes, Courtney folded her hands and laid them atop the table. "If I thought you were truly sorry, I'd accept your apology. I don't think you're a bit sincere. Furthermore, I think you've been downright rude. You somehow have it fixed in your mind that I have designs on your man, if, in fact, he is your man. But you're dead wrong. We simply met on the flight from L.A. There's nothing more to it."

Emotionally upset and not wanting anyone to see her cry, Courtney rapidly rose to her feet. "Thanks for befriending me, Jonas. Sorry the innocence of it has been misinterpreted. If you both will excuse me, I'll see if I can get back my original table."

Arlene and Jonas jumped up at the same time.

"Please, Courtney, stay," Arlene pleaded. "I feel like a first-class heel. I am sorry. And you're right on in your assessment of me. I allowed jealousy in and my claws to come out. You're a beautiful woman and I felt threatened."

Courtney would have liked nothing better than to tell Arlene she *was* a first-class heel, but that would only have added more fuel to the fire.

Jonas came around the table and stood next to Courtney, taking her by the hand. "Don't go. I invited you to join me and I was sincere. Everything will be okay."

Looking from Jonas to Arlene, Courtney tried to make up her mind about whether to go or stay. The compassion in her heart overruled her head. Arlene had apologized and Courtney thought she should just graciously accept it and move on. Besides, she hated seeing Jonas looking so miserable over what had occurred.

He was such a nice man and she had no desire to cause him pain. "Thank you both." Courtney sat back down.

Jonas looked relieved by Courtney's decision to stay put.

A shadow suddenly fell over Courtney.

"Mind if I join your party?" a familiar voice asked.

Chapter 7

Knowing she had to be dreaming, Courtney was afraid to look up. The voice she'd heard had sounded like Darius's. That wasn't remotely possible. She was in Hawaii and he was back in California.

Was she losing her mind? No. She'd already lost it the day she'd met Darius.

"Please do," Jonas said, wondering who the newcomer was. By the strange look on Courtney's face it fleetingly crossed his mind that this could be the man she had confessed to running away from. Then he recalled her saying the man didn't know how she felt about him. Still, he had to wonder.

Looking totally bewildered by the handsome stranger, Arlene nodded her assent.

"Everyone but you has agreed, Courtney. Are you going to answer me?"

Knowing she couldn't possibly control hr raging heartbeat until she identified the voice, Courtney slowly looked up at the man standing over her.

It *was* Darius, looking as fine as he always did. He was dressed in an expensive-looking white-linen, two-button, one-pocket blazer and matching pants, pleated in the front. A gold shirt was opened at the collar and his loafers were an interesting shade of brownish-gold, similar to autumn leaves. Darius was a very classy, trendy dresser, one who obviously didn't believe it was fashionable for men to go without socks.

Darius posted his hand on the chair next to Courtney's. "May I?"

Courtney's eyelashes fluttered wildly. "What…are…you doing…here?" she asked Darius before politely introducing him to Arlene and Jonas.

Her stammering was adorable. If he unnerved her like this, maybe she cared about him as much as he'd come to care for her. "Looks like Monica did as I begged her to."

His being there made some sense to Courtney now that he'd mentioned Monica. If he'd ended up at the same resort where she was staying without knowing she was there, she'd have to believe they were destined for each other. "Monica and I haven't been able to connect."

"When she couldn't reach you, I asked her not to let you know about my plans. I told her I wanted to tell you in person. She agreed, but not without a bit of arm twisting."

"Really now! Seems there's a lot I don't know about you, Mr. Fairfax. Like why you intentionally withheld pertinent information from me during our business encounter. Why don't you tell me the truth?"

"That will require me to sit down," Darius remarked, nodding in a friendly manner to the other occupants. He gathered that they were more intrigued than polite in allowing him to join them. As he'd come up on Courtney, she hadn't looked as if she were in an ideal situation.

Two was company and three was more often than not a crowd, Darius knew.

As soon as Darius sat down, their Samoan waiter, Tunga, was right at his service. Name tags worn by each member of the waitstaff disclosed their place of natural origin. Darius wasn't interested in eating anything at the moment. Courtney's presence was quite fulfilling enough. "Nothing, now, thank you. I'll call you when I'm ready."

The waiter inched back. "Okay, sir." Tunga turned and left in haste.

Slipping his arm around Courtney's chair, Darius put his mouth near her ear. "We threw my sister and her fiancé an unforgettable engagement party, Courtney," he whispered. "Candice and Roderick couldn't have been happier. I knew you didn't know she was a blood relative." He looked a little uncomfortable. "It was intentional."

Courtney appeared shocked. "Why?" Figuring Darius didn't want the others privy to what was being said between them, she adopted his same low tone.

"As a client, I wasn't required to divulge any personal information other than my ability to pay the bills. I hadn't heard of your company before so I just left a few things unsaid. If I'd said the event was a surprise for my sister, would it have made a difference? Would I have gotten any less than the best catering services money can buy?"

The table was once again visited by Tunga, this time delivering the appetizers. He spoke quietly with Jonas and Arlene, who'd given him their dinner choices. The other couple never looked his way and he took it as a signal to move away until he was summoned.

As Courtney thought about his questions, she wondered if Darius had a valid point. In fact, her knowing might have made a difference. Had she known he wasn't the one getting married, would she have relaxed her professional demeanor because she was so attracted to him? He hadn't lied outright, but he hadn't been forthcoming with the entire truth.

"I came to distrust you, perhaps without just cause," she said. "I didn't know what to think of your decision to hold back important information or how to let it go. Maybe you didn't fully trust me, either. Is that why you wanted to design and personally handle the invitations and the mailings? It would've revealed that you weren't the groom."

Courtney didn't think the job would've suffered if she'd foolishly mixed business with pleasure, but it wasn't something she was absolutely sure of. Affairs of the heart and business weren't always a good combination. She wasn't merely attracted to Darius. Courtney truly believed she was in love with him.

"That was purely the artist in me at work. I certainly planned on having you find out that I wasn't getting married. I'm not one who likes to mix business and pleasure. But I had a hard time hiding my attraction to you, so I made everything about business. With the exceptions of the few times I slipped up, like when I held my fork to your sweet lips."

He looked at her pouting mouth as if he'd like nothing better than to taste it right now.

It was hard to ignore him staring intently at her mouth, but Courtney didn't know how to respond to his provocative remarks about her sweet lips. "You mentioned Monica. How does she *really* fit into all this, Darius?"

"Monica and I had a heart-to-heart near the end of the reception. I knew you were upset with me from your demeanor earlier and I wasn't sure why. I finally decided to ask Monica about it. When I mentioned my feelings for you, she told me how she thought you might feel about me."

Tears came to her eyes. "I feel so foolish." She swallowed hard. "Monica had to be the one to tell you where I was, but I don't necessarily see it as a betrayal. She wants to see me happy." She looked down at the floor and back up at him. "How *do* you feel about me?"

"I think you already know, but I'll tell you, anyway. I care, Courtney, a lot. What I feel for you is deeply personal and it has nothing to do with business. You look and possess the character of the ideal woman I long ago created in my mind and heart. As for Monica, she fought hard to make the decision to tell me you were leaving for Hawaii. I felt I should talk to you myself, in person. I wasn't able to get on the same plane you were on because it was full, but I caught a flight a short time later. I've been here awhile but I had to get some sleep. I had one of those nonstop talkers seated on the aisle seat in first class. I had the window seat."

"You must've paid an arm and a leg for a last-minute reservation."

"If I'd had to, I would've paid whatever the fare was.

"Sorry if I hurt you by not mentioning that Candice was my

sister. I'm so proud of that beautiful girl. She was in her element last night. You should've seen the angelic glow on her face when she and Roderick were the only two on the floor for their first dance as an engaged couple. She beamed as brightly as a beacon in the night."

"I can imagine. She *is* beautiful. I saw Roderick come in with you." Courtney purposely didn't mention Monica's comments encouraging her to check out the man who was as tall and nearly as gorgeous as Darius.

"Roderick's crazy about Candice. He's a plastic surgeon with a Beverly Hills address, but he prides himself on serving patients who aren't the least bit wealthy, especially if what's needed is more out of necessity than cosmetic. My sister is a pediatric nurse-practitioner. They met at the hospital she works at in Hollywood."

Courtney smiled. "Is she crazy about her husband-to-be?"

"No doubt about it. They fell in love instantly. I didn't believe in love at first sight before them." *Then you came along and reaffirmed the possibility.* "I didn't believe in miracles, either. But I began to consider the possibility the same day we met. I want to know all there is to know about you. Think we can get to know each other now that our initial working relationship is over? I desperately want to know exactly who you are and what makes you so personable and self-assured."

Courtney blinked back the tears in her eyes. "What about the future work you discussed with Monica, J.R. and me?"

Leaning in, Darius gently pressed his lips against her cheek, momentarily losing himself in the sweet scent of her. "I strongly believe we can work together. That project is a great one, and it's an altogether different set of circumstances. You will be working with me, not for me. We'll be equal partners."

"I can't believe you're here, Darius."

Is this the stuff fairy tales are made of? I'm so afraid I'm going to wake up and find out I've only been dreaming.

"I'm here in the flesh, Courtney. You can pinch me if you want."

Courtney blushed hotly. "I'd rather kiss you instead," she stated boldly.

Darius got out of his chair and knelt down before her. Cupping her face in both his hands, he brought her head down and aligned their lips. As his lips came together with hers, his tongue searched and found hers. The kiss deepened and their mouths caught fire.

Surprised by the flaring passion between the couple, Jonas cleared his throat. "Is it safe to say you two already know each other? Or is this somehow a chance meeting?"

Courtney giggled. "We know each other, obviously with a desire to get to know each other better."

Arlene looked completely relieved by the romantic situation, no longer fearful of losing Jonas. "Are you two ever going to eat anything?"

Courtney looked down at her untouched appetizer of petite egg rolls. "Eventually," she remarked softly. "But I feel pretty full right now."

"That makes two of us." Darius got to his feet. "Come on, Courtney. Let's take a walk."

Darius reached into the inside pocket of his blazer and pulled out his wallet. Removing a twenty-dollar bill, he laid it on the table. "Thanks, guys, for sharing."

The couple walked in complete silence for a short distance. As they slowly strolled down the coastline, Courtney had the urge to get her feet wet. Darius wasn't dressed for frolicking in the water, but she really wanted to step into the surf. Removing her arm from his, she bent down, took her shoes off and set them aside. Blowing him a kiss, she took off running toward the water.

Courtney played hopscotch in the tiny rippling waves, which were nowhere near the size of the swells crashing along the coastline earlier in the day. Seemingly oblivious to everything around her, the young woman let herself go. Mindlessly, she slipped a little too far out, where waves rose higher than she'd calculated. When an unusually warm splash of water reached up to her waistline, it was too late to do anything about it. Instead of fretting, she laughed as if nothing out of the ordinary had occurred.

Darius stood stock-still and watched Courtney enjoying herself.

He had expected her to run out of the water when her dress was completely soaked. Instead, she surprised him by throwing her head back and laughing as if she didn't have a care in the world. Apparently, she didn't have a care, he thought, loving her free-flying spirit.

"We should go inside and change into swimwear," Courtney yelled to Darius. "I'd love to get back into the water. It's not even cold."

Darius nodded. "I guess it takes a while to cool off after an entire day beneath the hot Hawaiian sun. Ready?"

Courtney's laughter rent the air. "Here I come."

As Courtney ran toward Darius, he was prepared to catch her in his arms. Worried about ruining his clothes, she ran right past him. "Don't want to get you wet," she yelled.

Hand in hand, the couple walked back toward the main entrance of the resort and exchanged room numbers.

By the time Courtney reached her room to change into a swimsuit, jetlag had her by the throat. A nap wasn't the solution to what ailed her. She needed several hours of sleep and more than half the night was already gone. Finding it hard to keep her eyes open, she made her way into the bathroom. Disrobing was a task for her, proving just how tired she was.

Standing inside the glass-enclosed stall, Courtney hung up her wet sarong behind the showerhead. Positioning herself under the warm spray of water, she slowly lathered her body with strawberry body wash.

Instead of drying off her body and donning her bathing suit, Courtney slipped into the plush hotel robe. Making her way into the bedroom, she fell across the king-size bed, trying to remember Darius's room number. The fog in her mind was so thick she ended up picking up the phone and asking for him by name. As much as she wanted to be with him, she knew she had to cancel. "It would be much worse to accidentally fall asleep on him," she told herself.

The phone rang and rang. Thinking Darius was probably showering, too, she decided to call him back in a few minutes. As soon as she hung up the phone, she took off the robe and slipped under the bedding nude. Within minutes of tossing her head back on the plump pillows, Courtney was out cold.

Darius had heard the phone but not until the final ring. He'd been out on the balcony eagerly waiting for Courtney to call, celebrating his good fortune with a glass of wine. Already dressed in his swim trunks, he was disappointed that he'd missed her call. No one but Candice and Jasmine knew where he was. It had to have been Courtney calling. He'd left instructions with Jasmine only to contact him in case of an emergency.

Sitting down on the bed, next to where one of the phones was located, he dialed Courtney's room. Darius allowed the phone to ring five times before disconnecting. *Maybe Courtney has had a change of heart,* he thought. "No, that doesn't make sense. She seemed happy I came…and it was her suggestion to change and go back outdoors."

At a loss over what to do, Darius stretched out on the king-size bed and flipped on the television set, hoping Courtney would call back.

Rolling over in the bed, Courtney squinted at the bright green digital numbers on the clock radio. "5:10 a.m.," she rasped in a sleep-filled voice.

The memories of last night slowly began to seep into her mind. That she'd fallen asleep, failing to reach Darius as promised, caused tears to fill her eyes.

She sat upright in bed. "What if Darius leaves because he thinks I don't want to be bothered with him? Will he understand how tired I was?" She didn't know how understanding he was, but she sure hoped he was as reasonable as he appeared to be. "It's too early to call him. God, how can I wait another hour or two? You'll just have to," she remarked, answering her own question.

Courtney tried gathering her wits as she got out of bed. After putting on the robe and tying the belt loosely around her waist, she headed straight for the balcony. She had been looking forward to a sunrise and a sunset in Hawaii. She'd already seen a sunset, but she wasn't sure of the exact time the sun came up in this seemingly faraway land. She was determined to sit out on the balcony until shining rays of golden beauty streaked across the sky.

A slight breeze swept over Courtney as she pulled back the sliding-glass doors. It was a little cooler than she'd expected, but it felt pretty good. "The sun will be hot as Hades soon enough. I may as well enjoy this cool breeze while I can."

Seated on the side of the bed, Darius contemplated the same issue that had run through Courtney's mind. *Was it too early to call her room?* He had picked up the phone several times to call. While keeping himself busy in the wee hours of the morning, he'd read the hotel service directory from cover to cover, along with several other informative materials in his suite.

Courtney wasn't in the same area of the resort as Darius. According to the map, however, her suite wasn't far away. He'd laughed when he'd located her suite, having considered asking her to stay with him, since he had two bedrooms.

Unable to wait another second to talk to Courtney, Darius dialed her room number. He said a silent prayer as the phone started ringing.

Courtney had moved one portable phone out to the patio, snatching it up on the first ring. "Darius," she called out, knowing it couldn't be anyone else but him. "Please forgive me. Jetlag caught up to me and there wasn't anything I could do to ward it off. I called your room but didn't get an answer. I planned to call back but Mr. Sandman had other ideas," she explained, without taking a single breath.

Darius laughed. "This is good news. I thought you might have had a change of heart about getting together again. I'm glad that wasn't the case."

"Hardly, Darius! I was just afraid it was too early to call you when I woke up twenty minutes or so ago. I went out last night like a bad lightbulb."

"What are you doing now?"

"Lounging on the patio, waiting for the sun to come up. Want to join me?"

"Say no more. See you shortly."

Darius was out the door before he realized he only had on his robe. There was nothing unusual about going outside in a robe;

beachgoers did it all the time. Thinking Courtney probably had hers on, too, he let himself back into the room and riffled through the dresser drawer for clothes to change into later. Grabbing his swim trunks, he walked out again. She might think he was presumptuous, but he'd been too blessed so far to succumb to the stress of indecision. If she wanted him to get dressed, Courtney wouldn't hesitate to tell him—and he'd do whatever she asked.

Courtney ran into the kitchen and started the coffee brewing. Fearing she might miss the onset of sunrise, she rushed back out to the patio, but left the sliding-glass doors open so she could hear the door, then settled back down on the chaise. Knowing Darius was on his way had her beaming, yet she was nervous. She wondered if she should get dressed. "I should at least put on my underwear."

That decision made, Courtney dashed into the bedroom. Removing bikini panties and a T-shirt from her unpacked suitcase, she slipped them on in a hurry. Just as she came out of the bedroom, the knocker thudded against the door, and the coffee machine signaled that the brew was ready.

Courtney looked through the peephole then opened the door wide.

At the sight of her, Darius pulled Courtney to him and kissed her passionately. "Good morning. Is being here with me as surreal to you as it is to me?"

Standing on tiptoes, Courtney's lips grazed his bottom lip. "Every bit as much. I know exactly what you're talking about." Grabbing Darius by the hand, she pulled him in the direction of the patio. "We don't dare miss the Hawaiian sunrise."

"What about the coffee I smell, Courtney? I'll pour us a cup if you don't mind."

"Fine, but hurry. We don't want to miss out on a spectacular light show."

Darius had been to Hawaii and had seen quite a few sunrises, but he'd never stayed on Oahu. Maui was always his destination. Courtney was right to expect something magnificent, but he expected it to be more spectacular with them sharing it. His past trips to Hawaii had mostly been stress busters from work and he'd come there with his sister twice for relaxation and fun. No other female had been on his Hawaiian vacations. Since Courtney had mentioned that she'd never been to Hawaii, he hoped this turned out to be a wonderful experience for both of them as a potential hot new romantic couple.

Within minutes of Darius coming out onto the patio with two mugs of hot brew, the bright orange-colored sun slowly peeked up over the ocean. It was not disappointing to either one of them. Her loud gasp gave Darius a good indication of how she felt.

"It's so beautiful!" Another gasp of astonishment escaped her lips. "The Creator paints a masterpiece 365 days a year, all over the world…and at different times. Can you even begin to imagine what sunrises and sunsets are like around the globe?"

"I've experienced them in different parts of the States and in Mexico, Europe, Asia and Africa. Still, there are many places I've yet to see."

Feeling bold, Courtney tossed her arms around Darius's neck, bringing his mouth down to greet hers. The kiss was fleeting but memorable. "That was so nice," she said. Blushing, she pulled her head slightly back, her green eyes connecting with his topaz gaze. "Tell me something. How long do you plan to be here?"

"For as long as you are. That is, if you want me to stay on until then."

"I want," she cooed. "I don't dare take anything for granted, but I'd like to know how much of our time we should devote to each other."

"As far as I'm concerned, every waking moment, but only if you feel the same way. I came here because of you and I'll leave whenever you're ready for me to. What we seem to have won't end once we get back to the mainland. Will it, Court?"

She smiled, blushing at the same time. "If that's what you want."

"It's exactly what I want," he assured her, kissing the tip of her nose.

Turning away, Courtney walked over to the railing, where she leaned forward and gazed up at the sun. It was customary to wish upon a star. Since the sun was a star, she closed her eyes, wishing for their time spent together to be totally awesome. She wanted to leave Hawaii in a committed relationship. Marriage wasn't part of her wish, but she couldn't help wondering if that, too, was in their future.

Returning to the chaise, Courtney moved over to the left, as far as she could get. Patting the empty space, she looked up at Darius. "Lie down with me, please."

Instead of responding verbally, Darius acted upon her softly spoken request. Cozying up alongside her, he brought Courtney's head in to nest against his broad chest. She felt cuddly and warm to the touch and he loved holding her in an intimate embrace.

The couple lay in silence for nearly a half hour. Then her stomach growled.

"I'm hungry. What about you?" she asked, cutting into their tranquility.

Darius nodded eagerly. "I could do with some breakfast. I'll call room service. What do you want me to order for you?"

"I'd like a large glass of chilled pineapple juice, eggs scrambled soft and turkey links or patties. A bowl of sliced strawberries, mangoes or pineapple would be good. And a slice of wheat toast with lots of butter and either grape or strawberry preserves."

Taking a minute to think if she wanted anything else, Courtney snapped her fingers when she came up with it. "Add to the order Corn Flakes or Raisin Bran, two percent milk and a banana. Want to share a pot of breakfast tea?"

Darius wasn't a big tea drinker, but he wouldn't think of turning down Courtney. "No problem with the tea."

Before going inside to order their breakfast, Darius kissed Courtney thoroughly. Closing the sliding-glass doors behind him, he thwarted the strong urge to go back for another kiss. Thanking God again for his good fortune, he moved toward the desk phone, thinking about what he wanted to eat for breakfast.

A couple of minutes later, Darius pushed the doors back and poked out his head. "About twenty to thirty minutes, I was told. Mind if I take a quick shower?"

"Go right ahead. I plan to get in there when you finish."

Their eyes suddenly met in fiery collision. Neither one dared to voice their X-rated thoughts.

With all kinds of naughty visions running through her head, Courtney imagined Darius in the nude. The body of a Greek god, she thought. Then she recalled reading that the majority of Greek males weren't especially tall. As erotic visions kept invading her head, Courtney got up from the chaise and went inside.

Tiptoeing down the hallway, with the guiltiest look on her pretty face, Courtney stopped outside the bathroom. Putting her right ear to the door, she listened as the water pelted down over Darius's honey-colored nudity. His body was probably as smooth as his baby-soft face. The man's skin didn't appear as if it were acquainted with a razor.

How did he like his shower? Hot, tepid or cool? Did he prefer to towel or air dry?

The door suddenly opened and she literally stumbled into Darius's hard body. There was no way he could misinterpret what naughty-girl shenanigans she'd been up to.

If only the floor would open up and swallow me whole, I'd have an escape.

Feathering his fingers through her hair, he laughed. "You could've come in and joined me. I wouldn't have minded."

Courtney felt the hot color rise in her cheeks. "It's not what you think."

"Okay," he said, deciding to leave it alone. The look on her face told him she was embarrassed enough—and he was flattered. "Has breakfast arrived yet?"

His question was answered by a couple of sharp raps on the door.

"I'll get the door." Courtney scurried away, glad for what would be a short reprieve. In a minute or two they'd be seated across the table from each other.

Could she look him in the eye and not show her shame at being caught in the act?

Never in Courtney's life had she listened at the door as someone showered.

Did that make her a pervert?

As she released her fear of caring about what she'd done, her laughter trilled. No matter what she did or how she acted, she was cold busted. She asked herself if she had it to do over, would she do it again—and the answer was *most definitely*.

Still dressed in their robes, Darius had showered, but Courtney hadn't taken hers yet. Once he'd completed his morning routine, he had put his robe back on, planning on dressing in the swim trunks or the colorful Hawaiian shirt and white shorts he'd brought along. The arrival of breakfast had caused a change in plans.

The room service waiter rolled a metal cart into the room and over to the table, where he set out the numerous breakfast items. Once he received a nice tip from Courtney, he left, rolling his cart with him.

Courtney and Darius took a seat, eager to dig in.

Courtney poked at her eggs with the tines of her fork. "Perfect," she said. "I can't tell you how many times I've ordered softly scrambled eggs only to get them hard." She took a forkful of the fluffy eggs, smiling with satisfaction at the great taste. "Delicious! Is everything on your plate okay?"

Darius grinned at how breathless she sounded. Courtney grew more adorable to him by the minute. "It looks fine. Mind if I say a blessing before I begin?"

Another moment of shame assailed Courtney. Praying before every meal was how she'd been raised. The times she'd previously dined with Darius had shown he'd been taught the same religious practices as she had. "Sorry about that."

Once Darius finished a humble prayer of thanksgiving, Courtney lifted the silver teapot and poured a hot cup for both of them. Sprinkling the Splenda in her cup, she added one of the thick lemon wedges and stirred. She chuckled when he added milk to his tea.

Perhaps she'd try milk in her tea one day, but not today.

The couple lingered over breakfast, learning more about each other. Darius had graduated from the University of California, Los Angeles, UCLA. She'd earned a degree from the Culinary School of Los Angeles. "I also have a teaching degree. And I'm a big basketball fan. The Lakers, of course. I try to attend as many home games as I can. Monica and J.R. are embarrassed by me at times. I'm a screamer."

"I love the Lakers as well as the Kings."

"You really like hockey? That's not a black man's sport."

He peered at her over his glass of cold milk. "I don't limit myself to the passions of only one ethnic group. I enjoy skiing, too. Did you know there are several African-American ski clubs in southern California?"

She looked surprised. "As in snow skiing?"

Darius chuckled. "Swooshing down the mountainside is amazing. When I don't have time to go to Utah or Colorado, I hit Wrightwood or Big Bear. Waterskiing is also a favorite of mine."

"I know about Big Bear but not Wrightwood. Are they near each other?"

"They're in totally different directions but not that far apart. Want to try skiing with me this winter?"

Courtney pointed her fork at her chest. "Me, skiing? Are you serious?"

Darius cracked up at her expression. "I think you'd eventually come to like it."

Courtney laughed nervously. "It's not quite summer yet, so why don't we have this discussion just before winter sets in. Okay with you?"

Darius chuckled under his breath. "Sure, but I don't think I'll like your answer any better then. It's okay, though. I don't push my lifestyle on anyone. As a matter of fact, I love your free spirit. However, I'd like for you to tag along for fun. If you don't want to try skiing, you can watch me. There's nothing more beautiful than a mountain getaway in winter. We can have a snowball fight and build a snowman. Imagine sitting by a cozy fire after sunset. Sipping on a hot drink while roasting marshmallows can be a blast."

Loving the images but not ready to make a promise she might not keep, she smiled warmly. "I guess we'll have to wait and see. As for the present, we have an entire Hawaiian island to tour." She threw her hands up over her head. "Are you up for that?"

Darius grinned. "You don't know how ready I am for anything you want to do. I came here hoping to spend lots of quality time with you. We're going to do just that."

"All right! Let me take my shower so we can get on with our second day in Hawaii." Courtney jumped up from the table and headed toward the bathroom.

"Mind if I listen at the door to hear water running off your sweet body? At the same time, I'll use my vivid imagination to conjure up more erotic visions. I'll bet the sounds of water against your body will be melodic."

Courtney stopped dead in her tracks. He was laughing but it didn't sound like mockery. Turning on her heels, she ran back to the table. Leaning down, she kissed Darius breathless. "You have a smart mouth and a sharp wit to match. I'll have to remember to stay on my toes."

"All you have to remember is that Darius has a real love jones for Courtney."

"Hmm, that sounds delectable."

But Darius had said he had a love jones. He hadn't said he was in love.

Courtney suddenly grew quiet, wondering how long their affair would last after they returned home. There was nothing she wanted more than for their relationship to continue to grow, hopefully into the lasting kind. Well, she thought, maybe there was something else she desired. At the moment, Darius was it, the whole enchilada.

"Be right back," she told him.

"Wait a minute. I just had a great idea."

Curious, Courtney turned back to face him. "What is it?"

Darius's wide grin showed off his beautiful white teeth. "I think I'll keep it under wraps. You'll have to wait and see. I'm going to slip out of here and go to my suite. Go ahead and get it together. I'll meet you back here for our swim. Is that enough time for you?"

Courtney nodded her approval. "It's more than enough time to do my thing." Without further comment, Courtney sashayed out of the room, feeling very optimistic about the day ahead.

Chapter 8

Courtney's laughter rang out as splashing water hit her dead in the face as they played in the surf. Darius was having a good time making her his bull's-eye. Retaliation would come when he stopped flinging water long enough for her to get in a few good licks. Her hands weren't as large as his, but she knew how to use the heel of her hand to power-shove water at him with vigor.

As Courtney looked around, she noticed that there weren't many people on the private beach. It was still very early. Being practically alone was just fine with her. She liked being away from probing eyes. Courtney laughed, thinking of how nice it would be to skinny-dip in the ocean with the man who occupied so much space in her mind and heart.

Swimming up behind Courtney, Darius wrapped his arms tightly around her, wetly kissing her earlobes, nibbling at them like they were a favorite sweet treat.

Squirming around until she faced him, her eyes softly connected with his. "That feels so good, but can we include my lips in this? Did I ever tell you I like kissing you…"

Darius's lips crushed against hers, muffling her words and setting her on fire. His tongue probing her inner mouth was so sweet. He loved kissing her, too. Darius couldn't begin to tell her the dozens of ways he'd already made love to her inside his mind and daydreams and night visions. Courtney would think he was crazy if he mentioned too soon how much he'd fantasized about the two of them making love.

This was the kind of woman a man took his time with, lots of it.

Darius finally allowed Courtney to come up for air, at which time he glanced at his waterproof watch. "We'd better lie out in the sun to dry before we go sightseeing."

Taking Courtney by the hand, Darius led her ashore as she kicked up water all the way to the chaise longues. Plucking the towel sticking out of her straw bag, he gently dried off her face, hands, arms and legs.

Removing his towel draped over the chaise longue, she returned the favor by tenderly drying him off. The sensations she felt coursing through her body had her tingling all over. Kissing the palms of each of his hands after she'd dried them off, she saw reflected in his eyes the enjoyment he received by the same special attention he'd given her. Leading him over to the chaise, she adjusted the seat back to a position she thought would be most comfortable for him. "There you go. Take a load off, baby," she joked.

Minutes later, Courtney looked over at Darius, who appeared to have dozed off. Careful not to disturb him, she removed the brush and wide-toothed comb from her straw bag then sat up straight. Her wet hair was already pulled back and she took off the small black band and began thoroughly brushing it out.

Taking from the satchel a small curly hair attachment and a container of hairpins, Courtney repositioned the band around her hair and securely pinned the human hairpiece into place. Nice and simple, she thought, smiling, hoping Darius didn't mind store-bought hair. Store-bought or not, it was her hair simply because she'd paid for it in cash. She laughed inwardly at her own silly ruminations.

Putting the hairbrush and comb back into her satchel, she then removed a small purple kit filled with makeup and skin-care products. After cleaning her complexion with a premoisturized pad, she skillfully applied a light layer of oil-free suntan lotion.

Using a wide makeup brush, she dusted transparent mineral crystals over her entire face. Glad that Darius wasn't witnessing her quick makeup application, she continued by applying blush to her cheeks and painting ornamental lip gloss onto her lips.

Feeling as if someone were staring intently at her, Courtney looked to her left.

So much for lack of witnesses. What must Darius think of my primping?

Darius was all smiles, his eyes flirtatious—and she just couldn't help giggling.

Grinning, he blew her a kiss as he got to his feet. "You're beautiful without makeup, but it *can* help in highlighting natural beauty." He stretched his arms high. "As soon as I dress, I'll run ahead and get my rented car. Meet you on the driveway at the main entrance." Walking over to Courtney, Darius gave her a staggering, passion-filled kiss.

Darius removed from his bag natural-colored leather sandals and a royal-blue-and-white-flowered Hawaiian-style shirt. Then he slipped into some white shorts.

Turning her back to him, Courtney took off her bikini top and slipped on a pink-and-blue backless sundress. The sexy dress was far more casual than the sarong she'd worn to dinner, but it looked just as good on her fine-toned body.

Darius stayed rooted in place for the fashion show, only because he couldn't get his feet to work. Now that Courtney was dressed, he turned away and started up the beach. As though he didn't quite believe she was actually there in the flesh, he looked back at her every few steps to confirm her very real presence.

Darius had never once thought of himself as a confirmed bachelor. Love had just eluded him. Up until now, he wasn't sure he'd ever meet the right girl, the kind of woman a man was proud to take home to meet his family. She had met his only sibling and he was now very eager to meet her parents and grandparents. Darius believed that working through the family was the key. He had a good idea that Courtney's parents and possibly her grandparents had to approve of any man she dared to consider a partner in a committed relationship. He'd seen her grandparents, but he hadn't been officially introduced to them. Once Courtney was totally comfortable with him and their relationship, he'd ask to meet her family, if she didn't suggest that first.

The shining metallic blue Mercedes convertible 350 CLK was not at all the kind of car Courtney had thought Darius would have rented, but it certainly suited him. The expensive automobile looked as if it had been designed with him and his dynamic personality in mind.

Leaving the engine running, Darius rushed out of the car and ran around to open the passenger-side door for Courtney, kissing her tenderly. Once she got in and settled down on the plush ash-gray leather seat, he hurried back to the driver's side and slid behind the wheel.

"Ready for a set of brand-new adventures to begin?"

Courtney nodded. "I am, even though I believe the new and exciting experiences started for us last night. You have no idea what it meant to me to have you here."

Darius grinned. "I know what seeing you did for me, so I may have some idea."

Slowly, Darius rolled the Mercedes down the driveway, barely able to wait to open it up on the highway.

Glancing over at Courtney, he appeared genuinely pleased to see her bright green eyes wide open with wonder and expectation. He could tell that she was ready to drink in everything in their path. The beautiful plants, trees and colorful flowers would more than likely hold her spellbound. Though palm trees were plentiful in California, they also lined every street, avenue, drive and boulevard in Honolulu.

Twenty minutes later, Darius parked the car in a large lot at another Hawaiian resort, Serenity Point. After raising the convertible top, he jumped out the car and hurried to open the door for Courtney.

Looping her arm into his, he began walking. "Orin Stabler is the man I have an appointment with here at Serenity Point. This shouldn't take too long."

Her curiosity was piqued, yet she decided not to ask questions.

"I want you to come to the meeting with me. We're here to check out the best locations for the movie project I discussed with you, Monica and J.R."

Courtney felt a bit put off as she palmed her forehead. "You didn't come here for me. You're here on business." A dash of anger found its way into her tone. "I feel utterly stupid, not to mention naive as hell. What could ever have made me think you'd come all this way to see me?"

Darius's surprise at the unexpected outburst showed in his eyes. The hurt in her voice sent anguish surging inside him. "Wait a minute, Court. Traveling to Hawaii *is* all about you."

Feeling he'd duped her again, Courtney eyed him strangely.

Seeing that she still doubted his reason for being there, he inwardly flinched at the way she coldly stared him down. "I only got the idea of Hawaiian weddings after thumbing through the airline's monthly magazine. My feelings grew stronger after I got here. I'd almost forgotten what an idyllic place this is."

Courtney couldn't ignore the sincerity in his eyes. Once again she'd put her foot in her mouth, but how could she withdraw it gracefully?

Darius took both her hands. "Please believe me, Courtney. If you weren't here in Hawaii, I'd be at home or wherever you were. Let's not start our relationship out with distrust. I'm trustworthy. If you don't hang around, you won't find out for yourself."

Feeling more foolish than she had only moments ago, Courtney stood perfectly still before Darius. Giving in to her desires, she wound her arms around his neck, kissing him full on the mouth. "I'm so sorry. I really dove off the highest cliff on that one, didn't I?"

He gently kissed her forehead. "I've got you. Just hang on to me tight and I'll bring you safely back to where we were before this got started. Trust me, Court."

"I'm holding on and I'm trusting. My feet are back on solid ground."

Darius smiled brightly. "Are you feeling steady enough for this appointment? If not, we can try to reschedule."

"I'm fine. Let's go and find your man. I promise to listen and be quiet."

He smoothed her hair with his palm. "Your voice in this is important to me. If you have something to say or questions to ask, please speak up. I value your input."

Courtney laughed nervously. "Thanks. I'm happy you feel that way."

"If we hurry, we can still make it on time."

Courtney began running. She then turned around and started running backwards, causing Darius to laugh heartily. "Come on, man. You're falling behind."

"I don't think so, beautiful girl. I feel I'm neck and neck with you on everything. And I do mean everything."

You'd better rethink that phrase, Darius, since I'm already madly in love with you. Are you running right beside me in that arena? I'm not so sure. Oh, but how I wish.

Orin Stabler was an average-looking man—tall, well-built and blue-eyed. Orin firmly shook Darius's hand. A light kiss to the back of Courtney's hand instantly charmed her. "All ready for the tour of Serenity Point?" Orin asked.

"In the interest of time, we'd only like to see the area where weddings and receptions are held. We'd love to come back another time for a full tour."

"Very well. Please follow me."

Orin tossed out pertinent information on Serenity Point as he walked with Darius and Courtney. "We are often booked solid for one social event or another, mostly weddings and anniversaries where the couples renew their vows. This is an extremely popular spot. What dates are you two looking to get married?"

Courtney blushed heavily, but the query didn't fluster Darius in the least. "No date has been set yet, but a June wedding is a must."

Courtney was impressed by the fact Darius hadn't bothered to correct Mr. Stabler and tell him the wedding was for a movie.

Nor had Darius bothered to tell Mr. Stabler who was actually getting married. Well, he'd done the same with her when he'd

failed to mention that the engagement party was for his sister.
Darius Fairfax did have a unique way of doing things.

Courtney knew she couldn't fault him for that.

"June is a very busy month, when wedding dates are at a premium. Folks from every corner of the world flock to Hawaii to exchange wedding vows then. If you're talking about this June, Serenity Point is booked solid. While we do have cancellations, rarely do they occur in June. We keep a waiting list just in case there is a last-minute change in plans. You'd be surprised by the number of couples who are willing to put their name on the waiting list."

The Serenity Point wedding area was breathtaking. It was up high and at the very edge of a craggy cliff. It gave Courtney the feeling of standing at the ends of the earth. Getting married at earth's end was something to give deep thought to, Courtney mused, especially when it felt like you might fall off the edge.

As hard as Courtney tried to keep from seeing her and Darius standing at the edge of the cliff, waiting to say *I do,* she failed.

The wind rustling through the layers and layers of white satin and tulle her imagined gown was fashioned from made a soft whooshing sound. The wreath of white orchids and white and pink plumeria gracefully circling her head trembled under the force of the breeze. A beautiful attached tulle veil hid from the groom's topaz gaze the happy face and misting green eyes of his ecstatic bride.

Darius gently nudged Courtney. "Where are you right now?"

Feeling slightly off-kilter, Courtney stared openly at Darius, trying to get back her bearings. "At the edge of the cliff we just left. Did you get the feeling of being at the ends of the earth? I sure did. Thinking I might fall off was kind of unsettling."

Nodding, Darius smiled, yet he appeared a bit concerned for his companion. She actually looked as if she might have seen a ghost. "I think I experienced something similar. I suddenly got a crazy, floating sensation. At the same moment we stood looking down, I had the foolish notion I could fly if I jumped off the ledge."

Cringing at the mere thought of Darius's lifeless body lying in the ravine below, Courtney shook her head, trying to clear her mind. "It may be a great place for a wedding for someone, but not for me."

Darius was glad Orin Stabler had left them to experience the setting on their own. To him, Courtney appeared ready to take flight. "I'm ruling out this property. Let's get down from this cliff."

"What's next on the agenda?"

"One more stop and I promise you we'll be all play. I have another site I want to check out. Okay with you?"

"Fine with me." Just being with Darius was enough for Courtney. The man made her feel very special.

"The sooner we get business out the way the sooner we can get into playtime." He extended his hand to her. She took it and got to her feet. Pulling her into his arms, he kissed her. "What about a romantic dinner for this evening?"

Courtney smiled broadly. "I love the idea. The resort has lots of fine restaurants. Or do you have somewhere else in mind, Darius?"

"Leave it to me, sweetheart. I can deliver, big-time." Darius had a pretty good idea where to take her.

"Ooh, in that case, I'm all yours." Courtney was positive Darius could deliver.

Courtney's mouth fell open as she gazed upon the Eternal Gardens. Every kind of tree, plant and bloom imaginable appeared to tumble out of every nook and cranny of this extraordinary place. White benches provided seating with a view and water slowly trickled from a gold pitcher a stone goddess held in both her hands. A few steps away Cupid aimed his bow at the heart of a beautiful finely chiseled maiden.

"These gardens have been here for forty years or more," Mr. Kyoto said. "Refurbishing of the statues and upkeep of the grounds occur regularly. Some of the finest artists in the world created the dozens of statues in brass, cement, stone and other materials. Brilliant landscape designers are responsible for all the live plants, flowers and trees. Step over here so you can see why people choose this place to exchange their vows."

Tears sprang to Courtney's eyes as she viewed the colorful wedding mural painted on large boulders. Each huge rock depicted a certain part of the ceremony, from walking down the aisle to the exchange of rings. She'd never seen anything like it. These breathtaking gardens induced serenity.

"At the end of the ceremonies, either white doves or colorful butterflies are released into the air. Some couples opt for both. It is one of the most heartrending parts of the event and the most popular wedding package offering," he explained.

"I can see why," Darius responded. "This location is also tops."

"When are you two planning to marry?" Mr. Kyoto queried.

"We haven't set a date yet. We're here to check things out." He didn't bat an eyelash.

Courtney was quiet on the way back to the car. Her mind was filled with visions of weddings, romantic nuptials in Hawaii. She'd attended numerous wedding ceremonies, those she'd been contracted to handle and those of close friends and business associates.

As she recalled how Darius had responded to Mr. Kyoto's query about their wedding date, she smiled softly. He could've said the real reason he was checking out wedding locations, but he hadn't. He'd let Mr. Kyoto continue to think he was checking out sites for them.

How nice was that?

Then she thought about what that meant.

She'd been upset at him and disturbed by him for not sharing with her that Candice was his sister and now she was praising him for not correcting Mr. Kyoto.

"To get some sightseeing and fun time in, North Shore is where I'd love to take you. Any objections?"

She clapped her hands excitedly. "Of course not. I read it's the ideal spot for surfers. The entire area sounds like it'd be an exciting adventure."

On the way to the car, he challenged her to a race. She took off running as fast as her legs could carry her, their laughter sailing on the air. Being with him was fun and she hoped it didn't have to end with Hawaii. No matter how hard she tried to beat Darius, she couldn't. His strides were longer and her legs were much shorter than his.

Reaching the car first, Darius leaned against the passenger-side door, grinning like a Cheshire cat. When Courtney finally arrived, half a minute later, he opened the door for her. "That was a little unfair."

"Have you considered that I might've let you win?"

Darius threw his head back and laughed. "Whatever it is you want to believe!" His arms circled her waist. "Don't you want to give the winner a prize?"

Amusement danced in Courtney's eyes. "What kind of prize?"

The award he'd love to have and what he'd actually tell her were totally different things. Darius wiggled his eyebrows suggestively. "A spine-tingling kiss?"

Courtney thought the boyish expression on his face was so cute. "I can handle that." Pulling down his head, she kissed him, but only with a fraction of the passion she had in her. After all, they were in public. The sweet kiss stirred her from the inside out. She gave him another one, putting far more fervor into it this time.

Once Darius's passenger was settled in and buckled into the seat belt, he flew around to the driver's side, eager to make more beautiful memories with her. Pulling out of the parking lot, he turned right onto a tricky, winding road. As he headed for the highway leading to North Shore, glee was practically leaping out of him. She made him feel so naturally high. It was a great day so far and he hoped the rest of their stay in Hawaii would be just as exhilarating. There were a lot of places he wanted to show her.

Darius loved seeing Courtney's hair blowing freely in the wind. Her cheeks were flushed with healthy color and she looked happy. She was pretty, a wholesome-looking girl, but he wouldn't go as far as to describe her as the girl next door. Recalling that he couldn't stand his next-door female neighbor, Darius laughed inwardly. Jenna Wade drove him crazy back then. Candice accused him of having a crush on her, but his sister had no idea. Jenna wasn't a very nice person, period.

Darius parked the convertible. He then leaned across the console and removed from the glove box a map of North Shore. Spreading it out on his lap, he began studying it intently. Looking at the clock gave him an indication of how much time he and Courtney had spent together since just before 6:00 a.m. It was now thirty minutes past noon. Doing some quick calculations in his head, he figured out how much time they could spend on the North Shore before they had to get back in time for his evening plans. Right after his appointment with Orin Stabler, he had called the hotel and had the concierge make reservations for a very special dinner.

"Why do you have the map out? We're here. I saw the signs for North Shore. We drove right past it."

He tapped his index finger on the map. "This is an event map, which tells the monthly happenings in the different areas of Oahu. There's so much to do on this island. It's lunchtime. Are you hungry?"

"Not yet. I had that big breakfast. I want to watch some surfing. Can we do that?"

"I know the perfect spot."

Darius parked right on the sand at Sunset Beach, just like every other car in sight. "This is one of the hottest spots for surfers. Looks like a lot of people are riding the waves. This should be a blast," Darius said. "Man, look at the size of those crazy swells!"

Unable to believe the spectacular view before her, Courtney jumped up and down, squealing in delight. The water was cobalt-blue, a much darker bluer than the portion of the ocean surrounding the resort. Quickly stripping out of her sundress to the bathing suit beneath, she took off running toward the surf. "You won't beat me this time," she yelled back at him.

Laughing, Darius started up the beach after her, pretty sure he could catch up to her. Instead, he made the decision to let Courtney have a moment of glory.

"Come on, slowpoke," she shouted at Darius. Just as she was about to run into the ocean, she suddenly thought about towels, hoping the ones they'd used earlier had dried out by now. "Under this hot sun, we probably won't even need the towels. Stop looking for trouble," she advised herself.

Darius finally caught up to Courtney. "Why did you stop?"

"I was thinking about the towels we used earlier. I doubt they're dry, but then I figured we wouldn't need them, not with the sun as hot as it is."

"Maybe *you* didn't bring an extra set of towels, but I did. They're in the trunk. I'll go get everything."

Darius was sprinting away before Courtney could ask him what he had meant by *everything*. Knowing dry towels weren't an issue, she rushed into the surf, kicking up the water the way she loved to do. The ocean was very warm and she was thrilled.

Downtime was good for her, Courtney considered, as she frolicked in the water. Being dead tired all the time wasn't a good way for anyone to live life. Taking a week of vacation every six months wouldn't hurt anything, she thought. Extremely capable people worked for her. It was high time she started relaxing and trusting more in her employees, who were a fantastic group of workers. Courtney actually thought of them as family. The Party People was made up of very conscientious and caring folks.

Swimming up behind her, as she was none the wiser, Darius tenderly grabbed Courtney around the waist. Tilting her head back, he trailed kisses up and down her throat and then his tongue caressed her neck and ears. Turning her around to him, he took possession of her mouth. "Your kisses are the best, so sweet," he said as they were forced to take a break for air.

Lifting Courtney into his arms, Darius carried her farther out into the ocean. Waves repeatedly crashed over them, knocking the couple back a few steps, but he wasn't daunted. He wouldn't take her out past where she couldn't stand up. Even though she boasted that she was a strong swimmer, he'd never knowingly put her in any danger.

Courtney asked Darius to stand still, then she climbed onto his back and let him plod his way though the constant onrush of waves. Giggling and howling all the way, she was just as excited once he turned back and started back in.

At the shoreline, Courtney dismounted from Darius's back, following him to where he'd spread out a blanket and the dry towels. Her eyes grew huge with surprise when she saw the picnic basket. "How in the world did you manage this?"

"It's the idea I mentioned in your suite, but decided to keep it as a surprise. Sit down and open up the basket so you can see what's inside."

Courtney lifted the basket's lid and removed a large, double-layered plastic container. "Fresh fruit, cheese, crackers and sandwiches of some sort are packed in here. Oh, there's a bottle of wine and glasses in here, too." She giggled. "But you already know that." She leaned over and kissed him hard on the mouth. "This is so sweet. Thank you."

"You're welcome. I ordered the picnic lunch from food services so you'll have to give them credit. Are you ready to eat now, 'cause I sure am."

"Yes, my dear man! Jumping in the ocean stirred up my appetite. We can watch the surfers while we eat. This is so romantic."

Darius chuckled. "Just being with you is romantic. Thanks for agreeing to hang out with me. I don't know what I would've done if you'd sent me packing."

"I don't think that would've happened."

The attraction I have for you is too strong.

"I admit that I was surprised to see you. How could I have ever guessed I'd see you in Hawaii in a restaurant? I heard your voice first, but I just couldn't believe my ears." Her eyes suddenly glowed with unshed moisture. "Thanks, Darius, thanks for coming here. This trip is already memorable for me. It started the first second you appeared."

"I pray this is only the beginning of our making memories together. Courtney, I've never pursued a woman like this. I knew it was a crazy idea. I do crazy very well."

This is a first for me. And I truly hope you're the last. I have a lot to say to you and so much I want to show you. I vow not to rush you into anything. I plan to get us right the first time.

Second chances aren't always granted.

Chapter 9

The skill of the surfers amazed Courtney. She'd been to several surfing competitions in Malibu but nothing she'd witnessed equaled this. The waves alone were much bigger and stronger than those in southern California. The surfers also looked super strong. They appeared to be in fantastic shape.

As Courtney spotted a youthful-looking female on a surfboard, perhaps a teenager, she went bananas, pointing her out to Darius. "That girl's out there hanging with the big boys. Can you believe it? Look at her ride that killer wave! She's just as skillful as the men. The guys don't have anything on her. And she's still upright."

"So I see. I wonder if the others are intimated by her. She's good."

"They probably cheer her on. I read something about a yearly women's surfing competition on the North Shore. I think Sunset Beach was for men only, until the ladies started to protest and got something of their own going. I like their spunk."

"You would. You're spunky just like them," Darius remarked.

She gave him a sideways glance. "Does that bother you?"

"Strong, independent women turn me on." He chuckled. "Let me rephrase that. The independent woman I'm here with, the one I'm wildly attracted to, turns me on. I love to see females prosper and I think they should demand equality. You already know how proud I am of Candice. I hope she'll continue with her education and become a doctor."

"Has she talked about becoming one?"

"It was her childhood dream, so it surprised me when she went into nursing. However, maybe she'll keep at her studies and eventually reach her ultimate dream."

"Is doctor a more prestigious title than nurse-practitioner?"

Darius took his turn giving Courtney a sideway glance. "You may be twisting my words. Whatever Candice does, she does it extremely well. She earns prestige, no matter what title she bears. My sister has already won numerous awards in medicine."

Courtney thought they should change the subject. Darius seemed a little agitated with her. That was the last thing she wanted. Their vacation had only just begun. "Since we're spending every waking moment together, where are we dining this evening?"

"I've taken care of it, but I want to surprise you. What about taking a tour of the Dole Plantation? We have enough time. They give away sample goodies out there."

Courtney smiled. "Sounds like my idea of fun. Is it far?"

"We can be there in fifteen minutes or so."

The brochure Courtney read from was fascinating. "The information in here says Pineapple Express originally operated as a fruit stand in 1950. Dole opened this place to the public in 1989. Today Pineapple Express is one of the most visited tourist attractions in Hawaii. Imagine that. There's the train depot right there."

"Let's make a run for it." Darius smoothed his hand down over his hair. "After the train tour, we can explore the plantation gardens on our own, unless you have something else in mind."

Courtney grinned. "You make great plans. I like what you've chosen so far. I'm really looking forward to our secret rendezvous this evening."

"Romantic rendezvous," Darius corrected her. He was excited about it, too, and planned to do his very best to make it yet another memorable time for them.

Darius and Courtney quickly boarded the train. She instantly saw how vast the acreage was just by looking slightly ahead. An up close view of the ripening fruit showed off its vivid colors and suffused the air with the sweetest smell.

As they rode along inside the slow-moving train, Courtney and Darius listened closely to the narrator telling the group about the villages of old.

"Laborers came from all over the world to work the fertile fields of these islands," the narrator explained. "If you're anything like me, you love to see how other cultures live. I love my native Hawaii, but I travel to distant lands whenever possible."

Darius leaned in to Courtney until his shoulder grazed hers. "I'm sorry we won't get to the art gallery and Gunstock Ranch today, but we don't have time for either one. After walking through the gardens and the gift shop, we have to get back to the resort."

"Don't be sorry. I've had a wonderful time. I've already ventured farther than I would've done if I was alone. You've been the perfect guide. What's a Gunstock Ranch? I've never heard of it."

Darius laughed. "It's a ranch. Actually, it's more than that. Let's get up early tomorrow and get there. Do you like to go horseback riding?"

Courtney raised both eyebrows. "Put it on the same list as skiing. However, I think I'd like to try it. Can we ride the same horse?"

"The best riding experience is solo. The ranch owners will have a gentle horse for you to ride. Most places offering horses to ride take skill levels into consideration." He smiled broadly. "The thought of you seated behind me with your arms tightly around my waist is kind of electrifying."

Courtney envisioned a different scenario. "I'd rather sit in front of you. How's that for stimulation?"

"You've been electrifying me all day long." Darius couldn't wait to see her face later on tonight, once the surprise was revealed.

The mixed bag of sensations coursing through Darius made him want these delicious feelings of togetherness to go on forever. Looking into her beautiful green eyes made his heart dance. Courtney tasted as sweet as honey and he loved her full lips, soft and pliable against his.

At the moment, Darius couldn't imagine kissing anyone but Courtney. This savvy, independent woman made him happy, happier than he'd ever remembered being. The staggering kiss they'd shared earlier had made him feel as though her very pulse ran right through him, giving him the precious gift of life.

How could that be? How could a spirit other than his own get inside him?

It was time to go. If they didn't leave now, he feared they'd be late and his surprise for her wouldn't be fulfilled. Making wild, passionate love to her was the thought that jumbled his brain all day long, but there was so much more for them to learn about each other. If and when they made love, he wanted it to be a total experience, an unforgettable one.

Standing in front of the mirror nude, Courtney held up one dress after another. Although she loved the sarongs, wearing something sexier was more appealing to her. The look on Darius's face would tell her if he was pleased by her attire. His facial expressions often gave away his thoughts.

Holding up a white-crepe halter-style dress, she stared into the mirror at her image. "Now, this one is hot." With her skin now tanned, the stark white material was striking against her darkened flesh. She laid the dress aside in the consideration pile.

Pushing her hands up through her hair, she swept it atop her head. "Sophisticated is exactly what I'm after!"

Pulling out small amounts of hair on each side of her face to twirl with a curling iron was an option, she thought. Courtney recalled the nice compliments she'd received when she'd worn her hair up in the past. The idea of going to the salon and letting them handle it slipped through her mind. A glance at the clock told her there wasn't enough time for that. Darius was coming for her at six-thirty. If she knew where he was taking her, it might make her clothing choices easier, but she didn't have a clue. When she'd asked him the dress code, he'd told her to dress to impress, also mentioning elegance.

Knowing she could accomplish both impressive and elegance, Courtney laughed. Most of her traveling attire was beachwear and leisure items, but a smart lady never got caught unprepared. She hadn't expected Darius to show up in Hawaii, but she was ready for whatever he had in mind.

The basic black, after-five dress looked as good against her tanned skin as the white one had. It was backless and bashfully sexy. A slightly ruffled bodice made the outfit elegant. Pairing her evening attire with a diamond pendant, matching earrings and gold shoes, she felt confident she could pull off a terrific look no matter which dress she chose to wear.

Talking about dress to impress, Courtney thought, Darius had followed his own advice to her. His black Brooks Brothers suit was tailored to fashionable perfection. The deep lavender silk shirt and a multicolored, complementary tie highlighted his smooth honey-colored complexion. Black Stacy Adams shoes rounded out his great, sexy look.

Pleading for mercy from his rapidly beating heart, Darius brought Courtney into his arms. "You look fabulous, sweetheart. This stunning white dress was made especially for you. I'm proud to be seen with you."

Lifting his hand, she kissed the back of it. "Thank you. You're so sweet."

A white stretch limousine awaited the couple on the driveway of the resort's main lobby, the same area where Darius had picked up Courtney this morning. Her eyes darted everywhere as the driver of the limo swept them through the streets of Honolulu. The city was alive with lots of activity. Sunset was a little over an hour away.

Less than twenty minutes later, with Courtney's curiosity heightened tenfold, the couple was treated to a grand departure from Honolulu's Aloha Tower, en route to the luxurious *Star of Honolulu* for an elegant dining experience.

After they boarded the smooth-sailing ship, a young man came to direct the couple to the exclusive captain's welcome reception located atop the luxury liner's uppermost deck.

The handsome forty-year-old captain, Simi Tanaka, stood at the center of the deck, where he held a cordless microphone. His white, stiffly-starched uniform was decorated with an array of colored ribbons. Gold bars and black emblems graced his shoulder pads.

"Welcome aboard the *Star of Honolulu,* where you will be embraced by panoramic sunset views of Waikiki. Feel free to stroll along the decks or share a toast at one of the lanai bars. As you can see, our top observation deck has breathtaking vistas.

"Please enjoy yourselves and relax as you dance to the fantastic live music," the captain continued. "Fabulous appetizers and delectable entrées are served by our outstanding crew. Thank you for choosing us for your romantic Hawaiian sunset cruise."

The beautifully tanned Hawaiian man bowed at the waist, nodding his farewell.

"Cocktail and beverage service will begin any minute now. Then we'll be greeted and entertained by a troop of hula dancers," Darius explained to Courtney.

Courtney appeared pleased as she checked out the surroundings. "This *is* some surprise. I could never have figured out this treat. Thanks, Darius, for all the wonderful activities you've lined up. I can't imagine doing these things alone, which means I would've missed out on so much. I feel so special."

He kissed the tip of her nose. "You are very special to me. Please don't forget that."

Courtney reached for his hand and squeezed it. "I don't think you'll let me. Did you enjoy the captain's presentation?"

Darius chuckled. "He was long-winded, but I'm sure the speech is part of his job."

"It *was* informative. The part about live music certainly sparked my interest."

"Let me tell you a bit more. The *Star of Honolulu* is certified to go beyond Diamond Head to view the magnificent Kahala Gold Coast. Depending on sea conditions, the captain reserves the right to alter the route. This ship can carry fifteen-hundred passengers."

"Did this information come from all the reading you've done or have you taken this dinner cruise before?"

"I've taken a sunset dinner cruise here, but it was on a ship similar to this one. This is my first time aboard the *Star of Honolulu*."

Darius led Courtney across the deck to where he'd spotted a table with a perfect view of the stage. He pulled out her chair. Once he sat down, he moved his chair closer to hers. Leaning over, he kissed her neck. "I love your perfume. It smells like romance."

Raising her eyebrows, Courtney dazzled him with a smile. "I'm scared to ask how romance smells. Samsara by Guerlain of Paris is the name of my scent."

"It smells just like you. You've chosen well. I love the way it lingers on your skin."

Courtney liked being this cozy with Darius. They were out in public, but it seemed to her they only saw each other. He had barely moved his eyes off her face since they'd boarded the ship. She loved the attentiveness, loved the way his eyes deeply connected with hers. No man she'd dated had ever made her feel like she was the center of his existence.

Darius made her feel all sorts of alien sensations. This was only her second day in Hawaii and they'd spent most of their time together.

No man and woman spent that much time together if they didn't really have a genuine attraction for the other.

She was convinced of that much.

Courtney immediately turned off her thoughts as the hula dancers appeared on stage. Seconds later, upbeat, gentle music filled the ship's four decks.

These Hawaiian women were naturally beautiful, black hair flowing down their backs. Swaying with each provocative dance step they took, the movement of their gyrating hips and tender hand gestures was hypnotic. Courtney was mesmerized by the native attire and the beautiful fresh leis covering the crowns of their heads.

Darius was enchanted by the brilliance of Courtney's emerald eyes and her broad, expressive smile. Megawatts illuminated the evening, but the woman he was with outshone them all. Her personality was like a sparkling gem.

Hoping Courtney wouldn't mind, Darius twirled around on his finger one of her loose curls. "Your hair feels soft and satinlike." He closely studied her features.

The desire to kiss her suddenly hit Darius's heart—and his lips followed. Keeping his eyes on her, he pulled his head back. "There isn't anything I don't like about you. You're pretty, physically fit, mentally sharp and astutely business-minded. To top it off, you possess a great sense of humor. Last but not least, compassion seeps from your soul." He grinned. "Do I need to say more?"

"You've made things crystal clear for me on that issue."

However, there are several things I don't have any clarity on. Hopefully, before this trip is over, I'll know exactly who you are, Darius, inside and out.

As Darius tenderly stroked her arms, Courtney tried wishing away the fire burning deep inside her. Her flesh was melting beneath his circling fingertips. Coupling the sensuality of the moment and the romantic atmosphere, this experience ranked number one in her diary of life.

A waitress and waiter stopped in front of the couple's table, causing Darius and Courtney to look up.

"Good evening, sir, madam. Welcome aboard. Whenever you're ready for dinner, we'll escort you to the main dining room," the young lady said.

Darius leveled his gaze on the female. "I preordered a dining package through my hotel. It comes with special seating arrangements and a seven-course meal."

The waitress smiled brightly. "Great choice! You and your companion will dine at a private window table in the Art Deco Super Nova Room, which is complete with grand piano bar, lounge and private lanai terrace. I'll go look up your reservation. What's your last name, sir?"

"Fairfax," he responded, "Darius Fairfax."

Promising to return ASAP, both waiters left. "You really went all out for us this evening, Darius. I'm beyond impressed."

"As long as I can keep that beautiful smile on your face, I'm happy."

"I can't help smiling when I'm in your company." Leaning forward, she kissed him tenderly on the mouth. "Thank you again."

"You're welcome." Darius suddenly looked troubled. "I'm surprised that guests' reservations aren't checked out before they're escorted to the captain's reception. The way things are being handled seems chaotic to me."

Courtney closed her hand over his. "Does it bother you that the staff took it for granted that we'd be in the main dining room as opposed to dining in their top restaurant?"

Darius shrugged. "That could be part of it. But why offer different level packages and not know who purchased what? Guest names should be checked against the reservation listings where the package selection can be identified instantly."

He started to tell her the package also offered a spectacular revue, "My Hawaii Lei of Memories," champagne and a professional photo, but he'd leave that as another surprise.

"Don't let it spoil our evening."

Darius's eyes brightened. "The only thing that could spoil this night is if you and I weren't here together." He kissed her softly on the mouth. "No more dark clouds."

As promised, the two staff members returned to Darius and Courtney and immediately escorted them to the fabulous Art Deco Super Nova Room.

Darius had his arm around Courtney's shoulder as they followed a few steps behind the two employees. "Is it too cool for you, Courtney?"

"It feels wonderful. It's been so hot." As she winked at him, her eyes and smile grew flirtatious. "Would you give up your suit jacket if I asked for it?"

Darius was surprised by the question, yet he was intrigued. "I'd lay it over a puddle of water for you to step on, if you asked. What chivalrous thing would you do for me?"

He'd turned the tables on her, but Courtney was not at a loss for words. "I'm not wearing a jacket, but I'd give you my sweater. If it were raining bullets, I'd fall on your firm body to keep you from harm's way. If you needed CPR, I'm your girl. I'd do my very best to save your precious life."

Even though Darius had only been playing with Courtney, her sincere response had him spellbound. Just the thought of her offering mouth-to-mouth resuscitation to him caused a stirring in his loins. "You'd do all that for me?"

Courtney nodded. "And much more. You're definitely worthy of saving." She lifted her hand and gently stroked his cheek. As though drawn in by an invisible magnet, her lips seared onto his in a passionate kiss. "If you ever need saving, I'd love to rescue you."

The Art Deco Super Nova Room lived up to the hype. The staff made sure Darius and Courtney were settled in before taking off again, and instructed them to sit back and relax. The appetizers would be the first course served.

Courtney's repeated gasping made Darius believe she was just as pleased by the private dining room as he was. He took her hand until they reached the window table, where he pulled out her chair, then his. Desperately wanting to be alone with her, he dismissed the waiters, saying he'd summon them shortly.

"This place *is* the color of romance," she gushed. "Earlier you said I smelled like romance. Though I thought it was kind of weird, I'm now envisioning it in the decor. The blending of soft pinks and bold reds is perfect. Pink and red votives nesting in red glass candleholders are a nice touch. I love this dining room."

It didn't take long for the couple to grow comfortable in their quixotic setting. Losing themselves in the romantic atmosphere, Courtney and Darius stared adoringly into each other's eyes. Jazz played softly in the background.

"I'd like to dance," Courtney said. She couldn't bring herself to tell him she desperately wanted to feel his arms around her, but she'd been thinking of it constantly.

Darius got to his feet and extended his hand to Courtney. Before leading her to the dance floor, pulling her to him, he hugged her tightly. "May I have this dance?"

Courtney grinned. "You may," she responded, loving his style.

The moment Darius wrapped her up in his strength, Courtney

wished she could stay in his arms forever. Closing her eyes, she laid her head against his broad chest. Wondering what the rest of the evening held for them, she let her imagination run wild. Heated thoughts of Darius and her making passionate love sent her temperature soaring. The dinner cruise was wonderful, but she was eager to be alone with him again.

Darius lifted Courtney's head. "I love you, Courtney. I fell in love with you pretty quickly. I'll never forget how vibrant I felt in your presence on our first meeting. I have not been involved with anyone in over a year. Random dating was more suitable to my busy schedule. Meeting you has changed my feelings entirely. I want only to be with you. I hope in time you'll come to feel the same way."

I already feel the same way. With her voice lost to her, Courtney looked up at Darius, hoping her eyes would convey to him the message of love in her heart. She loved him as much as it was possible in a relationship so new. There was room for her love to grow into something permanent. Darius was a real man and a perfect gentleman. *Did she have fears?* Yes, but she believed all her fears could be overcome.

In the back of the limo things heated up between Courtney and Darius. Unable to keep from touching each other, anxious hands roved the other's body. She was already caught up in the burning flames of desire and Darius wasn't worried about landing in the inferno, not even if it meant getting burned.

Although the glass enclosure was up and the driver couldn't see into the back of the limo, neither one of them wanted to take the foreplay to the ultimate level. Their intimate rendezvous should be kept private.

The moment the limo came to a halt outside the area of the resort where Darius's suite was located, the couple couldn't scramble out of the stretch fast enough. Darius cupped his hand under Courtney's elbow and directed her to the elevators. His suite was located on the thirty-fifth floor, where the bird's-eye view was spectacular 24/7.

As they rushed into his suite, she didn't know about Darius, but she had high hopes of the foreplay continuing. She wasn't the kind of woman who took lovemaking lightly, but the love she felt for Darius made her confident that this wasn't a rash decision. Whatever else happened during the course of the remaining hours of the early morning was up to him. He had to want her as much as she wanted him. The decision to make love or not was in his hands. Courtney would be comfortable with whatever went down. He had emotionally professed his love for her and she loved him back.

Darius poured two glasses of wine and took one over to the sofa where Courtney was seated. Once she had a good grip on the glass, he sat down beside her.

Tangling up his fingers in her hair, his mouth came down on hers. Helping her up from the sofa, Darius held on to her hand as he led her into the bedroom. He gestured for her to sit down on the bed and she complied. He immediately joined her. Closely studying her dress, he tried to figure out the easiest way to separate it from her body. His hand searched for a zipper.

Knowing what he was doing, Courtney stood up and pulled the dress up and then over her head. "Is this what you were trying to do?"

His breath caught at the sight of her bare breasts. "When did you burn your bra?"

"I never owned one." She massaged each of her mounds. "Never had much to hide away in a bra. I also love the girls being free. Does my size bother you?"

Instead of vocalizing his response, he walked over to her. Wasting no time in covering her rounded flesh with his mouth, he suckled gently. Briefly, he raised his head and looked at her. "Sweet, Courtney," he whispered softly. "You taste so sweet."

Courtney's hands visibly trembled as she unbuttoned Darius's shirt. She had already loosened his tie in the limo during the heated moments of the ride back. She was eager to glide her fingers through his thick chest hair. She also craved to taste his honey-colored flesh. Just as he'd done to her, she dipped her head and slowly circled a nipple with her tongue. His flesh hardened beneath her lips. "How does that feel, Darius?"

"Indescribable," he said, his tone husky with passion. Not sure if she'd go as far as removing his dress slacks, he decided to save her the trouble. Unbuckling his belt and lowering his zipper, he slid the pants off his hips and down over his thighs, lower legs and feet.

Courtney gasped even harder. His thighs looked as if they'd been carved from solid granite. She fought hard to keep her eyes off the bulging outline inside his briefs, but she failed miserably when her eyes went straight there.

Seeing that his manhood was already hard, she swallowed hard. Freeing his sex from the restraints of his silk briefs steamed up the tender flesh between her legs. It would be a bold move on her part to strip him bare, but, as it was, she'd already indulged in quite a bit of risky behavior. She couldn't help wondering what Darius thought of her audacity.

Was it a turn-on or a turnoff for him? Whatever was flip-flopping through Darius's half-crazed mind, he didn't look like he minded her unleashing her naughty-girl side.

"Come closer to me, sweetheart," he encouraged soothingly. "I want to hold you in my arms until they're too tired for me to lift up." He guided her over to the bed and encouraged her to lie down. As he stretched out beside her in the king-size bed, he gently brought her into his strong arms.

The couple seemed resigned to allowing nature to take its course. With her head on his chest, he stroked her hair, smoothing it back at intervals. Having her nestled in his arms made Darius feel as if he had it all. Their relationship was brand-new, yet he felt like he'd known her his entire life. He *had* known her. She *was* the woman in his dreams.

He kissed the top of her head. "Are you comfortable?"

"I can't remember when I last felt this content," she whispered softly.

Courtney allowed herself to think of the boldness she'd displayed only minutes before. The part of her she'd shown Darius was new to her. She hadn't bared her breasts to any man, nor had she undressed one as if her life depended on it. "Did I shock you? If so, are you disappointed in how brazen I've been?"

Darius rolled up on his side. "You suddenly sound unsure of yourself. Did you stun yourself?"

"As a matter of fact, I actually stunned the hell out of myself.

The last thing I want you to think of me is that I'm fast and loose."

"Don't you think I know that?" He gently sucked on her bottom lip. "Nothing you've said or done would make me think anything negative about you. Maybe we both got a little carried away, but I don't regret anything we did. And I don't want you to feel any distress, either. Our responses were natural for two people who really care about each other. Can you believe and accept that?"

Unable to look up at Darius, Courtney only nodded. She was comforted by his comments, but she still felt a sense of shame. Perhaps it was a natural reaction, but she should've been a little less eager to show Darius how much she wanted him physically.

Without saying a word, Darius slipped out of bed. His sudden departure made Courtney feel even worse than she had. She began to feel abandoned.

Darius was gone less than a minute. Coaxing Courtney to sit up in bed, he helped her into his personal bathrobe. "Is this better?"

Feeling like a child, tears slipped from Courtney's eyes. "Can you forgive me for starting something grown-up I couldn't finish?"

"Shush," he whispered. Darius reclaimed his position in bed, pulling her back into his arms. "Close your eyes and let's just hold each other the rest of the night."

Chapter 10

Courtney awakened in bed alone. Her first thought was of Darius, wondering where he was. As she peered into the darkness, she saw that the bedroom door was ajar. Then she saw a light, appearing to come from the end of the hallway. The Bose clock radio read 4:00 a.m. She had obviously fallen asleep. Had Darius slept, too, or had he been up all this time?

Still cloaked in Darius's robe, Courtney slipped out of bed and went into the adjoining bathroom. Once she finished using the restroom, she stood over the sink and splashed cold water on her face. Slightly distressed at the unusual puffiness under her eyes, she wished she had access to her special formula eye cream.

Courtney walked back into the bedroom and went through the door leading to the front of Darius's suite. Seated in one of the plush chairs, he looked intent. Quietly, adoringly, she watched the man she loved probably more than was safe. It appeared he was studying a journal or day planner of some sort.

Feeling he was being watched, Darius looked up, his smile lighting up his face. "Doing okay? I didn't want to disturb you. You were out like a light."

Was that an accusatory tone she heard coming from him? Did he blame her for falling asleep on him?

Courtney knew that she was looking for any little thing to sabotage what they had going. It was hard for her to admit that she was just plain scared. Worry that she might have gotten in over her head was driving her fears. Darius Fairfax was the kind of man she hadn't run into before. He was debonair and worldly and she imagined that he knew his way around the ladies pretty well.

Will I become one of his casualties of love? God only knows. I don't have to be a victim. I could end this now and quietly disappear from his life. That might make it easier on him, but it would be one of the hardest things for me to do, since I love him.

Darius crooked his finger at her. "Come on over here with me, Courtney. Can I get you something? Is it too early for a cup of coffee or tea?"

"No coffee or tea, but thank you for asking." She cringed at how polite and businesslike she sounded. Still, she thought she should get dressed and get out of his suite. Her demeanor was totally different from earlier, before fear had crept in. If nothing else, she and Darius should be able to remain friends.

Courtney finally made her way across the room and sat in the chair on the other side of the round mahogany table. "Sorry I fell asleep on you."

Darius had wanted Courtney to sit on his lap, but he had no intention of pushing the issue. She looked fearful—and he hoped it wasn't him she was scared of. Things might have gotten a little out of hand earlier. It hadn't changed his feelings for her.

"No apology necessary. We fell asleep on each other. I'm not sure who passed out first. All I know is we must've needed it. We'd been going strong since a little after 5:00 a.m. yesterday morning. I wouldn't trade a second of the time we shared. There are no words to explain how much I enjoyed lying next to you in bed. Feeling any better about what happened between us?"

Hoping the telltale signs of blushing didn't show up on her cheeks, Courtney frowned slightly. "Could we *not* go there? I assure you I'm fine."

Darius nodded, thinking the mystified expression on her face was so precious. Getting up from his seat, he went over and knelt down in front of her.

Courtney had a flashback to when he'd knelt down before her in the restaurant. That had been a joyous moment for her. Darius had come to Hawaii to be with her and nothing could ever take away the euphoria of that momentous experience.

Locking his fiery eyes on to hers, he took her hands in his, kissing the back of each. "Do you know how happy I am to be here with you? There's no place I'd rather be. I've been so happy you haven't rejected me or my reason for coming here."

Courtney did her best to shake off her somber mood. He didn't deserve sullen treatment from her. Men didn't come any more sincere than Darius. He wasn't just blowing egotistical smoke her way. She sensed that he really cared for her and was there only because of her. Leaning forward, she rested her forehead against his. "I feel it, too, Darius. Happy feels good. What were you doing when I first came into the room?"

He stretched his hand out and retrieved his personal calendar from the table. "I was checking my travel schedule. The next couple of months are crazy busy. I have nine out-of-town business trips planned, most of them out of state." He opened the planner to share the penciled-in dates with her. "I'm off to Vegas for three days as soon as I get home from here. I have an important meeting in New York right after I get back from Vegas."

Darius pointed out the dates on the calendar for his upcoming meetings in San Diego and San Francisco. Portland and Seattle were within the same time frame. Chicago, Pittsburgh, Philadelphia, Washington, D.C. and Memphis were all on his agenda.

His hectic schedule worried and frightened Courtney. She wondered when he'd ever find time for her, for them. It seemed as if their relationship would take a backseat to his business. She felt the optimism over them becoming a super couple beginning to slip through her fingers. There was no way he could maintain a heavy travel schedule and manage to spend quality time on a personal relationship.

Darius was concerned about the troubled look on her face. He had an idea that the trips were at the core of it. "Think you can make any or all of these trips with me? I'd love to have you come along. There's so much else we could explore in new settings."

Courtney shook her head in the negative. "Impossible, not the way my business is booming. I have a pretty full work schedule, too."

"Can't your grandmother and Monica run things for you in your absence?"

Courtney cut her eyes sharply. "Would you allow someone else to run your business for you if I asked you to travel with me on behalf of my company?"

"Ouch!" He flinched. "I see what you mean. I'm sorry for being so insensitive. I'm aware that your business is just as important to you as mine is to me. I know there's a lot of travel involved in my work, but it shouldn't affect my committing to us."

Who are you kidding, Darius? I doubt if commitment is possible on the run.

"Let's not borrow trouble at this stage of our relationship, Courtney. I promise I won't leave you unattended, if that's a concern. I want to be with you and I can't make myself any clearer. This is where trust will have to take over. I need you to trust me."

Courtney felt foolish again. Her negative thinking would eventually get her into big trouble if she didn't get a grip on her fears. *Go with the flow,* she told herself.

This kind of love affair is brand-new for me, but it can't possibly blossom into something magical and beautiful if I continue to stunt our growth.

Sensing that it was time to change the subject and steer things onto a lighter path, Darius picked up a manila folder from the table. "This is my screenplay, the one with the wedding ideas. Want to look it over?"

"I'd love to read it. Thanks. I feel honored." Surprised that he wanted her to read it, Courtney took the folder from his hand and eagerly opened it.

Glad he'd put the smile back into her eyes, Darius chuckled inwardly. "Before you start reading, what do you want for breakfast?"

Promises to Keep

Deciding to put him to the test, Courtney laughed. "Do you recall what I ordered for breakfast yesterday?"

Darius stroked his chin, looking kind of smug. "Let me see. You ordered Raisin Bran or Corn Flakes cereal, two percent milk and a banana, turkey sausage, softly scrambled eggs, wheat toast with butter and fruit preserves and a pot of breakfast tea. How did I do?" He snapped his fingers. "Wait a minute. You also asked for sliced fresh fruit and a glass of pineapple juice," he said, teasing her with a Caribbean accent.

"Not bad," she joked, knowing he'd gotten everything right on the money. "This morning I only want pancakes and sausage."

His eyes widened. "Is that it?"

"Well, not exactly." Getting up from the chair, she plopped down on his lap. "I also want maple syrup. I love it heated, but I'd love to start with the hot, sweet taste of your luscious mouth." She pressed her lips into his, then allowed her tongue to coil with his as she tasted the delicious mouth she'd come to crave. She lifted her head. "Think we can wait on breakfast for a little while?"

Darius looked puzzled. "Yeah, but why wait if you're hungry now?"

"I'm hungry all right, but not for food. I'm starving for you."

Courtney got up from his lap. Connecting flirtatious eyes with his, she loosened the belt and let the robe fall open just enough to give him a glimpse of her bare thighs. Mimicking what she'd seen him do to her a few times, she crooked her finger—and began backing up in the direction of the bedroom.

The time for child's play and uncertainty was over for Courtney. She craved Darius in the worst way, desired to gorge on him for breakfast, lunch, dinner and also make him her in-between and late-night snacks.

If overindulgence was a sin, Courtney would be guilty of committing a big one.

Unable to believe what was happening, Darius looked at her with questioning eyes. Feeling concerned that she was acting on what she thought he wanted as opposed to her own desires and needs, he wasn't quite sure what to do. He certainly didn't want her to feel rejected. With that in mind, he got to his feet.

* * *

In the bedroom, Courtney wrapped her arms around Darius's neck. She saw uncertainty in his eyes. She knew it wasn't about anything to do with him, recognizing and understanding that his concern was for her. Courtney realized that he was worried about how she might feel later if she went through with something she wasn't absolutely sure of.

"It's okay, Darius," she tried to assure him. "I'm ready, ready for you and me. You said you needed me to trust you—and I do. I honestly believe in you. And I trust myself to make the right decisions in my life. I'm the only one accountable for my actions."

Darius heard the steadiness of conviction in her voice. He wanted so desperately to do the right thing by her. Just like her, he held himself accountable for everything he did. Darius didn't take possession of a woman like Courtney without honorable intentions. He had no way of knowing the outcome of the relationship, yet he was very clear on the outcome he desired.

Just in case they did come together physically, he began thinking of a way to retrieve a condom, without her being any the wiser. Once they reached the bedroom, he had her sit on the bed. Telling her he'd be right back, he dashed into the bathroom and opened his shaving kit, where he always stored extra condoms. Getting to his wallet was not an option for him at the moment.

Lifting Courtney in his arms, Darius carried her into the bathroom, where he turned on the shower full blast. Taking no time to disrobe, he settled them under the downpour of water. As her laughter rang out, he sighed with deep relief.

Courtney came out of her robe first, then made a dramatic show of stripping him of his, hoping he'd enjoy her fumbling attempts at seduction.

The condom was in the pocket of Darius's robe, but he was just relieved to have it close at hand. He'd never think of making love without protecting both parties.

With unsure hands, she fleetingly touched his intimate zones. Darius's soft moans and his helping her move her hands over his body let her know he was feeling it, too. As her hands grew bolder, the experience became even more delicious and fulfilling for her.

Swapping control, Darius began taking matters into his own hands. Picking up the drenched robe, he removed the foil packet from his pocket. As Courtney's eyes grew larger than saucers, she watched him place the condom, astonished that his manhood was much larger than she'd imagined.

Darius tenderly lifted her into his arms, holding her securely. "Wrap your legs around my waist, baby," he huskily encouraged. Turning his back to the water, he moved closer to the shower's back wall.

Fear once again welled up in Courtney, but in a matter of seconds it failed to be an issue. Darius's hands stroking her bare buttocks and gently touching her inner treasures made the fear fly free of her mind and body. There were so many mind-numbing, amazing sensations assailing her that she could only concentrate on the wild pleasures he was so lovingly bestowing upon her starving body.

For however long our relationship lasts, Darius Fairfax is about to become a part of my physical being, literally.

In the next instant, Darius had Courtney's back against the wet tile. Slowly, he made his way inside the woman he loved with his whole heart and soul. Careful not to hurt her or rush things, he took his time to allow her to adjust. With all the conviction he'd heard in her voice, he still wanted to give her a chance to call the whole thing off.

Inch by inch, Darius continued burying his protected manhood inside Courtney. She felt so tight to him and the incredible feeling sent his body into delectable spasms. His mouth had clung to hers from the moment he'd lifted her—and he had to come up for air, repossessing her lips only seconds later. Courtney had kept him breathless from the first moment he'd met her, a sensation he wouldn't mind feeling for the rest of his life.

With her femininity exulting in every deep thrust, Courtney had nowhere for her head to go but backward, so she moved it from side to side. Feeling every minuscule sensation coursing through her body, she gave herself up to Darius.

As Darius felt himself about to explode inside her, he returned to foreplay to bring her to the same point, hopefully at the same time he let go. Seconds into the sexual play, her nails dug into his back. Feeling her tightening up around him, he looked into her eyes. She was just as ready to climax as he was. Several more deep thrusts toppled the couple over the edge, causing them to feel like they were dancing wildly on air.

Darius continued to kiss Courtney passionately as she lay limp in his arms. Knowing he was responsible for her being lax as a rag doll made him ecstatic. Although she hadn't said a word, her screams ripping through the air certainly indicated how she'd felt.

Darius removed from the caddy a bottle of body wash before standing Courtney on her feet. Making sure she was steady, he began lathering her body. Instantly, he became aroused again. Wanting Courtney again so soon had his heart throbbing hard. Darius could only wish she'd come to want him as much.

Feeling sexy and complete, Courtney finally opened her eyes and looked at him. "You are amazing!" She immediately noticed the sexy glint in his eyes. "I'd love more breakfast. Are you feeling hungry again, too?"

"Ravenous!"

The alarm clock sounded at noon. Darius was lying on the edge of the bed, so all he had to do was reach his hand over to silence the shrill sound. Leaving on the accompanying soft music, he peered down at the beautiful, sleeping woman whose head used his chest as a pillow.

The memories of several hours ago sailed through his mind. He smiled as he recalled her saying he was amazing. Courtney was beyond amazing to him and he was thrilled by how she'd turned from an unsure woman to one with extreme confidence, making the transition in such a short period.

Hating to disturb her, but needing to go to the bathroom, Darius was careful in removing her head from his chest. Managing to lay her head on the pillow without her moving a muscle, he laughed inwardly. "The lady is out cold again," he whispered, slipping gingerly out of bed. Reaching the bathroom door, he looked back at Courtney. Stopping his forward progress was the angelic look on her face. It seemed to him she had found peace in sleep. Closing his eyes, he prayed for her serenity to continue.

Stretching her arms up over her head, Courtney looked around the room to get her bearings. Darius's suite, she thought, smiling. Even though she wondered where he was, she was sure he hadn't ventured very far away. Rolling over in the bed, she pressed her face into his pillow and caught a strong whiff of his cologne. Hugging the pillow closer to her, she moved over until she was in his spot on the bed.

Courtney looked up when the bathroom door opened. "There you are. I missed you."

No way could Darius have kept himself from smiling. She always seemed to know just the right thing to say to pump him up. "So that's why you're on my side."

Courtney laughed. "I didn't know we had sides. But I must confess, I don't like to sleep on the left side of the bed. Right in the middle is my preference."

Darius slipped back into the bed. He got in from the right, not wanting to disturb the comfort she appeared to enjoy. Scooting over, he lowered his head and gave special attention to each of her breasts.

Courtney squirmed under the heat of his sensuous mouth. "Still hungry, I see. Maybe we should order breakfast now."

Darius looked up at her. "Breakfast from room service?"

Courtney nodded. "We have to keep our strength up, don't you think?"

Darius chuckled. "Are you confessing to weakness? If so, how much do I have to do with your fatigue?"

Courtney rolled her eyes. "I'm trying to feed your stomach, not your ego."

Full from the pancakes and sausage she'd practically inhaled, Courtney pushed back from the table. "I can't eat another bite."

Darius laughed. "There's nothing left on your plate to bite."

Courtney had to laugh, too. "Did you really have to point that out?"

"What do you want to do today, Courtney? We've slept the

morning away so we've lost several hours of daylight. I've made all the plans for us so far and I'm interested in knowing what interests you."

Thinking Darius was so sweet, Courtney blew him a kiss. "Everything we did yesterday was a lot of fun. The cruise was romantic and way more than I'd expected for my surprise. Your holding me in your arms while we danced had me feeling so good. I'd like to go to the Polynesian Culture Center, but I hear it's an all-day affair."

"Not if we select the attractions we want to visit before going. From what I know, I doubt we could do the entire center in one day."

Courtney wrinkled her nose. "Maybe we could get an earlier start if we waited until tomorrow. Besides, I'd love to soak in the Jacuzzi. My muscles are kind of tight."

Darius and Courtney had had fun splashing water on each other. They had used one of the resort swimming pools first, then moved on to the Jacuzzi. Though she had admitted to him that her muscles felt a little tight, she hadn't explained which muscles were affected. He had an idea by the embarrassed look on her face at the time. In his opinion, Courtney had been too limp and relaxed earlier in bed for the kinks to be anywhere else.

While Darius kissed Courtney passionately, steaming Jacuzzi waters swirled around the couple who seemed oblivious to everything around them. Even though they were alone in the water, she figured she had to be somewhat reserved. All she really wanted to do was make love to him again and again. She was still in a romantic mood.

Darius kissed her forehead. "I can tell you're feeling better because you're a little more amorous. Ready to go back to the room?"

"That would be nice," Courtney responded, "but I haven't been back to my suite since we left the cruise. I need to change clothes and should at least check on things."

Darius nodded his understanding. "You're right. I'll go with you if you'll wait until I get ready. It won't take me long to shower again and get dressed."

"That's okay. We can do it at the same time and meet up later."

Darius didn't take to that suggestion. He wondered if she thought he might be tiring of her, but that wasn't happening. "What if I don't want us to be apart for a second? Am I asking too much of you? I don't want to crowd you if you want downtime."

Courtney had been worried about him getting tired of her. "I want to be with you every second, too."

Sighing hard, Darius gently posted his hands on both Courtney's shoulders. "When are you going to let my actions speak for me, speak louder than your thoughts? Have I given you any indication that I don't want to be with you? Why do you forget I flew all the way here to be with you? You're still borrowing on nonexistent troubles."

The spark of anger in Darius's voice and his deep sigh of frustration were not lost on her. To say she was sorry just might be another insult to him, she thought. She had to learn to be more mindful of his feelings, rather than apologizing so much. Instead of voicing an apology, she went into his arms, kissing him passionately, hoping he'd feel her heartfelt regret. Darius's ardent response to her kiss gave her some relief.

Dressed in lightweight attire—shorts and a sleeveless top—Darius drove along the coastline. The top on the car was up because Courtney had brought along his screenplay to read. In the close confines of the vehicle, she figured she could discuss with him any questions she might have. It was so hot that the short, summery shift she wore in sunny yellow was Hawaiian weather perfect.

Darius kept his eyes on the road as Courtney read. He didn't want her to miss out on so many beautiful sights, but she had insisted on delving into the screenplay. The coastline here reminded him a lot of the L.A. coast, so maybe she wasn't missing as much as he thought. Still, he wanted her to enjoy herself.

Courtney reached over and rested her hand on Darius's thigh. "I've only read the first twenty pages and I have to tell you it's incredible. It's so real. I can see these characters and the places you've written about."

"Thank you." A feeling of humbleness swept over him. "If anyone else close to me weighed in on my script, I might wonder how much of the assessment was due to bias. But you're far too honest for that. If you feel I've missed something essential or left out any key element, please let me know. The script will only be finished when I'm one hundred percent satisfied."

"I haven't seen anything questionable yet, but I have another hundred pages to read."

"I hate that you're missing out on so many of the sights, but I won't interrupt."

Courtney went back to reading and Darius kept a steady course down the coast. He then took a road leading to Pali Highway, which would take them to the Punchbowl National Cemetery, consisting of 116 acres honoring those who died during World War II in the Pacific campaign. It was given the name *punchbowl* because of its shape. Also located there was a breathtaking view of Honolulu from Puowaina Lookout.

Darius hoped Courtney didn't think it was morbid to visit a cemetery because there was a lot of history lying in an extinct volcano called Puowaina, meaning Consecrated Hill or Hill of Sacrifice. Ellison Onizuka, the first astronaut from Hawaii, rested there, having perished in the *Challenger* explosion.

Courtney looked up as Darius turned the car into the cemetery entrance, where they passed by a large mast. "Oh, my goodness, we're entering Punchbowl National Cemetery. This is one of the places I wanted to visit. I've read so much about it."

Darius pulled the car around to the back of the memorial where a parking lot was located. Once he parked the vehicle, he went around and opened the door for his companion. He noticed how carefully she'd handled his masterpiece as she put it away. Everything he'd seen of her so far told him she was an exceptional woman, a good one.

After locking the car and setting the alarm, Darius put his arm around Courtney's waist and guided her to the front of the memorial. "Let's check it out. I'm glad you don't think of this visit as morbid."

"Not at all, Darius. We're standing on consecrated ground. This is the final resting place of many of our American heroes. My grandfather and father have defended our country. It happened before I was born, but they've shared countless stories with me, unforgettable ones."

Seeing how emotional Courtney had gotten, he hugged her to him. "Don't cry."

"It's hard not to. I fully understand the significance of this place. I can't imagine not having the same reaction if we get to the Pearl Harbor Memorial."

"There's no *if* about it. I already planned to take you there. We have four days left. I want you to see as much as possible."

The couple walked all around the memorial, studying the plaques and much of the history on the walls. After reading many of the names of the fallen heroes, they signed the guestbook and then headed toward lookout point.

Walking along the wall leading to their destination, Courtney slipped her hand into Darius's. Her anticipation grew as they got closer. Her man was an excellent tour guide and he'd shared with her so much about the tourist sights on the island. There were certain places people came to Hawaii to see. They loved to hit the beaches and enjoy the nightlife, but they also had a thirst for visiting beautiful, world-renowned attractions.

The magnificent view before Courtney was more than she could ever have imagined. It was a clear day and she could see for miles and miles. The brochures, which had described this place as breathtaking and fantastic, certainly had it right.

Darius pointed outward with his finger. "That's the Honolulu coastline down there." He looked up. "Campbell Park and the Waianae mountain range are up there. I read that the state capitol building can be seen from here, but I can't make it out. Over there are Sand Island and Magic Island. I'm sure those names are very fitting."

"Look," Courtney shouted, "that's Diamond Head. I saw it earlier at the resort."

"That's Diamond Head, all right. It can be seen from many places on Oahu," Darius confirmed. "It's one amazing sight to behold. Look at the Ko'olau Mountains there to the left. It has been said that they appear to stand guard over the cemetery."

It suddenly began to sprinkle. Darius threw back his head and laughed when Courtney's hands went straight for her hair, the same hair she hadn't minded getting wet in the pool or in the ocean. "What's happening is known as the Moana sprinkles. We can consider ourselves lucky. Everyone doesn't get to experience this phenomenon."

"We've experienced it. Now let's get back to the car. Oh, my hair is all wet," Courtney cried. Realizing how silly she was acting, she lifted her arms up to the sky. "Rain down on me, special gifts from heaven. Soak me through and through."

Courtney had managed to surprise and impress Darius once again. He engaged her in a waltz and they danced around the lookout point, laughing as if they'd lost their minds. The sprinkles ended as quickly as they'd started, but the couple was already running for the car.

It took Darius longer to get down the mountainous road than it had taken to go up. Traffic was starting to be a problem, as well. Courtney looked as though she were about to fall asleep, so he turned down the radio until it could barely be heard.

Though her eyes were closed, Courtney was thinking about Candice saying that she and Darius were all the family they each had left. *What happened to their mom and dad? Were they dead?* On the way out of a cemetery wasn't the time to ask him about it. Maybe he'd tell her the story in due time. Then she let her curiosity get the best of her.

Reaching for the radio dial, she turned it off completely. "Is it by design that you haven't said much about your family, like your parents?"

Darius swallowed hard, tears springing to his eyes. "A car accident claimed their lives. My mother was driving under the influence of alcohol. Every time I started to tell you about them, I couldn't bring myself to do it. My mother was an alcoholic and they say it's hereditary. While I drink wine now and then, I never overindulge. Candice doesn't touch anything stronger than club soda. She's more fearful than I am of becoming an alcoholic.

I don't think so, but I allow her to conduct her life in her own way."

Regretting prying into his private life, Courtney reached over and squeezed Darius's thigh. "Now it makes more sense why you didn't order champagne at dinner last night. I'm sorry for your loss. I love you."

Courtney telling him she loved him overrode his sadness. Today was his future. He couldn't go back and reconstruct the past. If he allowed his grief to smother him, he'd have nothing to give to anyone else. He often felt the overwhelming sadness, but he tried restricting it to when he was alone. As for Courtney, he wanted to give her all the love and joy he had in him. Darius didn't want to make his grief a part of what they had.

"I love you, too, Courtney. I would have told you everything eventually, but some things are harder to express than others. Forgive me?"

"Nothing to forgive. You have a right to guard your inner pain. I do plenty of that myself. I wish I didn't, but I do."

"What *is* your pain? I want to know, but only if you want to share it."

"My parents' divorce was painful for me. I got over it after a while. Knowing they are friends eased the burden I felt. Mom just didn't love deeply enough. She had an agenda to fulfill and it meant more to her than staying married and being my mother."

"I still hear pain in your voice. I promise not to cause you any anguish."

Courtney stretched out on her bed and pulled Darius down on top of her. She lifted her head and covered his mouth. "You're staying the night with me, right?"

"Every single second of it. Do you want anything before it gets too late?"

"Yeah, I want you. If you're here all night, it won't get too late." Reaching for the button on his shorts, she worked it loose with ease and then lowered the zipper.

"You've got a point, lady."

Darius stripped away his shirt before she got a chance to reach for it. For them, time was everything. Gently pushing her dress up, he slowly took it off over her head. He didn't favor strong-arm tactics. No woman liked to feel roughed up while making love. Darius wanted to be a hero in her life, not a domineering force. If she felt free, she'd give herself freely and accept the same from him in return. Uninhibited love was the best kind.

Courtney straddled Darius, settling down just above his manhood. She felt the hardness of his abdomen as she got comfortable. Leaning forward until her mouth was in close range of his, she lazed her tongue across his bottom lip. Her fingernails circled his nipples and made them taut, ready for her to suckle.

After giving tender loving care to one of his nipples, she took care of the other. Using her tongue, she licked all the way down the center line of Darius's body until she reached the hairline of his manhood. Before she could make up her mind to go farther or not, Darius was lifting her off him and laying her flat on her back.

Tenderly working the moist flesh between her legs was every bit as pleasurable for Darius. As he inserted a finger into the core of her femininity, she tightly closed her muscles around it, delighting in the feel of his tender manipulation. Dipping his head between her legs, his tongue outlined her thighs and the area closest to her treasure trove.

Breathing hard in anticipation of what Darius might do to her next, Courtney tried to brace herself. If his tongue moved any farther to her center, she feared her body might come straight up off the bed. Closing her eyes, she begged for mercy.

In the next instant, Courtney's anticipation heightened tenfold. He was right there at the core of her passion, his moist tongue soothingly assaulting the lake of fire raging out of control. The writhing of her body was nearly more than she could bear. Feeling the flames of desire licking inside her, burning up her inner flesh, she was sure she couldn't hold on much longer. Her body was aching badly, throbbing hard for the ultimate release.

Courtney couldn't stop her body from rising toward his mouth to keep it in place. His lips closed completely around her intimate zone as he suckled hard and tenderly. That was her undoing. Her body spun into the kind of jerky spasms she'd never experienced before. The wild jolting might have scared her if it didn't feel so deliciously sweet. Believing she couldn't go any higher than she had already, her body shocked her, suddenly going berserk while bucking and shivering uncontrollably.

Screams of completion filled the air.

Courtney's fulfillment spurred Darius on, making him desperate to be inside her. As he forged a tender path into her moist canal, he already felt ready to detonate. Only a few deep thrusts later, he was sent reeling, falling off the precipice of ultimate desire.

Chapter 11

Horrified by the time on the clock, Courtney screamed, shooting straight up and out of bed. "This has got to stop!"

The screaming awakened Darius, scaring him momentarily, until he saw that Courtney appeared to be okay. He rubbed the sleep out of his eyes. "What's got to stop?"

Screaming again, Courtney pounded her fists into a pillow. "Staying in bed for days on end, that's what. First, we slept away nearly an entire day in your bed, and now we've slept in mine for the last several days and nights. We planned to go to Pearl Harbor, but now it's nearly three o'clock…and we leave tomorrow."

Darius laughed. "I don't think sleeping is all we've done, Court. You don't seem to mind being in bed when you're busy blowing my mind to shreds. Pearl Harbor's not going anywhere. If we can't manage to make it out of bed, Hawaii will still be here for us to revisit."

"Come back? I planned to see it all this time around. Who knows when I'll get back here?"

Darius pulled her into his arms, kissing her gently on the mouth. "Calm down. No way possible to do it all in seven days. I'll see to it that you get back to Hawaii. I promise."

Sticking her lip out in a pout, Courtney looked sulky. "It's easy for you to miss out on things. You've been here before."

Reaching his hand out, he mussed her hair. "You look so cute when you're pouting. I'll bet you're just as adorable when you're in a tizzy. Either way, it's sexy to me. What about a romantic dinner this evening in one of the resort restaurants?"

Just to mess with Darius a little, Courtney put a finger to her temple, as though she had to think about his suggestion. "I don't know. Everything we've done has been activities you've chosen. Can I get a little equal opportunity and treatment?"

If he'd thought for one moment that she was serious, he would have yielded immediately. "Don't you know this is a man's world, woman?" He poked at his side. "I gave up a rib for you so I could be in control…" The look on her face made it impossible for him to go any further. He burst out laughing. "Fell for my bull, didn't you? What do you have in mind for this evening? I'd love you to choose for us."

Picking up a pillow, Courtney tossed it right at Darius's head, hitting the bull's-eye dead-on. "How's that for bull, Adam?" Ducking when the pillow fire was returned, she fell down laughing, glad he'd missed her by a wide margin. "Some glasses might've helped," she teased, trying to gain control of her laughter. "What about Tokyo-Tokyo?"

Darius's eyebrows lifted. "What about it?"

"I'm trying to see if you'd like to eat there. According to the dining brochure, it's a fine, romantic place to have dinner."

"I thought you wanted equal opportunity and treatment. Why are you asking me?"

With his message loud and clear, she jumped off the bed. "We're having dinner at Tokyo-Tokyo at six-thirty." That said, she picked up the nightstand phone. "Tokyo-Tokyo, please. Thank you." Once an employee came on the line, she made reservations.

"Courtney Campbell, party of two." She stuck out her tongue at Darius to emphasize how she'd taken firm control.

She hung up the phone and stretched out on the bed. "If I didn't have to worry about my hair, I'd love to swim in the dolphin cove for about an hour. But if I get my hair wet now, I'll never get it together by dinnertime."

"What about all those cutesy hair clips I saw in the bathroom? Why can't you just use one of them?"

Embarrassment staining her cheeks over his discovery of her hairpieces, Courtney screeched. "Even if you saw the fake hair, you shouldn't have let me know. I feel mortified now."

"If they make you feel that terrible, why you do buy them? Also, you invited me to stay here with you, so you could've hidden them away. Don't kid yourself. I know fake hair from real hair when I see it or feel it, but the pieces you have are good quality and I don't think they'll be obvious."

"TMI," she exclaimed, "too much information. Let's change the subject."

"Okay."

Sometimes the finality of Darius's *okay* irritated her, yet she also appreciated that he didn't care to indulge in meaningless arguments. "Okay," she mocked.

Darius completely ignored her petulant mocking. "Ready to forgo gorgeous hair and fulfill your desire of swimming in the private lagoon with six bottleneck dolphins? Or are you chicken, scared they'll take liberties with your sweet, tender flesh?"

"As you've been doing?" she shot back in a whip-cracking tone.

"Enough of your insolence, woman. You're not to be ignored, are you?" Intending to silence her impudence, rolling over on top of her, he kissed her mouth shut.

Tokyo-Tokyo was everything Courtney had expected from what she'd read about the five-star restaurant. The establishment exuded peace and harmony. The menu boasted a seamless blending of global inspirations with Japanese traditions.

Wearing a sophisticated white strapless sarong, one highlighting her shapely figure, Courtney looked smoking hot. She had beautifully accessorized the sexy dress with gold-and-white open-toed sandals.

Despite the couple of hours of supervised swimming with the dolphins, Courtney had managed to pull off a fashionable hairstyle for the evening. Darius didn't comment again on the fake hairpieces and she hadn't brought it up, either. However, he did tell her he loved her classy hairstyle.

A fragrant white ginger lei caressed her slender neck. Courtney wore no perfume, allowing the pure scent of her lei to take center stage. A trio of gold-tone hoops dangled from each of her delicate ears. Her skin had tanned to a warm bronze, harmonizing with the stunning, soft-white dress.

Darius noticed that she had not stopped smiling since they'd sat down, her eyes darting all over the place. "Really impressed with your choice for dinner, huh?"

"Oh, yes! I love the authentic Japanese decor, especially all the red. I've never seen red marble pillars with gold and bamboo framework. This place is magnificent."

Darius eyed her with such deep, pleasurable feelings. "You're pretty magnificent yourself. For at least the tenth time, I love your dress and love you in it. White always highlights your blushing innocence. I remember how much I loved the white pantsuit you wore at the club, the night we met Rest Assured."

Courtney blushed. "*You do?* How sweet. I remember everything I've seen you in, too. We do look good in white, especially with these glowing golden-bronze tans. I noticed all the female heads turning to look at you when we walked in. The fact we're both dressed in white might have prompted a few of the admiring glances."

Darius cast Courtney a charming, sexy smile. "Heads turned because we're such a striking couple." He winked at her, causing her libido to react to his blatant sexiness. "Our attire may or may not have had anything to do with it. They weren't only looking at me. I spotted several swiveling male heads. What do you say to that, Miss Campbell?"

"We *are* a stunning couple, Mr. Fairfax," she easily acquiesced.

Surprised by Courtney's rapid-fire agreement, Darius smiled brightly, amazed at how one woman could make him feel so utterly wonderful and sexually wicked.

Leaving well enough alone, Darius picked up one of the menus left by the seating hostess. The couple then put their heads together to decide what to eat for dinner.

Darius pointed at one entrée that piqued his palate. USDA prime strip-loin Shabu Shabu was thinly sliced beef accompanied by vegetables. The dish was cooked at the table in a paper pot of dashi broth and served with spicy sesame and savory ponzu sauce. "This sounds good. I'm sold on it."

Courtney fingered an entrée with the same cut of strip-loin but preferred it sukiyaki style. The thinly sliced beef was cooked in homemade sukiyaki-style sauce, with tofu, vegetables and shirataki noodles. "I'll have this, but I'd first like to order a sushi appetizer."

Darius looked over the menu's sushi offerings. "They have a sushi platter for two. It comes with California, Rainbow and Philadelphia rolls, spicy tuna and jumbo shrimp tempura. Are you okay with that?"

Courtney nodded. "Let's order. I'm starved."

Walking off the calories wasn't necessary, since what Courtney and Darius had eaten wasn't sinfully caloric. The magic they felt between them had drawn the couple outside for a romantic walk on the beach. Stockingless, Courtney removed her sandals and allowed her feet to flirt with the calm Pacific waters. It didn't take much for her to convince Darius to remove his shoes and socks and unite his feet with hers.

Upon hearing the soft, melodic music coming from one of the resort establishments, he turned to face Courtney and brought her into his arms. Slowly, dancing her around in the shallow water, he looked down into her eyes. He then looked up at the moon. "You are so beautiful. The moonlight loves you. I wish you could see it dancing in your eyes and hair."

Courtney suddenly felt breathless, speechless. Darius said so many things that made her heart and spirit skyrocket somewhere over the rainbow. This time was no different. While offering her lips up to him, she pulled his head down to make the impassioned connection.

As the couple walked on, Courtney sighed hard. "I sure hate to go home tomorrow, but I miss my family, my work and my employees. Monica and I normally talk every single day, even on the weekends, and I miss our girl chats."

Darius's eyes empathized with her. "I'll bet you do. They say all good things come to an end, but our good times aren't ending here. I hope to keep you just as content as you've seemed to be throughout the past week. This is only our beginning, Courtney. As for Monica, I'm sure you two will have a lot to talk about once you're home."

Courtney's eyes gleamed. "You're right. I can't wait to tell her all about us. She's probably going to lose it. Want to know something?"

"What?"

"J.R. told me this would happen."

"You're kidding. What did he say?"

"It was the day we all had brunch together. When you went off to fill your plate, J.R. told us you looked at me like I was the queen of your heart. He also said you'd end up reneging on your commitment just to be with me. What do you think about that?"

"He was right on target, but I can't believe I was so transparent. Maybe I'm not as cool and smooth as I thought." He laughed at that notion.

"Wrong! They don't come any cooler than you, but you weren't offensive. Charming is what I call it. You were mildly flirtatious, but I never dreamed it was serious. Believing you were getting married kept me on high alert and determined not to fall for another woman's man, especially a client. The problem is, I'd already fallen—hard. I'm sure I lost my heart to you on the first or second meeting."

"I'd like to think it was at first sight, at the same time I lost my heart to yours." Lifting Courtney into his arms, he carried her over to a nearby playground.

To keep her dress clean, unworried about his suit, he sat down on a swing and pulled Courtney onto his lap. "Let's see how high we can make this baby fly. We may get it up there, but it'll never go as high as we've been for the past six days. I love you."

"I love you, too, with all my heart and soul."

As Darius attempted to make the swing fly as high as possible, Courtney's thrilling laughter rang out loud and clear.

* * *

Bound for Los Angeles, flight 126 had taken off right on time from the Honolulu airport. The jumbo jet had already clocked over an hour into the six-hour flight. Breakfast was in the process of being served.

Nudging her first, Darius turned to face Courtney, whose head had been stuck in his screenplay since shortly after takeoff. She wanted to commit the plot to memory. "The flight attendant is taking breakfast orders. Do you want scrambled eggs and ham or a vegetable omelet?"

Courtney made eye contact with the cute male attendant. "Vegetable omelet, please. May I also have more orange juice?"

"Beverage service will begin again shortly, but I'll see if I can get it to you before then," the male attendant responded.

"I can come up to the galley and get the juice if that'll make it easier," Darius suggested. He wanted Courtney to have whatever she wanted when she wanted it.

"I don't think it'll be a problem," the flight attendant said.

"Thanks."

Since the couple wasn't seated in first class, Darius knew once the aisles were jammed with serving carts he'd never make it to the galley. He had tried to use his frequent flyer miles to upgrade Courtney's ticket to first class, but he was told it couldn't be done at this point. Instead, he opted to sit in coach, which called for many fewer miles. Once the check-in was completed, he was told by an airline employee the unused miles would be credited back to his account.

"Let me get out," he told Courtney. "I want you to get your juice."

Reaching over, she laid her hand on his arm. "It's okay. I can wait. Let's give the guy a chance and see what happens."

"Okay."

Knowing his one-word response was the end of the orange juice issue, Courtney chuckled inwardly. She was almost getting used to the abrupt way Darius ended a discussion simply by agreeing with her. She had an idea that getting an angry rise out of him might prove impossible. Courtney had no desire to make him resort to such a destructive emotion. Darius was a well-adjusted, happy, fun-loving guy.

In a matter of minutes, the orange juice arrived. A short time later, breakfast followed. Courtney wanted to hurry up and eat so she could get back to the screenplay and finish her second read. Darius had written a story filled with loving relationships. Eager to take in his lovely words once again, she planned to read every chance she got.

The limousine Darius had arranged for pulled up in front of Courtney's house. He got out of the car, grabbed her luggage and walked her to the door. The limo driver would have taken her things, but he wanted to see her until the last second.

Courtney disabled the alarm, pushing the door back for Darius to enter. "You can just leave the bags here in the foyer. I'm not unpacking tonight. I'll take care of everything in the morning." She slid her arms around his neck. "Thanks for everything. I'll miss you tonight. I love you."

"You don't have to miss me. I can come back or you can go home with me."

Courtney laughed. "I love your idea, but I'm too tired to go any farther. Come to dinner tomorrow evening around six? I've decided to take two more days off to chill out. Besides, I want to finish the screenplay before I go back to work. Thanks for letting me keep it until I finish up."

"Not a problem. Listen, you haven't been to my place yet. Let me get dinner. I promise to let you rest. I'll pick you up...and bring you home whenever you're ready."

"I'm easy," she joked. "Call me and let me know you're on the way."

Pulling her to him, he kissed her thoroughly. "Sleep tight, love. Dream of us."

Courtney smiled bewitchingly. "I'll do that. You do the same."

Courtney thought of asking Darius to call before he went to bed, but she thought better of it. Tears filled her eyes as she watched him walk to the limousine. Blowing a kiss at his back, she knew her days and nights alone would never be the same again.

Missing him and craving his touch like crazy were only going to get worse during his absences. Closing the door, she reset the alarm and rushed off to her bedroom.

Seven days in paradise was over all too soon for us.

Seated on the sofa inside Courtney's home, Monica listened closely to what her boss and friend was saying. She was thrilled to see Courtney looking so happy, yet she thought her voice belied a trace of doubt.

"A shadow suddenly falling over my restaurant chair had me wondering what was happening. I heard his voice before I saw him, but I told myself no way he was there. Then I looked up. You can't imagine my surprise. It's how our love affair began."

"I'm not so sure it started then. Are you forgetting what J.R. said to us at the restaurant, when he was up in your business about Darius?" Monica asked.

"I *do* remember. One evening I told Darius about J.R.'s prediction. He said he thought he was smoother and cooler than that. He was surprised at his transparency."

"J.R. definitely called Darius's feelings for you. He turned out to be right."

Courtney looked a bit apprehensive. "I'm trying hard not to be worried about us. Early one morning Darius showed me his travel schedule. In two days he leaves for Las Vegas. Right after he gets back from there a whirlwind of traveling begins for him. Most of his business meetings are out of state. I'm afraid he won't have enough time for us."

Now, after less than twenty-four hours at home, Monica heard the tinge of doubt in her boss's voice growing into a mountain of it, all over her romantic liaison with Darius. "You sound as if you don't trust him to make time for the two of you. What I want to know is why? How many men would've pursued you to Hawaii if they didn't really care?"

Courtney shook her head in the negative. "It's not him I don't trust. It's me. I've never been in love before. Maybe I thought I was, but now I know I wasn't. What I've experienced with Darius doesn't even come close to anything I've ever known. We shared a uniting of spirits."

Monica appeared concerned. "You say you love him, but deep apprehension is starting to suffuse your voice. It'll end up taking over your entire being if you don't come to grips with the fear. What else are you afraid of?"

"That Darius's feelings of love for me may only be in my mind. I couldn't bear for him to end it with me. It seems like the best thing to do is get out while I can. I couldn't handle being rejected by him."

Monica put her arm around Courtney. "You've got to give up the fear, dear friend. Darius has shown me he is a man of genuine integrity. If only you'd seen his eyes. As he talked to me about his feelings for you, his eyes shone with brilliance. Have you discussed any of this with him?"

"Are you kidding? He'd think I was a lunatic if I brought it up, especially after the wonderful time we had together over the past week. Please, Monica, promise me you won't say anything to him about my fears. It's actually very juvenile on my part."

"I agree with you there." The hurt in Courtney's eyes made Monica wish she'd bitten her tongue. "I'm sorry I said that, but this isn't a teen crush. You two are grown folks. If Darius doesn't know how he really feels about you, how do you propose to know for him? You're not inside him."

Courtney nodded. "You're right. How do I continue to get in deeper with him when I'm so fearful of eventually losing him?"

Monica lifted a few strands of Courtney's hair and let it fall back to her shoulders. "I can't answer that for you, sweetie. Follow your heart. I don't think it'll lead you astray. As you said, you haven't been in love before. The hurt you felt from the last relationship was from disappointment more than anything else."

"Exactly," Courtney cried out. "Disappointment *also* hurts."

"It does hurt. Unfortunately, some of us go into relationships with unrealistic expectations. Instead of allowing things to unfold naturally, we throw all this junk in the way. I see you tossing everything into this matter, Courtney, including the kitchen sink."

Courtney managed a watered-down smile. "You make too much

sense. Thank you." Courtney scratched her head. "I'm supposed to see Darius tonight, but I'm toying with the idea of canceling. Maybe we need a few days apart to sort out our issues."

"*We? You* need to sort things out. You're the one with the issues. From what you've told me, Darius is in no doubt whatsoever over what he wants. And he wants you. Take it or leave it. You were so upset when you thought he was getting married. Now you know he's single and you're still upset. I'm sorry, but I just don't get it, Courtney."

Courtney wrinkled her nose. "You're not alone. I don't get it, either."

Feeling frustrated, Monica sighed inwardly. "If you don't show him you want him, then, yes, you will eventually lose him. If Darius thinks you two aren't on the same page, you'll give him no choice but to up and disappear. Trust me, he will start to sense your fears if he hasn't already."

"Okay," Courtney stated calmly, not wanting an argument to ensue. She changed the subject abruptly. "Did you bring the contracts we discussed?"

Accepting that the conversation was over, Monica reached down and patted the leather shoulder-style briefcase at her feet. "They're all in here." She looked closely at her boss. "Are you sure you want to work? When you called last night, you scheduled off two more days, saying you were worn out. What's up?"

Courtney sucked her teeth. "Working helps keep me sane. You know that. I just need you to bring me up to speed on the concluded events and those coming up."

Monica shrugged. "If that's what you want to do, boss. I'll start by saying there've been no major snags at the office. Everything's running smoothly. There were times we could've used your expertise, but you've taught us how to figure it out. We eventually took care of every issue."

"Good to hear." Courtney produced a much brighter smile this time.

Chapter 12

Inside the shower stall Courtney felt relieved to know her employees had run her company effectively in her absence. Because of the favorable report Monica had shared, she decided to stay away from the office for two additional vacation days. She also decided not to cancel her dinner with Darius.

How many times had he warned her about borrowing nonexistent troubles?

Courtney knew he'd given her the same advice more than he should've had to, and she had to start acting her age. Lose the fears or lose Darius—those were her options. She had to let the two of them be led to whatever was their destiny.

Having washed and conditioned her hair, Courtney sat on a stool in front of the bathroom's large mirror. Firmly holding the blow-dryer in her hand, she guided the plastic comb-style attachment through her wet hair. The beauty shop she patronized was closed on Mondays, making it impossible to get an appointment.

While drying her hair, she thought about what she'd wear that evening. She was excited about seeing Darius's place, imagining that his high-rise condo was posh. He owned a single-family home, as well, but touted it as having too much room for one person, though he planned to move back there at some point. Currently, it was leased out to a couple with three children.

Having set aside her earlier bout of apprehension, Courtney kissed Darius passionately at the door. Wearing white jeans and a purple top, she looked well rested and relaxed. This was a casual evening and she chose comfortable attire.

Lifting her arm up, Darius twirled her around. "You look hot in anything you wear." He moved his hand down over his outfit. "Looks like we continuously have the same ideas in clothing choices. We've both chosen white again."

Darius also had on white jeans, pairing them with a black short-sleeved polo shirt.

"We do have this *white thing* in common. You look great, as always." She kissed him again. "Mind that I brought along the screenplay? I've written down a few questions to ask you while we eat."

"I'm flattered. I'd love to answer your questions. How far are you into it?"

"I'm nearly finished. I read a lot this morning and I got back to it after I took care of my hair."

Courtney had put the manuscript in her briefcase, retrieving it from where she'd set it near the front door. "We can go now."

Darius kissed her on the mouth. "By the way, your hair looks beautiful. All yours, right?" he joked.

Forming a fist with her free hand, Courtney feigned a punch at Darius's arm. "As I told you before, all of it is mine. I had to pay for the fake hair."

"That's right, you did," he said, taking the briefcase from her hand. "I got this."

Touring Darius's high-rise condo was a real treat for Courtney, who noticed he'd used pretty much the same materials as in his office. The glass, chrome and silver decor created a coordinated look throughout the spacious home. Polished and brushed silver vases, African sculptures, small artsy statues and picture frames served as accents. Splashes of black broke up the silver and chrome. Stainless steel predominated in the kitchen and laundry room.

"Where do you want to eat, in the kitchen or dining room?"

Courtney had noticed on the walk-through that both tables were set. The kitchen table had more casual dinnerware, whereas the formal one was decked out in fine china.

"Either one is okay with me—wherever you'd be most comfortable, Darius."

"Since the meal is a casual one, let's use the kitchen. In there we can see the city lights from the picture window, once I pull up the electric blinds. I can practically see all of Hollywood from this high up. There are advantages to living on the twenty-fifth floor."

Feeling totally relaxed in Darius's condo, Courtney smiled. "I'll bet, especially when there are only twenty-eight floors in the building. I can't wait to see the view."

Taking Courtney by the hand, Darius led her to the kitchen. Pulling out a chair, he waited until she was seated. Leaning down, he kissed her ears and mouth. "Be right back. I'll get the food."

Realizing that her briefcase was in the other room, Courtney jumped up from the table and ran to the front of the condo. Opening the case, she removed the screenplay and rushed back to the kitchen.

Darius was busy setting out the salads and dressings when Courtney popped back into the room. "There you are." He spotted the folder in her hand. "Oh, I see. You had to go get your fix. I love your addiction to my story."

Courtney chuckled. "I *am* addicted to it. Lots of passion going on. But what I love most about it is the pure honesty between the couples. Seth and Shawn are my favorites. Rick and Tina and Bart and Constance are tied so far. I'm hoping nobody will start acting like a fool, but please don't tell me. I want to read it for myself."

Darius sat down. "Want to know what else is on the menu?"
She nodded.

"I hope I didn't mess up, but I grilled hamburgers and steamed a few ears of corn on the cob. I'm not much of a chef, but when I considered takeout, I decided I wanted to try to do it myself. The burgers were cooked on my stovetop's grill. I seasoned them with dry onion-and-mushroom soup mix."

Casting a skeptical eye on Darius, she put a fingernail to her temple. "I'm starting to smell more than burgers. If I've got this right, you've been talking to Monica. She knows I love hamburgers seasoned the same way. Give it up, Darius."

Looking abashed, Darius shrugged. "You got me. But I only wanted to please you. I told Monica about my paltry cooking skills…and she suggested the burgers, telling me I couldn't go wrong there. She also said you loved corn on the cob."

Laughing and crying at the same time, Courtney got up from her chair and slipped her arms around Darius's neck from behind. While hugging him cheek to cheek, she dropped kisses into his hair. "You are such a caring brother. Knowing you love doing things to please me means a lot. I only pray I can please you half as much. Thank you for being who you are. Please don't change on me."

Darius heard fear, but only in Courtney's last remark. It bothered him to know Hawaii hadn't rid her of all her anxiety about their future, but he wasn't giving up. The relationship had progressed to an intimate level, but she still wasn't sure she could trust him. Besides showing his love for her, he needed her to put her trust in him. Without faith, their relationship wouldn't get very far. He shuddered at the thought.

The couple polished off their salads in silence. Darius's mind was busy thinking of ways to let her know he was for real. It wasn't too soon for him to reveal where he wanted the relationship to go.

One bite into the juicy hamburger made Courtney close her eyes to savor the tasty onion-and-mushroom flavoring. She nodded repeatedly. "You did super, Darius, for someone who has confessed to a deficiency in cooking skills. I taste something I can't identify. Did you use something other than the soup mix?"

Darius was impressed with her taste buds. "A couple of tablespoons of A-1 sauce and Worcestershire are part of the mixture. That didn't come from Monica. I just happen to love those sauces, especially on my steaks. I started to do rib-eyes, but I was worried about ruining them. I'll get braver as my confidence grows."

"I think you would've done fine with steak. However, I love

Promises to Keep

the burger and toasted sesame-seed buns. Don't count me out for another if there are any left."

"I fixed six, so there are plenty left. Instead of Monica, I might call you for a few cooking tips."

"Anytime.

"About the script," Courtney began. "It seems the story is about love at first sight and how to convince a stranger you love him or her. Am I getting the drift?"

"Very much so. I wanted to portray love at first sight. Once the couple get over their hesitancy about the novelty of their feelings and realize that the feelings are real, they can progress to marriage quickly. At first, it was more about working the story line around June brides. I reworked it to show how love can blossom when you least expect it. It's more appealing featuring both aspects."

Courtney looked curious. "Is there a particular reason that you did the rewrite?"

Not so long ago, he'd thought she wasn't ready for anything more from him in this relationship. He could answer her question in all honesty. But he still felt the timing might be wrong. Darius seriously had marriage on his mind, strongly believing Courtney was the woman for him. She was his soul mate.

"Remember when I told you I didn't believe in love at first sight until after Candice and Roderick got together? I now know it can happen, so I changed the screenplay to reflect that." He failed to tell her he'd done the rewrite after he'd fallen for her the same way. They'd discussed this matter before. Darius didn't think it was a good idea to rehash it because of her resurfacing uncertainty.

His answer made her feel slightly disappointed. Courtney had hoped he'd changed the story line because they'd fallen in love the same way. Somehow she didn't get the feeling he'd done the rewrite as far back as the beginning of Candice and Roderick's relationship. Still, she kept her disappointment to herself.

"I see where you're coming from. The two elements really spice up the story. I like both concepts. When do you think you'll be ready to start shooting?"

"Hopefully soon. As you know, my upcoming travel schedule is heavy. It will prevent me from pulling the shoot together as quickly as I'd like. Meyer and I are still working out the details of our arrangement. The wording has to be fine-tuned. A final contract hasn't been drawn up yet. Both lawyers are considering individual demands."

"That's right, you're leaving for Vegas soon." She'd said it as if she'd forgotten. But it wasn't something she'd easily forget; his traveling schedule worried her a great deal.

"I had to move my trip up by a day in order to make another important meeting while I'm there. I actually leave tomorrow evening. We can do lunch and dinner before my nine o'clock flight, if you'd like. I'd love for us to spend as much time together as possible. I've been hoping you'd stay overnight."

"I can't," she said in a clipped tone.

His brows lifted at the sharpness in her response. "Why not?"

Knowing she had come off rude, she felt obligated to explain herself. "I have a lot of work to do. Monica and I had a meeting earlier. We accepted quite a few more catering events while I was gone."

"Are you saying you didn't know about those events when you decided to take a couple extra days off?"

Disliking the interrogation, Courtney shot her eyes at him. "I didn't know until we had the meeting. After Monica left, I decided to go into the office tomorrow."

Darius flatly didn't believe her. Had he not brought the traveling schedule up, he believed Courtney would have at least considered spending the night with him. "Is lunch and dinner out of the question, too?"

"Sorry, Darius, but I don't see either one happening."

Darius's eyes narrowed. "Let me get something straight here. In Hawaii, you asked me when I'd find time for us after you learned I'd be traveling a lot. I asked you to come with me and you turned me down, which I understand. I'm trying to make time for us—I'm not opting out, Courtney. Can you please explain why you are?"

Sighing, Courtney looked over at Darius. "You make the right decisions for your professional life and I'll do the same for mine. Okay?"

The obstinate look in her eyes and the rigidness of her jaw let

Darius know he needed to give it up. The last thing he wanted to do was argue with her when he had to go out of town. Nothing he could say would convince her of his sincerity. Darius believed she'd soon come to accept his love without conditions. He'd hold on tightly to that belief.

Darius reached out for Courtney's hand. "Let's go into the family room and relax and listen to music. I'll get the dishes later."

Not so sure she wouldn't demand to be taken home, Darius steeled himself for whatever might come next. He wasn't leaving town with Courtney upset.

"You cooked. I can at least stack the dishwasher." That said, she got up and began clearing the table.

Darius wondered how the sweetest girl in the world could be so stubborn, so unsure of herself—and him. Rather than have her do all the work, he pitched in, helping her rinse off the dinnerware before loading the dishwasher.

"All finished," Courtney sang out. "I'm going to the bathroom. I'll meet you in the family room in a couple minutes."

Rushing out of the kitchen and down the hall, Courtney slipped into Darius's bedroom. There were two more baths in the 2,600-square-foot condo, but she had other ideas. Searching through his walk-in closet, she took down one of his long-sleeved shirts and went into the master bath. After stripping out of her clothing, she put on the shirt. Neatly folding her attire, she laid them atop the wicker clothes hamper.

Although it was only eight o'clock in the evening, she strolled over to Darius's bed. Pulling back the plump comforter, she slid into bed and stretched out. Courtney knew she had hurt Darius by acting so selfish. He didn't deserve any kind of hurt.

Darius had carried the screenplay into the family room, decorated in gray leather. He began perusing it while waiting for Courtney to come back. Ten minutes later, he wondered where she was. Getting up from the sofa, he went in search of her.

Reaching the hallway, Darius noticed the powder room door standing open. Farther down the hall he spotted the second guest lavatory door ajar. Happy that she'd felt comfortable enough to use his personal bath, his feet sped up. He opened the closed double doors and walked in. If Courtney was in the bathroom, he wouldn't be intruding on her privacy since a door stood between the two areas.

Seeing Courtney lying in his bed made his heart thump hard. Deciding not to question his good fortune, he removed his shoes and lay down beside her, fully clothed.

"Hi," he said softly. Darius traced her full lips with his forefinger. "I missed you." His eyes lit up when he noticed that she was wearing his shirt. It felt good to know the evening wasn't going to end up as a total bust. Bending his head, he kissed her tenderly.

"Can we just lie here and cuddle for a while?" Courtney's green eyes appeared to plead her case. "All I need right now is reassurance, Darius. I don't want anything to get in the way of emotional love and I don't want our evening defined as merely physical."

Hoping she didn't think his feelings for her were just physical made him content to meet Courtney on her own terms. "Cuddling is warm and nice. I love you."

Courtney smiled. "I love you, too. Sorry about the way I acted in the kitchen. You were right. My intolerant attitude has nothing to do with the job. Your leaving tomorrow has me upset. Can I please spend the night in your comfortable bed?"

"Is it just a comfortable bed or the comfort you find in my arms?" he whispered.

Darius chuckled at how quickly Courtney had done a total about-face. A few minutes ago she'd said no to spending the night.

On her terms, he reminded himself. *Everything she did had to be on her terms.*

"It's about you and me. I want to fall asleep in your serenity-inducing arms." She kissed him passionately. "I used to sleep soundly until I met you. All of a sudden I can't fall right off to sleep. Last night I was awake for hours on end dreaming about you."

"Sleep and dream all you want, but please stay wrapped up in the warmth of my love."

Courtney closed her eyes. "There's no place I'd rather be."

A question suddenly popped into her head and her eyes fluttered open. "You mentioned a best friend the other day, but you didn't give a name. Who is he?"

"Sounds like you're assuming my friend is a *he*. Interesting assumption." Darius held his laughter. Courtney's expression was sobering.

"Then who is she or he?" Defiance in her eyes was clearly visible.

"It is a *he*. Raleigh Crestview and I have hung together since junior high. We were also roommates at UCLA. We graduated near the top of our class."

"Where does he live?"

"Up north, in San Francisco. He's a brilliant film editor. We've talked to him about editing the film, but he has a fiancée. Raleigh is not too keen about leaving her to come here."

"Smart man." Wishing she hadn't said that, Courtney mentally scolded herself, gauging Darius's reaction at the same time. As always, no reaction whatsoever.

"His fiancée, April Lowe, is a wonderful animator. My friend says she eats and sleeps animation. She's made quite a name for herself in the business. We've made plans to get together for a couple of meals while I'm in San Francisco. If April can land an animation project here in L.A., I see Raleigh jumping at the chance to join our team. He's worked with Meyer Chandler before."

"Think I'll ever meet Raleigh and April?" Courtney asked timidly.

"No doubt about it. Maybe you can fly up to San Francisco one evening and have dinner with us. You can either catch a red-eye back or the first morning commuter flight. Raleigh is really looking forward to meeting you. I also e-mailed him some of the photos I took in Hawaii. I've told him a lot about you."

"I've been talking a lot about you, too, over the phone. Grandma and Papa are so excited for me, for us. Being in love for them is like the paradise you often mention. Fifty-plus years of marriage is an amazing feat. And they're still happy."

Darius's wobbling emotions tugged at his heartstrings. "My

parents would've been married thirty-seven years if they had lived. It still isn't easy for Candice and me, but we get through each day. Grief can either make you stronger than strong or break you down completely."

"Thank God both of you are enormously resilient." Courtney's next thought didn't come easily to her. Losing the battle to stay awake, Courtney grew silent. Seconds later, she closed her eyes.

Knowing what the sudden quiet meant, Darius cuddled up behind Courtney, placing his arm across her belly. Hoping he could sleep with her right next to him, he kissed the back of her head. The excitement of having her at his place and in his bed for the first time had his adrenaline pumping hard.

Awakening around 4:00 a.m., Darius was puzzled by Courtney's absence next to him. Sliding out of bed, he put on his robe and strolled out of the room in search of her.

Just outside the entry to the family room, he stopped abruptly, his heart careening. Seeing Courtney stretched out on the sofa with a pillow under her head, reading his screenplay, made him feel good. She was so into his story and he saw that as a huge plus.

If women didn't get the profound messages in his scripts, he'd view the work as a failure. Women's fiction was a genre of remarkably raw, heartfelt and honest storytelling—and he loved it. There were so many issues females had to deal with on a daily basis and it made him want to write problem-solving stories they could relate to.

Every man wasn't a liar, a cheater and a freeloader. Every female wasn't bossy, unreasonably demanding and money hungry. If his stories could bring women and men together in respect, in truth and in love, leaving the bull completely out of their relationship, everyone would win. Darius believed in this theory with his whole heart.

Courtney looked up. "Hey, Darius, come on in." She sat up to make room for him to sit down. "I'm on the next to last page of your script. Can you believe it?"

"Your nose has only been in it every waking moment." Seating himself next to her, he laid his chin on her shoulder. "Seeing you reading my script turns me on. And it also makes me feel very proud. Something must keep drawing you back."

"Not just something. Many things keep me reading. Fantastic points of view from both male and female characters are one huge driving force. It's like you're speaking from the perspective of both genders. Your ideas on how to make a relationship work is amazingly brilliant."

"You think so?"

Courtney cast him a skeptical eye. "Come on, Darius. You know your stuff when it comes to writing about relationships. If every man and woman involved in a romantic liaison practiced your wise advice, wow, what a day for love. I've taken so many mental notes."

His eyes softened as they connected with hers. "Thank you." He paused. "I want to say something here. I hope you take it the right way."

Courtney chuckled. "Me, too. I haven't been batting a thousand lately."

"You are a complicated woman," Darius continued, "in so many ways. You're demanding, but you place demands only on yourself. If *you're* getting the messages in my work, I believe others will, too. Your vote of confidence keeps me wanting to go forward with the project. I imagine a few people stick to reading something they don't like, but the majority will toss it aside for something far more interesting."

Smiling devilishly, Courtney laid aside the screenplay. "Hmm, smart thinking. Since I need something far more interesting, I'll put away the script temporarily. What do you think is suddenly more interesting to me?"

"You and me, baby." Darius pulled Courtney onto his lap.

"It's all about us. I want you to leave me with another burning memory to ponder while you're away. Make love to me, Darius."

Courtney stayed Darius's attempt to get up. "Right here, right now," she whispered. Taking a throw from the sofa's back, she stood and had him do the same. After covering the cool leather with the throw, she lay down on it. Smiling wickedly, summoning him to her with the crook of a finger, she invited him to join her.

Sighing with pleasure, Darius gently lowered his body down on Courtney's, his mouth coupling with hers at the same time. Lifting his head, he adoringly watched her expression, his anxious fingers unbuttoning her borrowed shirt. "What happened to just cuddling, nothing physical?" he whispered softly.

Raising her head, she captured his lower lip, tantalizing him, moaning softly near his ear. Nipping and teasing his mouth gently, using her teeth and tongue, she felt his lower body rapidly stiffen against her belly.

He put on protection and entered her with heart-stopping tenderness, letting out a loud, pleasurable groan and following it up with a sigh of deep contentment. "Bad girl or good girl tonight?"

Courtney giggled. "When I'm beneath you, my bad girl persona eggs me on without end. No good girl routine exists for me, at least, not in this compromising position. All I can advise you to do is brace yourself. 'Cause not even I know what a bad girl might do in the feral throes of passion."

Darius laughed against her mouth, streaming a trickle of his breath into her lungs. "Naughty or nice, I like both personalities. That only I get to see the bad girl side of you is one hell of an added bonus."

Time for talking over, Darius gently thrust his manhood inside Courtney's femininity. His plunging movements were tender and steady. As he withdrew from her at timely intervals, she couldn't contain her body's nearly uncontrollable squirming in time to his thrusts. If her body's own propelling responses to his overpoweringly amorous lovemaking didn't calm down, she feared they'd end up on the floor. The sofa was wide, but it still had limited space, unlike a king-size bed.

Deep thrusts from Darius and Courtney's pivoting gyrations intertwined, pushing them closer and closer to the edge of no return. While continuing to heighten the mad desire for a blowout, simultaneous climax, they each fought hard to resist it. Neither wanted to see the lovemaking come to an abrupt end, yet they both felt an insatiable urge to leap off the precipice of passion together.

Breathing escalated as Darius's and Courtney's bodies began losing control. With no strength left to fight the sweetly tumultuous inevitable, they willingly gave themselves up to the exquisite explosion just waiting to happen.

Seconds after their bodies shook like a violent force of nature, a floating sensation descended, capturing the gale storm of passion and restoring serenity.

Chapter 13

Walking into the reception area of Darius's offices at high noon felt strange to Courtney. She'd only visited his professional digs when he was her client. As new lovers, things had changed drastically between them.

Jasmine smiled sweetly. "Hi, Courtney. It's great to see you again. Wow, what a rich, dark tan." Rushing from around her desk, Jasmine gave her boss's lady a warm hug.

Courtney knew Jasmine had no idea how much her warm greeting relaxed her. She hadn't known what to expect since she and Darius weren't dating when he'd left for Hawaii. Nor had she known if he'd made his assistant privy to their love affair. Outside of sharing his Hawaii-bound plans with Monica, he'd mentioned that only Candice and Jasmine knew where he was headed.

"You can wait in Darius's office if you'd like, Courtney. He's in the conference room finishing up a meeting." Jasmine's eyes twinkled with merriment. "My boss told me you and he are in love. Congratulations! I'm so happy for you both. He's a good man."

"Thank you. It seems we've made quite an impression on each

other." Beaming at Jasmine, Courtney took a seat in one of the chairs. "I'll wait here for him, unless that bothers you."

Jasmine waved off Courtney's concern. "Your presence is hardly a bother."

Darius came around the corner just as Jasmine completed her statement, but it seemed he hadn't heard her. Looking intent, he handed her a notebook. "Please type these notes up for me when you have time."

Darius quickly whipped his head around and saw Courtney seated there. By the expression on his face, something had prompted him to look behind him. "You're here. I hope I didn't keep you waiting."

Courtney got to her feet, smiling beautifully at the man who had everything she wanted. "Just got here, Darius. Ready to go to lunch or do you need more time?"

"I'll be ready in a second. I need to tell Jasmine a couple of things before we go." He pointed something out to her in the notebook. "Schedule another meeting with Meyer, our lawyers and me. The day after I get back from Vegas isn't soon enough, but I can't do it on the road. Since I'll be in and out of the office for the next couple of months, I want contracts finalized as soon as possible. The terms are coming together nicely."

"Glad to hear it. I know you're ready to get casting started. You two have a nice lunch. Will you be returning to the office?"

"No choice, not if I want to clear my desk. Courtney made reservations for an early evening dinner. I plan to head to the airport after we finish. See you later, kiddo."

"I'll be here. Bye, Courtney. Hope to see you again soon."

"Thanks, Jasmine. Have a great day," Courtney responded in kind.

Seated inside Miss Lilly's Country Cooking Restaurant, Courtney studied the menu. Collard greens and mustards were a favorite of hers, but she couldn't imagine greens fixed better than Grandma Alma's. In fact, she didn't spot any soul-food dish her grandmother couldn't prepare beyond anyone's wildest expectations.

"Cubed steak with onions and gravy, mashed potatoes

smothered in gravy and a cornbread muffin. I'd also like a side order of mustard mixed with collards," Courtney relayed to the waitress. "Thank you."

"Is that all for you, ma'am?"

"Isn't that enough?" Courtney laughed heartily. "I'm happy it's lunchtime. I'd never order this heavy a meal after seven in the evening."

The waitress laughed, too. "I know what you mean, but I eat Miss Lilly's food any time of the day and night. Sometimes I even call in a take-out order on my days off. Many of the other employees do, too."

Darius chuckled. "I wonder how many of you folks realize you're giving your paychecks right back to your employer."

"We all know it. I've seen you in here lots of time, sir. And when Ms. Jasmine calls the take-out orders in, she always says what Mr. Fairfax would like."

Darius raised an eyebrow. "You know who I am?"

"Only because I've seen you in here with Ms. Jasmine and heard her call you by name. You eat Miss Lilly's food a lot, too," she charged.

"Why do I feel so busted?" He looked at her name tag for the first time. "Marion, can I trust you to keep my eating habits a secret? You've already ratted me out to my girlfriend here, Courtney. Are you going to start keeping an eye on my weight?"

Courtney smiled. "Yes, if you're eating this kind of food too often. I want to keep you healthy. Maybe you should give Marion your order so she can get back to work. We're not the only diners in her section."

Thinking she'd stepped over the boundaries, Marion looked terribly embarrassed. "It's okay. I can wait."

Trying to keep her from worrying, Darius cast Marion a bright smile. He thought what she'd done was kind of cute and innocent. He knew she meant no harm. "I'll have the same thing Courtney ordered. I'd also like hot applesauce and green beans. Please top my steak and gravy with sautéed mushrooms. That should do it. Thank you."

"No wedge of cornbread and slice of sweet potato pie, Mr. Fairfax?"

"You really *do* know what I eat, don't you? That's incredible." He appeared astonished. "Please feel free to add those, too. Thank you."

Marion smiled at the couple before she walked away.

"Was that amazing or what?" Darius asked Courtney.

"It was also hilarious. You never know when big brother or sister is watching," she teased. "That she pays such close attention to her patrons is a tribute to her. She wasn't being mean or facetious."

Darius grinned. "I know. I can't wait to tell Jasmine what happened."

"Speaking of Jasmine, you said her boyfriend was a linebacker. What team does he play for?"

"Stefan Clayton plays for the Raiders. I keep hoping they'll become the dynasty they once were. I was young when the team moved back to Oakland. The absence of football in southern California is a huge travesty."

Courtney reached out and entwined her fingers with Darius's. "I wish you didn't have to go away. Every time I think about your trip I get sad. Promise to hurry back to me? I know I'll ache for you every moment of the day."

"Same here." The love in his eyes mirrored her own. "We'll get through this brief absence. Seventy-two hours will zip by. We lead such busy lives and the time will fly. You'll see how fast it'll go. If you need me, Courtney, call. Promise?"

"You have my word on it." Spotting the waitress, Courtney said eagerly, "Here comes the food."

The waitress unloaded the serving tray and set out the entrées. "Enjoy yourselves. You two are a stunning couple. It's been a pleasure serving you."

"Thank you," Darius and Courtney said at the same time.

Speaking each other's sentiments simultaneously had the couple cracking up.

Sniffing the delicious aromas, Courtney closed her eyes for a moment. "I can't wait to taste the steak. I never forgot the taste of yours. Eating off your fork had me thinking it was the closest I'd ever get to kissing you. Boy, was I wrong!"

"You actually thought that, Court?"

She nodded. "And a lot more." She took a forkful of steak, applesauce and mashed potatoes, holding it up to Darius's mouth. Leaning across the table, she first kissed him full on the mouth. "Delicious food for the tastiest man on the earth," she cooed. "Food tastes even better on your delectable lips."

Darius laughed heartily.

Courtney couldn't keep from sharing her thoughts with Darius. "Since I've confessed my feelings for you, I may as well tell it all. You took up residence inside my head the day I met you. And I could never think clearly enough to make sense of it all."

Darius loved what Courtney had said. "Now that I'm settled into your head, can I move into other places? Do you have any free space in your heart?"

Pausing to ponder Darius's query, she watched him eat. He made an art form of chewing slowly. He was obviously a man who appreciated a good meal. He once told her he respected the care put into meal preparations and the time it took to perfect a pleasurable outcome. She was willing to bet he wouldn't waste a thing on his plate.

"You're already moved in, Darius—lock, stock and barrel. You've filled up every empty space, including the heart chamber. Maybe I need to consider charging you rent."

Throwing his head back, Darius laughed. Totally taken by her sweet, humorous comments, his fingers nervously traced the back of her hand. Her engaging personality caused a thick fog to suffuse his mind. Women hardly ever made him nervous, but Courtney gave him the jitters and made him deliriously happy, all at once.

"I'm a much happier man because of your dazzling presence in my life. Please don't evict me."

Frowning, Darius wished he hadn't gotten a glimpse of the clock on the wall. Time was ticking away on them. In a few more hours, he'd board a plane bound for Las Vegas. A short distance away by air or car, yet a vast amount of space separating him from her. The thought of her in L.A. and him in Vegas wasn't a happy one.

Removing a photo album from a bookshelf in her study, Courtney carried the thick volume of Hawaiian memories into her bedroom. Already showered, dressed in a pair of white silk pajamas, she lay down on the bed on her stomach, situating the album out in front of her. Tears brimmed in her eyes before she ever opened the first page.

For several minutes, Courtney just sat there, recalling the breakfast he'd fixed, serving it in bed on this early sunshiny morning. Lunch at Miss Lilly's was a fond memory.

Thinking about the dozens of passionate farewell kisses Darius had given her before he'd slid behind the wheel of his car, she shivered with longing, wishing he could have hung around long enough to kiss her a couple dozen times more.

A million kisses wouldn't have been enough for her, Courtney knew with certainty. Darius staying behind with her was the only thing she'd continuously hoped for all day long. It was the only solution that would've brought her sweet solace.

Getting into her own car, Courtney had driven straight home. The blur of her tears had made it difficult to see at times. By the grace of God, she'd arrived back home safely. Closing her eyes, she prayed for Darius's safe arrival in Las Vegas and his entire stay.

Getting out of bed, Courtney knelt down on the side of the mattress. She immediately closed her eyes, supplicating on behalf of her family, close friends and all children, no matter where they resided. Her normal routine was to pray first for others. Asking God to meet the needs of those all around the world came next. Praying for her enemies was also part of her daily prayers.

"God, please take good care of Darius. Keep him safe. He is your child, just as I am. We know you love us. I pray for his safe travels and for the success of his business. I humbly and earnestly ask you to cover him with the blood of the lamb. Please, Lord, keep us all safe from hurt, harm and danger. I ask these things in your Holy name. Amen."

Chapter 14

Hastening into his hotel room, Darius set his black leather briefcase atop the Ergo desk. After tugging his upper body free of his sports coat and tie, he unbuttoned the top three buttons on his silk shirt. In dire need of relief from the physical and emotional stresses of the day, he silently prayed.

Deciding to take a quick shower before calling Courtney, Darius stripped down completely and rushed into the hotel bathroom. Turning on the water, he adjusted the temperature. A full turn brought him face-to-face with the wide wall mirror above the marble dressing counter. Standing stock-still in front of the looking glass, he slowly began to study the features peering back at him.

Happy eyes, he thought, thinking of Courtney. Smile could be a tad brighter; extremely well-toned physique. Body and mind physically and mentally sound, he assessed. Letting the water get as hot as he could stand it, he grabbed a white washcloth off the metal rack and began steaming his face.

Darius hit and missed spots on his body as he dried off with a white, soft, bath-size towel. Stepping out of the bathroom, he headed over to the bed and dropped down on the mattress.

Eagerly anticipating the sweet sound of Courtney's voice, he quickly dialed her number. The first three rings went unanswered. She picked up on the fourth.

Just as he'd imagined, hearing her voice brought instant joy to his heart. "Sweetheart, it's me. Are you okay?"

Needing to blow her nose, yet not wanting Darius to know she was sick, she looked helplessly over at the Kleenex box on her nightstand. "Thank God you're safe. I'm fine, now that I've heard your voice. Knowing you're perfectly okay helps me relax."

He didn't necessarily agree with the *perfectly* portion of her remark. His situation was terribly imperfect because of her absence. "What's wrong, Courtney? Are you crying?"

"I watched you go up the steps." Repositioning herself on her bed, Courtney sniffled, hating how her voice quaked with emotion. "Then, when you disappeared behind a security booth—you may think I'm super silly—I began to miss you terribly."

"Court, sweetheart, we miss each other. I guess we're both silly. My concentration is still on our vacation in Hawaii. The scheduled meetings today were real important, but I had a hard time sweeping memories of us out of my mind."

The tender tone of Darius's voice had Courtney heading for a total meltdown. She badly needed an emotional release for everything she feared. Rarely did she sob this brokenly or tremble so hard, but everything in her life had changed drastically. Her emotional state was a clear sign of turmoil, yet Courtney hadn't ever been happier or more content, just a few moments before Darius had phoned. Her emotions flip-flopped way too much.

Love caused unbelievable chaos for women—and for men who were in touch with their feelings.

God had come to her rescue, as He always did. Once again He had heard her burning supplications. Safe travel for Darius had been near the top of her prayer list.

Covering the mouthpiece with one hand, Courtney held the receiver a few inches away, doing her best to muffle her cough. Managing to regain some semblance of control over what might be a virus attempting to take hold, she cleared her throat. Moving the phone even farther away, she finally blew her nose as quietly as she could.

Darius had no idea what was happening on Courtney's end of the line. The silence concerned him. *Was she ill?* Whatever was distressing her, he wished she'd talk to him. "Courtney, should I call you back later, once you're up to talking?" He sighed. "You're not saying much of anything. You're acting odd."

Taking a deep breath, Courtney laid her head back on a bed pillow. "I'm up to talking now. If I seem odd, it's because I'm a changed person. Every time I consciously or unconsciously start thinking about us...about what direction our relationship is heading, I end up fantasizing about you." She didn't want to tell him she wasn't feeling well, not with him out of town. If he thought she was sick, the Darius she'd come to know and love would insist on hopping the first flight home. However, what she *had* said to him was the honest-to-goodness truth. *She did fantasize about him—quite a bit.*

Stroking his chin, Darius stretched out on the bed. "Maybe it's more than a mere fantasy. What if you end up with me as your protector? I don't want you wandering around lost, Courtney. As far as you and I are concerned, I'm rock solid."

As if God had known exactly what she needed to hear, she looked up to heaven and mouthed a silent *thank you.* To go forward with this conversation, or to let it be, buzzed inside her head. She and Darius *had* to come together on everything to do with their relationship, but it didn't need to be rushed. Yet they couldn't allow it to fall by the wayside and eventually fail.

Missing Darius more than she'd ever dreamed possible, Courtney flew across her bedroom to answer the phone. He was due back this evening and she prayed there'd been no change of plans.

Disappointment cruised through her upon seeing Monica's number on the caller ID, but only because she had hoped it was Darius. Not wanting her friend to know about her not-so-stable emotional state, Courtney decided not to answer the phone. In the next instant, feeling terrible about ignoring Monica's call, she grabbed the receiver. Remembering how she and Monica kept each other company during the hours of loneliness had caused her to change her mind.

Placing her hand over her heart, Courtney took a deep breath. "Monica. What's happening with you this morning? It's still very early."

"Calling to check on my best girl and see how she is. How're you feeling?"

Courtney sighed. "I may as well be honest. I miss Darius. I didn't want you to know how badly so I considered not answering the phone. But it's good to hear your voice. I've got a case of the sniffles. Other than that, I'm fine. And you?"

"I know you miss him. It doesn't matter how long he's been gone. J.R. can be gone just a half a day and I nearly lose it. When we're close to someone like that, missing him causes a real ache in the heart."

"Anyway, he's gone, and it's time for me to get my butt back to work. I'll be in tomorrow as scheduled, but I have to go to the dentist first. I developed a toothache late last night. I should make it to the office before noon."

"You should probably go straight home after the dentist. I'll drop by to check on you. If he calls in a prescription for antibiotics or pain, I'll pick it up. Stay put."

Courtney smiled. "You're a great best friend, Monica. I have a lot to tell you, but we'll chat later on."

"I'll have my listening ears on," Monica joked. "I'll call when I'm on the way."

"I've really been missing you, Monica. See you soon, dear friend."

"Count on it."

As much as her tooth was hurting, Courtney stopped by the drugstore to pick up her own prescriptions. The numbness had worn off already and the tooth was throbbing again. She'd had a two-surface filling, but Dr. Mai recommended a root canal. He was a fantastic dentist and would never do any unnecessary work. The root canal appointment was scheduled for the end of next week.

Courtney let herself into the house and went straight to the kitchen for a glass of water. Pulling from the refrigerator a bottle of cold water, she poured it into a glass. Tossing back one pain pill, she chased that with the cold liquid. The medicine bottle came with labels warning that it caused drowsiness, so she strolled back to the bedroom to lie down for a short spell.

Before her head hit the pillow, the phone rang. Monica, she thought. Hoping her friend wouldn't be upset with her for not calling, she picked up the receiver. "Hey, Monica, is everything okay?"

"I thought you were going to call me to get your medicine."

"I already picked it up. I needed it badly. This tooth is back to throbbing, but I did get a filling. The pain should subside soon."

"Glad to know you're okay. Listen, Darius called here for you. He thought you were planning to work today. I told him you were coming in until your tooth acted up. He said he'd call you on your cell. Have you heard from him?"

"Not yet. Let me check my cell. I keep putting it in my purse, though I can't hear it ring in there." Courtney hung up the phone, reached for her purse and rustled around in it until she came up with her cell. She flipped it open and saw that she had some messages. After scanning her call history, she counted three missed calls from Darius.

After listening to her messages, Courtney leaped off the bed. Darius had taken an earlier flight from Vegas and would be at her house any minute now. "Would he come, anyway, since he didn't get me?" she wondered to herself. "Please don't let that stop you, love. I'm here now."

Just in case Darius did show up at her door, she ran into the bathroom to freshen up. As soon as she turned on the water in the sink, the doorbell rang. Laughter welled up in Courtney. As she made a mad dash for the front door, she didn't care what she looked like.

Without asking who was there, Courtney opened the door and flung herself against Darius's body. Pulling his head down, she crushed her lips into his, kissing him hungrily, showing him how love-deprived she'd felt in his absence.

"I missed you, too," he said in response to what her kisses told him.

Darius was thrilled to see Courtney in such a good mood,

but he had an idea her euphoria wouldn't last long. His next traveling date had also been pushed up. He was leaving town again tomorrow afternoon. On the verge of seeing his dream come to fruition, he was at the beck and call of the money people, the ones who'd back his venture.

There was a lot of interest in his screenplay and Darius knew he had to ride the waves while they crested high. For the next month or so, he had to be available to everyone interested in backing his dream.

For all the work he'd put in on this project, for all the writing, rewriting and endless phone calls, he wanted Courtney more than anything else in his life. Success was great, but he was at a time in his life when he needed someone to share it with. Courtney Campbell was the only woman he'd ever imagined having by his side forever. While he was away from her in Vegas, his imagination had gone wild.

Holding hands, Courtney and Darius made it back to her bedroom. She had him sit down on the bed. Kneeling down in front of him, she removed his shoes. As she went for his socks, he stilled her hands, pulling her up from the floor. "Please sit down next to me so we can talk. There are a lot of new developments in my life."

Dread filled Courtney, but she didn't know why. *Yes, you do know why,* she thought. *This is where he tells you he can no longer commit to you. He'll use his busy schedule as a reason. You did let him know you were upset about it. The time has come for him to break your heart into a million little pieces, Courtney. You knew all along that heartbreak was waiting in the wings, but there were no indications of a beginning to the end.*

Yet this is the end.

Darius took hold of Courtney's hand. She snatched it away, surprising him. "Why'd you do that? A few minutes ago we couldn't get enough of touching each other. What's wrong all of a sudden, Courtney?"

"Just tell me what you came here to say, Darius."

The painful look on Courtney's face worried Darius. *What did she think he came there to tell her?* It obviously wasn't making her happy. "My travel schedule has been moved up again. I have to leave tomorrow afternoon and I'll be gone several days. I wish you could go with me. But I know that's not possible."

"Darius, you don't have to say any more. I get it. I really understand." Courtney wanted so badly to save face. Save face and lose the only man she'd ever love. What kind of alternative was that? One she had to take because she sure wasn't in a position to give out ultimatums. If she were in that position, she'd never make Darius chose her love or the love he had for his business. She could never do that to him.

He took a deep breath. "I'm so close to my goals. Right before my eyes I'm seeing my dreams come true. This has been a long haul, not to mention a long time coming. You know exactly what it's like to build a company from the ground up." He grinned boyishly. "I want to be just like you when I grow up."

Two of Courtney's fingers pressed to Darius's lips silenced him. "It sounds like we both did a lot of thinking while we were apart. We've had a great time together and I'll always be grateful to you for that…" The lump in her throat was hard to swallow.

"What are you really saying, Courtney?"

The exact same things you came here to say to me, Darius.

"I'm telling you our relationship is not working for me anymore. I can't do two things at once. Just like your business, mine also needs undivided attention. I thought I could run my business and handle our love affair at the same time. We've discussed making time for us. I can't. You can't do both. Both businesses are too important to let them suffer in our absence."

With the strangest look in his eyes, Darius got to his feet, hardly able to believe his ears. "Are you saying it's over? Are you ending our relationship?"

"We agreed on it from the start, Darius. If one of us wasn't happy, we'd say so. But it doesn't change what I feel for you. Nothing can ever change that."

"Exactly what *is* it you feel for me? It can't be love. You can't love me and walk away from us on a whim. Where's this garbage coming from, Court?"

Courtney could see how angry Darius was, his face distorted with rage. She didn't understand it, especially if his intent was to dump her.

Maybe he doesn't like me beating him to the punch.

Courtney scolded herself. It was wrong to reduce their love affair down to one beating the other to the punch. He was right, this *was* garbage. Still, she had to get out. If Darius didn't want out right now, eventually he would go. She couldn't make him stay.

Courtney totally dismissed the little voice telling her he had said no such thing.

Reaching into his pocket, Darius pulled out a white box with a tiny red bow on it. Thrusting it into Courtney's hand, he closed her fingers around it. "I don't know what's happening, but I pray that you come to your senses. Inside this package is something I chose especially for you. Unfortunately, I'm now attaching strings to it." He blew out a gust of breath, hating what he was about to say. "Don't open it unless you decide to choose me over everything else in your life. I love you, Courtney."

Courtney opened her mouth to say something, but Darius used the same method she'd used earlier to silence him. "Sending me away will be one of the biggest mistakes of your life if you love me. You're trampling on true love in the process. I hope you can't get me out of your head, 'cause I sure as hell won't get you out of mine. My love for you is incapable of dissolution."

Pulling Courtney into his arms, Darius kissed her passionately, praying she'd feel everything he felt for her. Moving her aside, he walked out the room, stiffening his spine. It was hard for him not to go back.

As Darius slammed the front door shut, Courtney's heart pumped hard.

A half hour later, still reeling from what she'd so foolishly said to Darius, Courtney stood in the middle of her bedroom, nervously fingering the small box. She didn't need to ask what had happened. She already knew.

She had sent away her one and only true love.

Walking over to the mirrored dresser, Courtney opened the top drawer and gently placed the box between the layers of her intimate apparel. Two seconds later, she took it out. Walking over to the bed, she sat down, staring hard at the box.

Curiosity was killing her. Her hands trembled as she went to remove the top. Suddenly, Darius's remarks rang loudly in her ears. Pulling back her hand as though she had touched fire, she dropped the box on the bed.

Don't open it unless you decide to choose me over everything else in your life.

After several more attempts at opening the box, she decided to adhere to the strings Darius had attached. She wasn't sure what he'd come there to say, but she hadn't given him a chance to say it. He seemed so sure about his feelings for her, yet she'd been so sure he was calling off their love affair. "How confused am I?"

No longer was she sure about anything, except her love for Darius Fairfax.

Chapter 15

"It's been three weeks since I ended it with Darius. Why am I still such a mess?" She peered into the compact mirror, fingering the puffiness under her eyes. Not a day or night had gone by that Courtney hadn't practically cried her eyes out. "It seems I was right about what I thought he'd say. If not, wouldn't he have called me by now?"

Seated at the table in Courtney's kitchen, Monica sighed hard. "I don't know what else you could possibly expect from him. You released him, set him free. He told you what he wanted from day one when he came to Hawaii to woo you. Darius is a man who knows his own mind. According to J.R., he's doing the same thing you are, pouring himself into his work. His movie, *Promises to Keep,* is starting production soon. He's been out of town a good bit, but he always calls or meets with J.R. when he gets back."

Courtney pushed her sandwich around on a plate. The title of the film wasn't the original one. He'd admitted to changing it during a rewrite. "Is talking to J.R. his way of checking on what I'm doing?"

Stretching her eyes in disbelief, Monica sucked her teeth. "I don't believe you just said that! It's so unlike you. Arrogance doesn't become you. If he was breaking up with you, why would he bother? But I'll answer your question anyway. Darius doesn't mention you, Courtney. He told J.R. you'd broken it off with him the day after it happened. He hasn't mentioned your name since, not to either of us."

"Period?" Courtney asked tearfully.

"Period!" Monica noticed the tears in her friend's eyes. "Really, why *did* you do this awful thing? I find it hard to believe you broke it off with him just because you thought he was about to do the same thing. Please tell me there's more to it than that. There has to be."

Crying hard now, Courtney shook her head from side to side. "When a man starts a conversation with 'Sit down so we can talk,' a woman knows something is up. Then he says 'There are a lot of new developments in my life.' What else was I supposed to think? I felt he was leaving me behind, up until he gave me that box. At that point, I no longer knew what was up."

"What box?" Monica screeched. "This is the first time you've said anything about a freaking box."

Courtney nodded. "I didn't mention it 'cause I haven't opened it." She went on to tell Monica about Darius's conditions.

"Where is this mystery box now?"

"It's in my lingerie drawer. I can't tell you how many times I started to open it. Can fear do this to me? Why can't I be stronger?"

"Fear has all sorts of power—powers we give it." Monica jumped up from the table. "We can talk more right after you open the box. And you *are* going to open it. If not, I intend to open it for you."

"No, you can't do that. Darius wants me to open it, but only when I'm willing to put him before everything else in my life."

Grabbing Courtney by the hand, Monica practically dragged her down the hallway and into the bedroom. "Get the box." Courtney gave her a skeptical look. "Now, Courtney. Get the box right now!"

After retrieving the box, Courtney came over and sat down on the bed next to Monica. As with every other time before, she had a hard time opening it. "I can't. If I open it, I'll have to follow Darius's instructions."

"Okay, Miss Campbell." She patted Courtney's knees. "Let's go over exactly what Darius said. I know you just told me, but I want to hear it again, word for word."

"He told me not to open this box until I decided to put him before everything else in my life. No, wait a minute—wrong wording. 'Don't open it until you choose me over everything else in your life.' That's it. That's exactly what he said."

Brushing back disheveled hair from Courtney's face, Monica couldn't help feeling sorry for her. "Don't cry, sweetheart. I can only imagine how this must hurt. But I believe Darius is hurting, too. If he said those words you just repeated, he wasn't breaking up with you. In my opinion, he came there prepared to give you a gift. Why would he even have a gift with him if he wanted to end it?"

Courtney grabbed a tissue off the nightstand and wiped her eyes and nose.

"To open or not to open the mystery gift is all up to you. Think about his conditions before you make the final decision. Are you ready to choose him over everything else? Are you ready to make Darius your number one priority?"

"Yes. I love him that much. I just have to get there," Courtney cried.

"Get where?"

Courtney looked at the time on the clock radio. "To Darius's office, his home, Candice's place, wherever I can find him—and I won't stop looking until I locate him."

Monica grabbed Courtney and hugged her tight. "Now you're talking the language of love. Go find your man, girlfriend. He's been all yours from day one."

Disappointed at finding Darius's offices locked up for the evening, she took the next elevator back down to the lobby. So many things had run through her head since she began the journey to find her man. *If he's still mine,* she thought, starting to feel unsure.

Parked on the street, Courtney got back into her car. Darius's home was only a few miles from his office and even a shorter distance from her place. Had she gone there first, maybe she wouldn't have lost valuable time. It then dawned on her he might be out of town. His travel schedule *was* a heavy one, she reminded herself.

Ten minutes later Courtney parked her car in Darius's driveway. She didn't know if he was inside or not, but she took a few more minutes to calm down. She had no doubt about how she felt about Darius, but he had a say in this matter, too. Maybe he'd had a change of heart after so many weeks of not hearing from her. "Well, you won't know until you get your butt inside and face the issue head-on. That is, if he's in there."

It took Courtney another couple of minutes to get out of the car. She then took a few steps, only to turn back. Once she finally reached the entry, it was another minute or so before she pressed in the doorbell. Standing back, shuffling her feet, she waited, hoped and prayed.

Darius finally opened the door, wearing a bathrobe. His hair looked damp, as though he'd just gotten out of the shower.

Every memory Courtney had of him naked rushed through her head. "Can I come in, Darius? Please."

Without saying a word, he opened the door wider. Stepping aside, he allowed her to gain entry. Having missed her like crazy, he'd much rather haul Courtney into his arms and kiss some sense into her pretty head. Missing her wasn't the crux of their problems. The last three weeks were the worst of his life, after the deaths of his parents. But a lifetime of living with a woman unsure of her feelings for him was disaster bound.

Reaching into her purse, Courtney removed the white box, handing it to Darius. As he took hold of the package, the puzzled look on his face didn't surprise her. "Since you came to my place with it already in your possession, I believe you intended it as a gift. So I'd like us to sit down and open it together."

Darius eyed her curiously. "Why are you here, Courtney? What changed in three weeks? Are you here to say you're certain of us now? If that's the case, I can't trust what you might *think* you're sure of. You have to *know* your desires without any doubts."

Courtney hated the misgivings she saw in Darius's eyes, but

she understood. "I accept your attached strings. I love you, Darius, only you. You are first and foremost in my life. I can succeed or fail at my business, but I don't want to fail you or us. Successes come and go. True love is forever."

The expression on Darius's face said she hadn't convinced him. His gaze strayed between her and the box. Dropping down on the sofa, he gestured for her to join him and she quickly complied.

Darius looked her right in the eye. "You're not ready for a man like me, Courtney. You should know by now that I don't do anything halfway. It's all or nothing with me. I love you. Unfortunately for me, you don't understand the depths of my feelings. Hell, at times, I don't understand myself. Yet I know, without a shadow of doubt, that I'm in love. You, on the other hand, aren't sure if you can ever love, period. I'm convinced you don't know what love is. Your fears constantly get the better of you."

"Darius, that's not fair. I admit to being overly fearful, but I've never been unsure about my feelings for you, not for a second. I fell in love within a heartbeat. I…I…choose…you…above everything…else in…my life. I do know what love is, Darius Fairfax. It's what you and I are drenched in. I can never love anyone but you. I know that without a doubt because you're the only man I'll ever love."

Seeing tears falling fast from Courtney's eyes was more than he could take. Lifting her up from the sofa, Darius swung her around and around until she begged him to stop. Seeing how dizzy she appeared, he carried her back to the sofa. As he sat down, he guided her onto his lap, kissing her with all the ferocious hunger pent up inside him.

Holding the gift in his hand, he slowly removed the top. As a smaller black velvet box was revealed, she gasped inwardly, her hands flying straight to her stomach.

Leaning in closer to Courtney, Darius kissed her tenderly. Before opening the lid of the velvet case, he fell down to his knees. "I love you, Courtney. I want to marry you more than anything in this world. There's more to marriage than love. It's a lot of work and it'll take both of us to make it a success. If you need more time…"

With her tears falling, Courtney's lips urgently pressed against his, kissing him until it was difficult to breathe. "I'll marry you! No time needed. I love you, Darius. I love you desperately and I want to spend the rest of my life showing you just how much."

Thrilled with Courtney's answer, Darius flipped the top to reveal a stunning diamond ring. "This is a perfect ring, perfect for you. I hope you like it."

Gasping hard, trying to catch her breath, Courtney's eyes continued spilling tears. "I love it! I've never seen anything like it."

The indescribably beautiful center stone was three carats. Delicately set inside two rows of brilliant diamonds, the solitaire diamond was surrounded by a three-tiered band of white and rose gold, each one encrusted with innumerable rare pink diamonds and brilliant white ones.

In awe of the engagement ring, Courtney couldn't find the right words to express its sheer beauty. "The entire setting is absolutely breathtaking. I'll wear it proudly. I love you deeply, Darius." Kissing him passionately, she tumbled off the sofa's edge, landing right in Darius's arms.

Slipping the ring onto her finger, Darius returned her passionate kiss. "I love you, too, Courtney. I can hardly wait for us to get married. I promise to be the best husband to the woman I love with all my heart and soul. Our spirits meshed immediately."

Courtney threw herself back into his arms. "I feel what you mean. It's time for us to celebrate our love and our engagement. Everyone will be so happy for us."

Darius kissed her again and again, leaving her breathless and hungry for more. "No one will be happier for us than you and me, love. We are going to celebrate our love eternally and all our promises to keep!"

Chapter 16

Twelve Months Later

A fabulous June wedding in Honolulu, Hawaii was close at hand.

Alma, Monica and Candice had flown to Hawaii a couple of days earlier to make sure everything for Courtney and Darius's wedding had been arranged according to the couple's wishes. Numerous lavish suites had been reserved at the Kahala Resort for the three women and the rest of the wedding party.

Courtney and Darius were expecting forty-five guests to attend the wedding and reception. The number of attendees, including the wedding party, was small, but the couple wanted an intimate affair. Family, close friends, coworkers and employees made up the guest list. The ceremony was scheduled to take place on a level cliff on Kahala Resort property, high above the Pacific Ocean.

Harrell, J.R. and Roderick had arrived yesterday morning. Maurice, Courtney's father, and her mother, Chelsea, had flown in with Courtney later in the day. *With her parents as close friends, there'd be no wedding-day dramas from them.*

Darius's best man, Raleigh Crestview, and his fiancée, April Lowe, had arrived around the same time as Courtney and her parents. As lifelong best friends, Raleigh and Darius supported each other through thick and thin.

Jasmine Parker and her extremely handsome linebacker boyfriend, Stefan Clayton, had also flown in early yesterday.

Seated on the side of the bed in her suite, trying to bring her prewedding jitters under control, Courtney smoothed her hand over the white summer-weight comforter. She thought of how she was alone right now, but this whole scenario was about to change.

Courtney had been nervous since the day Darius proposed to her nearly a month after their initial visit to Hawaii. During the past twelve months, the happy couple had been caught up in a whirlwind of romance and intrigue.

June had finally arrived, but Courtney's nervousness continued. Now that the most profound moment of her life was nearly upon her, she felt even more uneasy. Sixteen months had passed since the first day gorgeous Darius Fairfax had walked into her office, where he had tenderly handcuffed her heart.

Smiling brightly, Courtney stretched out fully in bed. Laying her head back on a pillow, she looked up at the swirling palm ceiling fan. Dreams of forever filled her heart, as sweet memories of her amazing love affair with Darius danced in her head.

As she envisioned her wedding day, Courtney prayed it would be everything they'd planned for. In front of family and friends, they'd finally exchange vows.

The elegant, sunset ceremony was only one day away.

"This is my last time alone as a single woman. From this day forward, Mr. and Mrs. Darius Fairfax will share the same residence and bed for the rest of their lives." Courtney giggled. "Does it get any better than this? I have a feeling it does. As much as we love each other, we will surpass every goal we've set for living happily ever after."

Missing Darius like crazy, Courtney fought hard to resist the urge to call him. Standing on tradition, the bride and groom wouldn't see each other the night before their big day. Rules didn't stop her mad desire to see him, kiss him and profess her undying love for him.

Courtney planned to have a light lunch around noon with her mother, grandmother and all her female attendants, but she still had four hours to while away. The luncheon would take place in her suite, upon the ladies' insistence. The women feared she'd run into Darius and the other men if they ate anywhere on or around the resort. The women planned a sleepover for her last night as a single woman.

Getting out of bed, strolling through the suite and onto the lanai, Courtney plopped down on a lounger. Looking out at the ocean, she thought about Darius and her swimming and playing in the ocean. That always made her smile. They'd shared so many wonderful memories on this isle of paradise. Courtney had fallen in love with Oahu.

Laughing, she thought about their brief swim with the dolphins. As cute and cuddly as the friendly mammals seemed, their countless teeth had kept her on edge. Darius had pegged her right when he'd called her a chicken. She'd never admitted her dread to him, but she knew he had sensed it big-time.

This last remaining day is for reflecting, she thought. *I have so much to think back on.* Courtney recalled only the good times. Her fears had been left in the dust, after she'd learned so much about love and trust from Darius. It was hard for Courtney to believe she'd been so worried about her ability to unconditionally love and trust a man.

"Hey, everyone," Courtney cheerfully greeted her guests. Enthusiastically hugging and kissing her family members and friends, Courtney silently welcomed the end to a lonesome morning. "Come in. Lunch will be served in approximately thirty minutes. Hi, Grandma, Mom. You look so beautiful."

Alma squeezed Courtney tightly. "Not as beautiful as you, my darling," Alma cooed. "How *are* you today, my one and only granddaughter? Still suffering the jitters?"

"Thanks, Grandma, for the sweet compliments." Courtney chuckled. "Jitters! You're way off base. It feels like a swarm of bees are building a hive inside my belly. These nasty jitters sting like crazy. Wish I'd brought my insect repellent," she teased.

Her eyes tearing up, Chelsea kissed her daughter's forehead. "You may hate hearing this, but you look a lot like me, my child. The older you get the more of me I see in you. Maurice often mentions it to me when we talk on the phone, but I hadn't seen any evidence of it until this trip. I kept stealing glances at you in L.A. Your dad is so right."

"Mom, I'm proud to look like you. I inherited my green eyes from dad, but I have your smooth complexion, not to mention those curving hips you love to sway. My lips are full and pouting just like yours. And our hair color is nearly the same."

"Maurice has reddish hair, too, so that one trait is a toss-up. You and Chelsea are the same height. No matter how you slice or dice it, both of you are beautiful women," Alma remarked, meaning every single word she'd uttered.

Even though Chelsea had left and initiated the divorce against her son, Alma loved her. Without Chelsea, there'd be no Courtney for the elder Campbells to love, cherish and pamper. No hard feelings existed among any of the Campbell women and men. Chelsea and Maurice had remained friends throughout the years. As each parent looked out for their daughter's best interest, it kept Alma humble and grateful.

Smiling beautifully, Courtney turned to face her other guests. "Monica, Candice, I'm so happy you're both here. Love the colorful, sexy sarongs you ladies are styling."

Seeing the women storing their overnight bags and extra pillows in a hall closet made Courtney smile warmly. She was pleased by the idea of a special ladies-only pajama party her friends had planned in her honor. Everyone expected a lively sleepover. Monica and Candice were in charge of fun and games.

Alma, Chelsea, Monica, Candice, Jasmine and April all had roles in Darius and Courtney's wedding. Chelsea and Monica were matrons of honor. Candice, Jasmine and April would act as bridesmaids. Alma, the family matriarch, served as the go-to person. To ensure that everything went as planned, she'd become the overseer for the entire wedding celebration.

Monica sniffed the white gardenia bloom in Courtney's tresses.

"Your hair smells like a spring day right after a fresh rain." She tossed her arm around her friend's shoulders. "Your alluring, gauzy white pants ensemble is how men define sexy. Guys would love to tug loose the drawstrings on your low-slung pants. You, my loving boss, transformed into an island girl on your first visit here thirteen months ago."

Loving her daughter's newly acquired smart eye for fashion, Chelsea nodded. "The white leather sandals are darling, too. Maybe you *do* have some of your mom's design talents. I noticed how much zestier your wardrobe is since I saw you last."

Throwing her head back, Courtney laughed. "Stop with the flattery, already! Darius has my head big enough." She quickly drew Jasmine to her side. "Besides, Mom, this stunning woman is also a top fashion icon. Look at her! She reeks of elegance in simple navy shorts and a dainty lime top," Courtney praised.

Pointing at Jasmine's petite feet, Monica smiled at the younger woman. "If we wore the same size shoe, I'd love to borrow those too-cute green-and-navy sandals. I met Stefan yesterday. Now that's a handsome guy you got. And he has the prettiest girl."

Jasmine blew Monica a kiss. "Thanks. You always say the sweetest things."

There was a light knock on the door and Monica rushed over to answer it.

"It's the food, everyone," Monica shouted back to the group, moving aside to allow room service waiters to roll in large serving carts.

The women held hands as Courtney whispered a blessing over the food.

"Amen," everyone sang out simultaneously.

"Ladies, let's dig in," Chelsea remarked. "Everything smells so good."

Courtney and her guests had fun laughing and talking trash while lifting off the silver serving domes to get a peek at the delicious-smelling delicacies.

Courtney held up the menu. "I'll go over foods ordered so we'll know what we're eating. There are several salads: Caesar, Waimanalo green, Chinese Hoisin chicken and Hawaiian fruit. For sandwiches we have grilled Ahi, Kahala chicken club, French dip, Pipikaula Reuben and veggie garden burger. There are also sides of steamed Asian rice, wok-fried vegetables and smoked paprika-seasoned fries."

Before Courtney finished the menu rundown, guests began filling their plates.

"For our drinking pleasure, we ordered tropical lemonades: pineapple, strawberry and guava," Alma enlightened everyone. "The mini bar is fully stocked if anyone wants something stronger. Or we can call room service for mixed drinks like Mai Tais."

"Mm, I see we have pineapple upside down cake for dessert." Monica pointed at a pink-looking tart. "What's in these, Courtney?"

"Those are fresh Kula strawberry tarts." Courtney shrugged. "That's all I know."

"And I don't need to know more," Monica said on a chuckle. "I love strawberry anything, including lip glosses."

Monica received lots of laughter on her comical remarks.

Once the ladies began eating, near silence descended on the room. Romantic Hawaiian music played softly from CDs Courtney had inserted into the player. Discovering how much it calmed her, she had really gotten into this type of music on her first visit. She loved hearing the ukulele. She found the spirited tones hypnotic and seductive.

April came over to the sofa. Sitting down next to Courtney, she handed her a white business-size envelope. "This is for you from all of us." Her hand gesture encompassed the other ladies. "We hope you'll love it."

Curious about the contents of the envelope, Courtney ripped it open from corner to corner with her forefinger. "It's a gift certificate for the resort spa. Oh, my goodness, this is wonderful. Earlier, I was thinking of scheduling a few spa services. Thanks so much to each of you. I can't wait to use this."

After looking down at her wristwatch, Chelsea reached her hand out to Courtney. "You don't have long to wait. Our spa appointments are scheduled twenty minutes from now. We'll all change into comfortable clothes and be on our way. Our bellies are full so we're ripe for a nap as soon as we return. That is, if we don't fall asleep at the spa."

"I've hardly had any sleep since we left L.A.," Candice shared. "Jet lag has already caught up to Roderick and me. Napping sounds perfectly divine to me."

Nodding in agreement with Candice's remark, Courtney made direct eye contact with April. "Have you and Raleigh decided when and where you're getting married?"

Pretty, ginger-complexioned April Lowe was very personable, possessing the kind of shapely body men loved to cuddle up with. She wore her wavy hair short, and the cute cut was perfect for her slender, oval-shaped face.

"He wants Jamaica and I want a northern California wedding. He doesn't know it yet, but we're getting married somewhere up north. It just so happens that his mother and I are on the same page on this. And Mommy Dearest gets whatever she wants from Daddy Dearest."

Loud laughter rang out from the others.

"Everyone is well aware of how mothers often get their way, especially with pampered sons they love and adore," April continued. "Raleigh is just the opposite. If he keeps on balking at Robin Crestview's relentless desires, Daddy, Walker Crestview, will step right in and settle the debate. Unlike Raleigh, Walker is a total sucker for Robin."

Alma raised an eyebrow. "How can you go into a marriage where your mother-in-law-to-be is manipulative and gets to have everything her way?"

"I don't have to live with Robin," April simply stated. "I love her son, but I don't see in-laws as a package deal. Neither does Raleigh. Don't get me wrong, he dearly loves his mother. It's the constant manipulation he has no stomach for. We've discussed over and over again his mother's role in our lives. She doesn't have one. This is our life and we plan to run it according to our desires. No one else but God has a say in it."

"Good for you, dear child," Alma commented. "Not many young women are as strong as you, nor do they think like you. I'm glad you and your fiancé have a good understanding of the role his mother *won't* play. I applaud and congratulate you."

All the ladies cheered and pumped fists to show their support.

Feeling a sense of sadness coming over her over at the thought of never meeting Darius's parents, Courtney rushed to her feet. "So everyone's getting a massage. We're going to have a blast. Let's hurry and get changed."

Scrambling for their overnight bags, flitting about in all directions, the ladies dashed off to change their clothes.

Staring at the phone in a trancelike state, Darius was practically worn down from fighting the urge to call Courtney. He'd been obsessing over talking to her since 5:00 a.m. He had quietly slipped away from the large group of men about twenty minutes before. Determined to have memorable fun, the guys, both young and old, had gotten kind of loud. The men had a blast trying to top each other with shocking X-rated jokes. Surprising to Darius, Harrell had more than a few shocking, comic yarns to relate.

No matter what he tried to do not to think about her, Courtney owned Darius's undivided attention. He'd had no idea how hard it would be to stay away from her in paradise. It was hard enough during his travels, when she hadn't gone with him.

Papa Harrell and Maurice stepped into the bedroom Darius occupied. He'd been fortunate enough to reserve the same two-bedroom suite he'd had before. Candice and Roderick had agreed to share his quarters at his insistence.

"Here you are," Harrell remarked. "Are you okay, son?"

Darius nodded, "I'm fine. Can't wait for tomorrow to get here. How'd you guys get through the night before the wedding, when you couldn't see the woman you loved?"

Maurice chuckled. "All brides and grooms go through the same tortuous tradition. I have no idea who came up with such a backward theory. Chelsea was determined to see me before the wedding…"

"Yes, she was," Harrell interjected, cutting his son off. "Until your mother and her best friend got wind of it. They tracked Chelsea down and brought her back just before she made it into the room where you were."

"She was only a couple of yards away from the holding tank," Maurice said.

"Holding tank? I know you're a police officer, but what does a holding tank have to do with anything?" Darius asked Courtney's father.

Maurice and Harrell burst out laughing.

"Nothing to do with what you're probably thinking," Maurice responded.

"Our bedroom served as the bridal party dressing room on our son's wedding day," Harrell told Darius. "Chelsea was kept holed up in there until the ceremony began. No one had heard her curse before then. I remember Maurice's mom cracking him up when she asked if he was sure Chelsea hadn't ever served in the U.S. Navy."

"If not, she sure knows how to cuss like a sailor, Mom told me," Maurice confirmed. "On my wedding day, Mom fussed with me nonstop about Chelsea's foul mouth. She later told Dad and me how my future wife was capable of cursing a blue streak. Up until she was whisked away to the wedding chapel, Chelsea hadn't stopped using the same offensive language. Interestingly enough, she rarely cursed during our marriage."

Maurice's eyes glowed with sentiment. "I recall the whole thing vividly," he continued. "It was the one day Chelsea was determined to see me. It was more about us being told we couldn't see each other than anything else. She has never let another person set any rules for her. Lady Chelsea governs her own life. I'll never forget the day we got married. Nor will I forget the day a U.S. Marshal served me with divorce papers."

"I'll never forget that day either, son. You looked like you just got a notice to report to duty in hell. The next year and a half was just like that for you—pure hell."

Maurice smiled at his father. "And you were there for me through it all. Thanks."

Darius saw the strange look in his future father-in-law's green eyes. The topic of conversation was so ironic. One day Chelsea was terribly desperate to see Maurice. Many years later, she'd become desperate enough for her freedom to strike out alone. Leaving her husband and only child behind, she'd begun a journey into the unknown. Darius thanked God the couple's friendship had survived the divorce.

The love and concern for their daughter had given Courtney the courage to survive.

Living the kind of fast-paced life Chelsea desired had been more important to her than her own flesh and blood. Darius wasn't into judging folks, but he had constantly wondered when Chelsea's conscience had flown the coop. Had she rediscovered her scruples in Paris or had she possibly regained her values between visits to L.A.?

Tomorrow, tomorrow, Courtney and I will belong to each other forever. Darius knew he had no choice but to wait until tomorrow, which seemed to him like a year from now. Alma and Monica weren't letting him anywhere near Courtney.

No use in me trying to get to the woman I love.

Fighting hard to hold in her emotions, Alma crossed the living room inside Courtney's posh, beautifully appointed suite. While carefully inspecting her granddaughter's fresh-flower wreath for her hair, delivered only moments before, she inhaled the delightful perfumed scent. Alma had smelled a lot of flowers but none as sweetly perfumed as the blooms found on the Hawaiian Islands.

Chelsea joined her ex-mother-in-law. "Your emotions are pouring out of you. Courtney's beautiful, isn't she?"

"She's more beautiful than any bride I've ever seen. The look in her green eyes shines brightly with love. We have young Darius to thank for that. Before she met him, she wasn't sure she'd ever find true love. For a brief time she'd almost given him up, but fate saved the day. Has she told you the story of how they met?"

Chelsea's eyes dropped to the floor. "I'm afraid not. It seems she only shares the intimate details of her life with Maurice, you and Harrell." Chelsea warmly hugged Alma. "I don't think I could've raised her to become who she is today."

"Paris is a long way off and an awfully expensive phone call. I know you two e-mail each other an awful lot."

Chelsea took both of Alma's hands into hers. "Thank you for taking care of my little girl, who is now a beautiful grown woman. I wasn't around to be her mommy, but if she'll let me, I'll be the best grandmother to her future babies. Hopefully, I can be just like the mother and grandmother you've been to Courtney."

Alma kissed both of Chelsea's cheeks. "Your daughter needs you. Go to her."

Waiting until the last minute to put on her dress, Courtney paced back and forth across the room. "I can't believe this day is actually here. I still feel like I'm in a dream."

"It *is* here, dear friend, and it's a dream come true for you and Darius."

Eyes wide with disbelief, Courtney shook her head from side to side. "Well over a year ago I believed he was engaged to marry someone else. We all know how *that* turned out. The thought still can bring me to tears. It was the day before I first found true love with Darius while Candice and Roderick celebrated their engagement during a reception we catered."

Monica wagged her finger back and forth. "Love started before then. Remember the wager J.R. wanted to make? Later in the day, he told me he saw in Darius's eyes the same profound love he felt for me when we first met."

Alma stepped up and hugged Courtney. "Papa and I saw it early on, too. Young Darius wasn't the only one who fell in love at first sight. You fell for him the same way, on the same day he turned his heart over to you. I can't tell you how many times my grandson-in-law-to-be has told me the magnitude of what he felt that fateful day."

Courtney eyed her magnificent engagement ring, easily dismissing the crazy hoopla surrounding the *mystery box*. Recalling how she'd boldly gone to his home to get him back brought tears to her eyes. Darius had fulfilled her every dream and fantasy by asking her to marry him. *Oh, what a feeling.* They'd shared countless romantic moments. This particular one had surpassed them all. She'd spent the night with him, but they didn't make love. Their entire night was spent spinning animated plans for the future.

On this beautiful day, a half hour or so before sunset, a light breeze from the ocean below swept upward, gently swirling around a flat cliff. The view of the cresting Pacific Ocean and surrounding mountains was awe-inspiring.

A white organza runner scattered with sea grass was laid out at the point where the bride and her party made their grand entrance. The runner ended a few feet behind the altar, which was inside a fairy-tale white gazebo decorated in countless Hawaiian blooms.

Orchid-filled crystal vases, majestically placed at both ends of the aisles, were affixed to glass hurricane lamps, hung alongside the pathway. At sunset, the antique gold lamps would instantly provide magical lighting.

Waiting patiently for his bride-to-be to walk down the aisle on Maurice's arm, Darius glanced at the ocean from his position on high. Handsomely dressed in traditional wedding attire, he looked fabulous clad in a long-sleeved white shirt and white linen slacks, a lavender sash at his waist, Courtney's favorite color. Plain white leather shoes completed his statement of Hawaiian tradition.

Darius hadn't forgotten a single detail of their wondrous Hawaiian romance and beyond. From the day they'd met until the day Courtney had said *yes* to his proposal of marriage, he could conjure up at will any memory of every moment in her arms.

Atop this spectacular cliff overlooking the ocean was where he and Courtney would soon be joined as one. Tears falling from his eyes, Darius thanked God for bringing into his life the only woman who'd ever appeared in his dreams. *Courtney Campbell, soon to be Courtney Fairfax, and I will spend eternity loving one another.*

Soft music floated in the air like a cache of butterflies playing tag in the breeze. Matrons of honor and bridesmaids appeared at the entry. Marching down the aisle in tune to the melody, it looked as if the breeze also danced melodiously with the couples.

The women wore lavender dresses. Sashes in a darker shade adorned their waistlines. Beautiful leis in purple and ivory had been given to each female in the wedding. The sterling silver plumeria necklaces and earrings they wore were gifts from the bride.

Central to the Hawaiian culture was an *aloha spirit,* a

commitment to treat oneself and others with kindness, respect and love.

Groomsmen escorting the bridesmaids also wore traditional Hawaiian attire, the material fashioned in the lightest shade of beige available. Sashes were in the same darker shade as those of the attendants.

The Hawaiian wedding song, "Ke Kali Nei Au," chosen by the bride and groom, signaled the bride's arrival. Getting to their feet, everyone looked back at the entryway. Music from the instruments stirred their hearts.

The touching, meaningful lyrics of the wedding song were first penned in Hawaiian in 1926 by Charles King. Later it was translated to English and sung by many artists. It was made famous by Elvis Presley in the movie *Blue Hawaii.*

Spotting eagerness in the faces of many of the guests, Darius immediately understood the deep emotions underlying those expressions. As Courtney drew closer to the altar, anticipation flared uncontrollably in his stomach. He suddenly felt sweat forming beneath his clothing. On any day but today, his wedding day, the clammy feel of his body would have driven him nuts.

Holding on to Maurice's arm, Courtney was stunning in a modern, designer-original holoku, a traditional Hawaiian wedding dress. This magnificent gown radiated a delicate essence of free spirit and romance. Diamond-white material added sparkle to the tiered dress, fashioned in tulle to rustle in the ocean breeze. A beautiful midlength train in the same tiered design was attached at the end of the low-cut back.

The stunning garland of flowers replaced the traditional veil. Surrounding the bride's head, the garland was intricately woven with pastel-colored plumeria, pikake tuberoses, white orchids and white ginger. White ginger was touted as the most fragrant of flowers.

All of a sudden Darius felt light-headed. As Maurice placed Courtney's hand in his, he just stood there, staring into her face as if he were seeing her for the first time. In a word, Darius was thunderstruck by his stunningly beautiful bride.

Kissing his daughter on both cheeks and shaking hands with Darius, Maurice claimed his seat in the front row.

Minister Onasuka took his place at the altar, looking out at the guests. His white, lightweight baggy attire billowed in the soft breeze. "Who gives this woman away to be united in holy matrimony with this man?"

Maurice, Chelsea, Alma and Harrell all stood. "We do," they said in unison.

Minister Onasuka nodded in respectful recognition of Courtney's family. "You may be seated now."

The minister turned his full attention on Courtney and Darius. "We shall begin the ceremony with the exchange of leis between the bride and groom. Like a wedding ring, the lei is an unbroken circle. It represents your eternal commitment and devotion to each other. The beauty of each flower is not lost when used to create a lei. The beauty of the bloom is enhanced because of the strength of its bond. May we please have the leis?"

An emotional Monica presented the leis to Courtney and Darius.

Staring into Courtney's eyes, Darius gently placed the lei he held around Courtney's neck, battling the urge to bring her into his arms and plant a staggering kiss onto her sweet lips. Fighting back her tears, Courtney stood on tiptoes to position the lei around his neck.

The minister read fitting scriptures from the Bible, all pertaining to marriage. "Instead of Courtney and Darius taking their traditional vows, the couple has written their own." He looked at the couple and nodded.

Turning to face one another, Darius and Courtney held hands.

Courtney gently squeezed his hands. "On this day, as our bodies and souls are united in the eyes of God and our family and friends, I promise to give you the very best of me each and every day." She allowed her tears to flow unchecked. "It is my desire for us to learn how to communicate effectively, in a way we both can be heard. Our grievances can't get between us if we don't stuff them inside to fester."

Courtney licked her lips and continued. "Whether it is a friendly chat, a loving one or the fire-and-brimstone kind, we must remember to let love rule our tongues. If one of us gets frustrated enough to want to leave the other, getting back to basics and remembering our good times and the holy vows we took can help us get through anything and everything. Until death us do part."

"Courtney, I love you more than I can express," Darius began. "Knowing I'll have the rest of my life to show you and tell you every day has me delirious. To love with all our might, come hell or high water, means to stick it out if we run aground. We will fight for this marriage until we get it right. I am in this union for life."

Overwhelmed, Darius paused for a second. "I love you as much as life itself so I can't imagine living a day without you. Yet I know it's impossible for two people to be together 24/7. As business matters take us on separate journeys, my love will be wherever you are. I know your love will be with me. Until death us do part."

Courtney and Darius joined their baby fingers together. *"Ola loko i ke aloha,"* the couple said in unison, tears rolling down their faces. "Love gives life within," they said at the same time, reciting the sentimental meaning of the Hawaiian phrase they'd uttered.

With their vows taken, Courtney and Darius looked up at the minister and smiled. It was a cue for him to reclaim the proceedings.

"May I kindly have the rings?" the minister asked.

Raleigh handed over Darius's ring and Monica gave him Courtney's.

Minister Onasuka held up the rings for everyone to see. "Like the lei, these rings represent an unbroken circle. Courtney, please place the ring on your groom's finger."

Courtney kissed this sacred ring before slowly slipping it onto Darius's finger.

"Darius, please place this sacred ring onto your bride's finger."

Darius slid the ring in place, kissing it afterward.

"By the powers invested in me by the great state of Hawaii, I now pronounce you husband and wife. God has blessed this holy union." The minister spread out his hands wide. "I now present to you, newlyweds, Mr. and Mrs. Darius Fairfax."

Sunset arrived at the same moment the couple was pronounced husband and wife. Just like magic, the hurricane lamps glowed with the brightness of a golden halo. Bowing out gracefully for the night, the fiery reddish-orange sun dipped down and kissed the ocean. Astonishing gasps came from every direction.

Darius engaged Courtney in a kiss that sent her reeling just before they exited the gazebo. "We did it! We pulled off our Hawaiian dream wedding."

Courtney gently caught her husband's bottom lip between her teeth. "Our wedding memories will last as long as our love, forever and ever."

He tenderly squeezed her waist. "I've had a hard time holding back a surprise, but here goes. I want our wedding spliced into our movie, *Promises to Keep*. Raw footage of the ceremony will blow viewers away. But only if you agree."

Courtney was terribly excited at the prospect, her breath coming in broken gasps. "Of…course I…agree," she sang out, dancing down the center aisle. "You and I are superstars."

"If only in our own eyes," he joked. "I love you, Mrs. Campbell-Fairfax." He winked at her, letting her know he was okay with her using her maiden name. She'd been a Campbell for twenty-eight years and she'd only been a Fairfax for several minutes.

A Campbell was what she was, all she knew how to be.

As Courtney and Darius reached the white stretch limousine, guests began tossing birdseed and flower petals. Peals of laughter and shouts of congratulations filled the air.

The grand reception was held in a clear-topped tent offering incredible views of the Pacific sky. With the ocean directly below the cliffside party site, a bride and groom couldn't ask for a more awesome backdrop.

A traditional Hawaiian band played soft instrumentals. The music's tempo was expected to pick up once dinner was served. Bringing lots of guests to the dance floor was the band's top priority.

Just as Courtney and Darius's reception was getting under way, the lovely couple arrived at the party tent. Before taking seats at the head table, they began working the room, happily greeting their guests. Bride and groom were plastered with lots of kisses and hugs during visits to each table.

Courtney and Darius then took a few minutes to walk around inside the tent to see all their visions fulfilled to specifications. "Everything is just as we envisioned it," Courtney told her husband, thrilled by all the beauty before them.

Turning her around to face him, Darius kissed his wife's forehead. "I would have moved heaven and earth to fulfill your every desire. I'm so happy you're pleased with what you see. Everything I've done and plan to do is for us, Court."

Smiling gently, Courtney leaned into Darius. "You *did* move heaven and earth."

"I can't take all the credit. We can't leave out Grandma, Monica and Candice. They each helped make our dream wedding a reality."

"I second that. Let's take a peek at our wedding cake," Courtney suggested.

Atop a large corner table sat a three-flavored cake of passion fruit, guava and coconut. The five-tiered masterpiece, decorated with white pikake and lavender pakalana flowers, was a Hawaiian favorite. Swirls of white and lavender butter cream and edible seed pearls had been artistically applied to each tier.

A loud noise prompted Darius to look behind him. "Oh, they're ready to serve dinner. We'd better get to the table. Otherwise, guests will think we left to get a head start on our honeymoon."

Courtney laughed. "We have the honeymoon suite tonight, but we'll be on a floating hotel tomorrow morning. I can't wait to cruise the rest of the Hawaiian Islands."

"That makes two of us, sweetheart. We'll have a wonderful honeymoon. We may not make it out of the cabin, but we can always order room service," Darius flirted.

"Breakfast, lunch and dinner served in bed. That means we'll have to keep a robe handy. Oh, what a glorious life we'll have for the next seven days!"

"Correction, Courtney. Glorious is ours for the taking eternally."

At that moment Courtney caught a glimpse of her parents, who looked very cozy. Maurice and Chelsea had been playful and flirtatious with each other on the flight. Courtney didn't know if they might rekindle their romance, but it was a nice thought.

Guests were treated to Asia-Pacific appetizers of sushi, oysters and seared salmon, followed by a salad. Also on the menu were entrées of filet mignon and steamed moi, a delicious local fish. Besides the wedding cake, a Hawaiian coconut-and-strawberry-flavored shortcake Napoleon with fresh strawberries and Mascarpone cream was also a sweet selection. Compliments of Roderick and Raleigh, a three-hour open bar was available to the Campbell/Fairfax family and guests.

The Hawaiian wedding song was played as Mr. and Mrs. Fairfax's first dance. Darius led his smiling bride to the center of the floor. Bringing her into his arms, he couldn't resist the urge to kiss her. The open display of affection caused a burst of applause.

Kissing Courtney deeply, passionately, oblivious to the world, the couple danced all around to the band's more upbeat version of the same song. Lifting her chin with two fingers, he looked into her eyes. "Are you as happy as I am, Mrs. Fairfax?"

Loving the sound of her new name, she smiled brightly. "Mr. Fairfax, Mrs. Campbell-Fairfax can't imagine being any happier. Well, maybe I could do with a little more happiness. Once we consummate this sacred union, no couple will ever rival our joy. It's been hard not to think of what'll happen tonight when we're alone."

Darius pumped his fist in the air. "We both know what'll happen. We just have to find the courage to slip out of here. The honeymoon suite awaits us."

Maurice came up to Darius. "Do I have permission to dance with your stunning bride and my beautiful daughter? You two make a striking couple. Congratulations again. We're all so happy for you. Papa Harrell will be coming for his baby girl next."

Making a sweeping hand gesture, Darius moved aside. "My pleasure, Dad."

Both men laughed. It was the first time Darius had referred to Maurice as *Dad*. It sounded like music to Courtney's ears.

Papa Harrell did come for his baby girl. Twirling her around the floor, the pride he felt in his granddaughter was evident on his handsome face.

"Speech, speech from the happy couple," several guys shouted.

Darius stood first and turned to help up Courtney.

To quiet the soft buzzing of voices throughout the room, Harrell tapped the side of the crystal goblet with the handle of a fork. "Quiet, everyone, so we can hear the speeches."

Giving Harrell a nod of thanks, Darius held up his and Courtney's entwined hands. "I'm sure there are many words to express how much we appreciate each of you, but at the moment all of them elude me." His comment drew peals of laughter.

"You all have flown so far from home to be with Courtney and me on the most important occasion of our lifetime. For that, we will remain forever grateful." He took a moment to gaze adoringly into the sparkling green eyes of his bride. "This beautiful, charming, witty and sometimes very stubborn woman stole my heart the first moment I laid eyes on her. A lot of people don't believe in love at first sight. I was one of them, until I saw love blossoming right before my very eyes. My lovely sister, Candice, and her fiancé, Roderick, caused me to have a serious change of heart."

Darius peered down the length of the table to smile at his sister. "Candice still can't believe I beat her to the altar, yet she's thrilled for us. Everyone present is very precious to us. These are everlasting friendships we've built and we can't thank you enough for your presence. I love all of you. Now it's time for me to step aside and let you hear from my stunning bride, whom I always have a hard time taking my eyes off."

Bending his head, Darius kissed Courtney full on the mouth.

Nervous, Courtney blushed like the newlywed bride she was. "I believe Darius covered the bases well. We know it was a huge sacrifice for you to fly to Hawaii to be with us on our special day. I want to thank all of you who pooled frequent-flyer points to help make this happen. We couldn't have done this without you. Dad,

Grandma, Papa and Mom, I can't say enough about you. There's not enough time to say it. You know what you've meant to my life and what you mean to me. Family, I love you dearly.

"Monica, my dear friend, I'd have a hard time running the office without you. J.R., I thank you for understanding when we work way past office hours. You're a great guy and you're the perfect fit for Monica. You balance each other well in every aspect of your beautiful marriage. I love you. April, we don't know each other very well, but I'm looking forward to becoming good friends with you and Raleigh. Jasmine, you are a pure godsend. Candice and Roderick, you've been my rock. I love you both. I can never forget you, especially since your reception brought Darius into my office."

Darius and Courtney bowed from the waist. "Thank you for all your love and support. We love each of you from the bottom of our hearts," they said in unison.

* * * * *

REQUEST YOUR FREE BOOKS!

2 FREE NOVELS PLUS 2 FREE GIFTS!

KIMANI™
ROMANCE

Love's ultimate destination!